The Merang Mysteries

The Murder Above Merangs (Book 1)
Fancy Death At Merangs (Book 2)
The Murder Away From Merangs (Book 3)
Copycat Death At Merangs (Book 4)
Summer Death At Merangs (Book 5)
<u>Books in the pipeline</u>
The Last Tango At Merangs
The books can also be read as standalone

The Murder Above Merangs

The Merang Mysteries, Volume 1

Carole Marples

Published by Carole Marples, 2024.

THE MURDER ABOVE MERANGS

First edition. March 3, 2024.

Copyright © 2024 Carole Marples.

ISBN: 979-8224561872

Written by Carole Marples.

To Chess and Pat for their feline inspiration

Dead Body on a Wednesday

Wednesday 15th April

The day of the murder started like any other Wednesday at Merangs. As usual, I arrived first. After nearly two years, the novelty of having my own confectionery shop hadn't worn off. I still couldn't believe my luck at having secured a prime spot on Buttersley High Street. And the extra room at the back, just perfect for a tea room, had been an added bonus. Maybe it was sad to say, but my entire life revolved around those two bright, sparkly rooms. But what if, because of the murder, it all came crashing down?

By 10 o'clock, I'd already set up the tea room, wiped down the glass cabinets in the shop and eaten two caramel soft centres before James sauntered in – over one hour late.

'Good afternoon,' I said to make my childish point.

He flashed a smile that would have melted most hearts. It crinkled the sides of his cheeks and reached up to his bright blue eyes. 'Petty doesn't suit you.'

I could have punched that self-satisfied smirk right off his too-handsome face. I should never have employed a friend who didn't need to work. 'It's not just you who's late. Shakira's not been with the delivery yet.'

'She's just parked her van outside.'

As I opened the door for our baker and her cake trays, she limped in, clutching a shoe to her chest. 'Look at this.' She thrust a red-soled stiletto at me. 'My poor Louboutin. The heel's snapped off.'

I sighed at yet another of Shakira's dramas. 'What happened?'

'A fluffy midget thing on a lead tripped me up.' She flicked the strands of blonde hair stuck to her lip gloss. 'Sent me flying. Something that small should have an alarm or something.'

James stuck his head out the door. 'It's crumb Armageddon out there. I'll bring in what's left. Go through to the tea room, Shakira. I'll join you in a minute. Coffee for two when you're ready, Hels.'

I gritted my teeth. *Is anyone going to do any work around here?*

Shakira stayed for over an hour, taking on board two double lattes and Monday's Viennese whirls. She was still there when Prue, the captain of my ship, sailed in at eleven.

Prue straightened her pristine pinny, surveyed the tea room and tutted. I followed her scowl to James and Shakira. He was leaning back in the seat with his endless legs stretched out. She'd perched hers on a chair. They must have felt the heat of our gaze, as they both suddenly looked up.

Shakira heaved herself out of the seat and flicked crumbs from her ample cleavage. 'I'd better be off now. I've got a pile of ironing and forty-eight Barbie cupcakes to ice before I pick up the kids and bury the hamster.'

It was not long after Shakira left when disaster struck. I'd just returned from the bank and popped my head around the tea room door. Water was pouring from the ceiling through the central chandelier and splashing The Silent Sisters seated nearby. It would take more than that to shift them from their usual table. A bucket stood under the downpour. Gulping in disbelief, I made a quick assessment. The marble-topped tables would be fine, but I might have to shift the Lloyd Loom chairs.

I jumped when Prue's distant voice called from the cellar, 'Helen, is that you? I'm looking for the fuse box thingy to turn off the main lights.' A haggard-looking Prue emerged. The criss-crosses on her cheeks had deepened into livid lines. 'Don't just stand there, you goose. Do something useful for a change.'

'Okay, keep your hair on.' Childish, I know, but she sometimes acted like I were twelve, rather than nearly thirty-two. *Surrogate mum, you may be, but I'm the boss around here.*

Prue called through to the shop. 'James, go bang on the door of the flat upstairs. See what's going on.'

'Don't you worry, Mrs Mayflower,' shouted Malcolm – one of our regulars. 'I've just arrived. Leave it to me.' Although not visible from the tea room, I could picture him drawing his short, stubby legs to attention.

'Do not fear, my dear; Malcolm the Man is here,' echoed James.

Prue bristled. James would pay for that later. Malcolm irritated Prue with his dog-like devotion, but she wouldn't have him ridiculed. She turned her attention to the two sisters and gently guided them to a dry corner. Meanwhile, I stared at their identical straw shopping bags, which had started the day all jaunty with their cherry bobbles and were now just sodden shapes beside the empty chairs.

'Towels!' called Prue.

I jumped to attention, flicked the fuse in the main shop, located the towels and mop, and put up the sign saying, 'The tea room is closed'. As I mopped, I worried away. Who would fix it? Who would pay? What if they couldn't do it straight away? It all went around like a song in my head.

Malcolm returned, sweaty and breathless. 'I ran as fast as I could.' He bent double, and his belly bobbed on his knees as he panted. 'It's a bloody long way.'

The flat had a private entrance at the rear of the shop, and we had no back door – except the fire door, which I'd forgotten about. As Merangs stood in the middle of Buttersley High Street, it was a bit of a trek, especially for the older man who was fond of his beer and pasties.

I patted his back. 'Take it easy, Malcolm. You'll wear yourself out.'

'I've banged on the door, but nobody's answering. Can we ring them? Don't you have the number?'

'No, but I think it's managed by the estate agents opposite.'

He looked towards Prue for corroboration, but she was busy thrusting food at the sisters. The shower had not affected their appetites. They were consuming cake with the deliberate rumination of hillside sheep. Their wet, grey hair with its peculiar sour tang, and the seeping straw bags, were the only indications of something awry.

Malcolm straightened up and wiped his brow. 'I need to see this through. I'll nip round to the agent's.' He set off again, and I continued with my ineffectual mopping. At least the water was only dripping now. Malcolm was soon back, wheezing but pleased with himself. 'The receptionist woman tried ringing the flat, but there was no answer. They've got a spare key. It's against all their rules, but someone's going to enter.'

His large, round face had turned purple, the strands on his otherwise bald head dripped, and the white nylon shirt clung to his chest.

I took his hand. 'Malcolm, please sit down before you collapse. No, not in the wet, obviously. You need hot, sweet tea.'

'Thanks, Helen, love. I've done all I can.' He jutted out his bottom lip. 'It's up to them, now.'

James continued out front in the shop. I took comfort from the ringing of the till, which was definitely number one in my all-time favourite top-ten sounds. Meanwhile, the rest of us remained in our mini-drama waiting for the next act to begin. I'd only tripped the fuse for the chandeliers, so we still had the lamps, which provided a soft, intimate glow.

The sisters had moved on to coffee and brownies, and Malcolm was cramming in a Victoria sponge as if he'd not eaten all week. Prue fussed with her beehive, returning imaginary strays to the mother ship and patting it all down as if reassuring a small mammal. On the subject of hair, the unwashed smell had become more pungent; the sisters were next to a radiator.

Suddenly, the dripping increased, accompanied by heavy, plodding thuds. *Hell, what have they sent? An estate agent or an elephant?* There was a crash as if something had been knocked over, and we all stared up at the ceiling. More thuds – they were manic now – and then everything shuddered as if a boulder had been hurled down the staircase.

After a few moments of calm, someone flung open the main shop door. *Don't mind the English Heritage paintwork, will you?* The tea room door shuddered as this someone progressed through the shop like a bull with no time to browse.

Within seconds, a middle-aged man in a baggy, grey suit appeared in the connecting doorway. His bulk completely filled the space. He took a moment to find his voice. Unexpectedly high, it held a distinct note of complaint. 'You'd better call an ambulance. No.' He spluttered and shook his large head. 'The police. No. I mean both.'

The man's legs buckled, and he lunged towards a chair. Prue and I jumped to his assistance, while Malcolm punched in the emergency number as if he'd been waiting for that moment all his life.

When the operator spoke, Malcolm pursed his lips and offered the phone to the agent as if handing over his firstborn. The agent sank further into his seat, but after wiping his palms, he took a deep breath and held out his shovel of a hand.

Once an Estate Agent, Always an Estate Agent

The estate agent cleared his throat, sat up straight, and spoke to the emergency services. 'I want the police, ambulance and undertakers—' He glared at the phone. 'Police, then. There's a body in the bath. Dead. I'm sure. No, I'm not there. I'm in Merangs, the shop below … No, I won't go check.' His eyes bulged, and his chins wobbled. 'Dead, yes, dead. I know what I'm talking about. My mother was a nurse, and she was very high up.' I blinked, picturing a nurse up a ladder tending her patients. 'Let me tell you, I know a dead body when I see one.' His voice had reached an unnatural pitch, almost as disturbing as the scene he described.

The rest of us gaped at each other, and the sisters clutched at their throats as if their own lives were in danger. I'd never seen them so animated.

'Oh, my word,' said Prue.

The agent stood. 'Yes, the address is: Merangs Confectioners, 44 High Street, Buttersley. Postcode is …' He rattled off the details with aplomb.

I imagined him later, back at the office, recounting events and saying with pride, 'Well, it never leaves you, the training, you know. Once an estate agent, always an estate agent.'

Nodding, the agent added, 'Yes, yes ... I will. I'll stay here until they come. Yes, thank you. Cheerio then, bye.' Perhaps he'd not got his leave-taking quite right, but then again, who could throw out the exact *mot juste* in a stressful situation? He sank back into his seat as if his energy was all spent.

James, hovering in the connecting doorway, made an inappropriate remark about not expecting to find a dead body on a boring Wednesday. 'A Friday's more likely, don't you think, Prue? It's all gone a bit slack by then.'

I'd been about to say his flippancy annoyed me, but Prue shooed him away. Not knowing what to do with myself, I fidgeted. An unnatural pall descended. I wanted to ask about the body without seeming ghoulish. I turned to Malcolm, who was drumming his fingers on the table and clearing his throat every minute or so. He would be waiting for Prue to take the lead, but she was too discreet to enquire. As for the sisters – well, let's just say my expectations were low.

It wasn't just that I couldn't phrase a question, but my small-talk system had completely shut down. It must have been the shock; I couldn't even steady my knees.

Prue handed the agent a cup of tea.

'Very kind of you, Mrs Mayflower. Thank you.' He struggled to take the delicate china cup. Prue can't have been thinking straight. The cup would have been beyond his beefy hands at the best of times, but given they were shaking uncontrollably, it was just asking for trouble.

It came to me; the agent was called Mr Klondike. He bought violet creams now and then for his mother, who lived in a nursing home.

I was wondering whether to enquire after his mother when he exclaimed, 'Death! It seems to be following me around.' White-faced, he peered over his shoulder as if the Grim Reaper had arrived. 'Death!'

Once more, the sisters' hands fluttered to their throats. Malcolm's fingers didn't miss a beat, but Prue's cup rattled in its saucer.

'What do you mean, Mr Klondike?' I asked.

'Mother died last week. I found her in her chair. They say it comes in threes.'

I managed some vague, sympathetic noises, and Prue offered the correct condolences. After that, there was no more conversation. We had a long and uncomfortable wait. The sisters' sour hair smell was now hitting the back of my throat.

James had left the tea room door ajar. At last, we heard the bustle of officialdom, but it was still a shock when a policeman appeared.

'Yes, Constable?' Prue's tone reduced him to a bothersome boy scout at the door.

He was tall, early thirties – the right age for me and quite good-looking. I wanted to assure him I'd washed my hair only last night. His colleague followed. Who had teamed those two up together? The second officer's head bobbed around the midriff of the other. He still had an authoritative air with his radio and jangly accessories, but even so, a bad-tempered child could have pushed him to one side if necessary.

'Are you the one who reported the incident, sir?' The tall one directed the question to Malcolm, who had half risen from his seat.

Mr Klondike raised his hand like a child in class.

The officer nodded. 'If you'd like to come along with us, sir. We'll take a look at ... er, that which you have reported.'

'If you want me to accompany you as well, I could, ahem, you know, just ...' Malcolm tailed off, apparently not quite sure what he could offer.

'Please remain seated, sir. We may require you later for any further information that may assist our inquiries.'

Malcolm sat back in his seat, hands on knees, nodding sagely, as if at the hub of an FBI investigation. He'd be demanding witness protection next.

I knew it wasn't about me, but the tall one hadn't even looked my way. Maybe green-eyed brunettes with corkscrew curls were not his thing?

Mr Klondike stood, and they all trooped out through the fire door. An odd-sized gang; the tall, quite good-looking one could have stayed. I tried to make eye contact with Prue, hoping she'd shoo the sisters away. Surely, there was no need for *them* to stay? Malcolm wasn't a problem. He often irritated me and was usually in the way, but at the same time, he was a comforting presence.

Prue moved towards the kitchen. 'I'm going to make some fresh tea. They won't be long and they'll probably be hungry.'

They were hardly our menfolk returning from a hard day at the coal face, but all the same, I cut more cake. Heavy footsteps trampled once more overhead, and I stared anxiously at the chandelier, but the dripping had stopped. Prue was right: they were back soon.

Mr Klondike was shouting some sort of protest. He charged in, threw himself onto a chair, and held his hands out to Prue. 'They don't believe me, Mrs Mayflower.'

The policemen followed at a more measured pace. The tall one's eyes lit up at the refreshments. The small one was 'over and outing' on his radio. Malcolm stood to attention, and I thought he was going to salute. Helping themselves to slabs of chocolate cake, the officers sat down with their tea. Mr Klondike remained slumped in his chair. That didn't seem right. In reading too many crime novels, I expected more action. A sense of urgency perhaps: sirens, yellow tape, figures in white suits, a pop-up incident room set up in five seconds flat? Anything, but all we had were two PCs tucking into afternoon tea. The tall one was not quite so handsome when cramming cake into his mouth.

'We have what we call a fluid situation,' said the small officer.

Is he trying to be funny?

'What precisely do you mean, young man?' asked Prue.

'Well, to be precise, the body that Mr Klondike saw or thinks he saw is no longer there.'

Arse and Alien Investigate

I told James to shut the shop. Sacrilege I know, but I needed him in the tea room with me. Mr Klondike was slumped across two chairs, emitting faint whimpers. The Silent Sisters whispered to each other behind their hands, and Malcolm paced up and down with his hands behind his back.

The police were in no hurry to move it forward, so I decided to take charge. 'Can we just establish the basic facts? Someone was in the bath, dead or alive, with the water overflowing for so long, it flooded through the ceiling.' I pointed to the large damp patch to emphasise my point.

James plonked himself down beside me. 'Maybe he was just showing off, splashing around.'

'Not everyone's like you, James,' said Prue. She stood in front of Malcolm. 'Please sit down, dear. You're making us all dizzy.'

I tapped a spoon on a saucer to reclaim the attention. 'Mr Klondike went to check and reported a dead body in the bath.' I was getting into my stride now. 'Male or female, by the way?'

The police swivelled in their seats to face Mr Klondike. Had they not even established this?

He shuddered. 'Definitely male.'

'And would that correspond with the tenant?' I continued.

'Okay, Miss Marple, we'll take it from here,' said the tall, no longer attractive one.

'Well, men, look sharp,' said Prue. 'I shall be leaving in exactly fifteen minutes.'

Both officers looked towards her but didn't seem to know what to say. They weren't to know we were on the wrong side of a hair appointment. Each Monday and Thursday, Prue's stylist engaged in some heavy-duty backcombing of the beehive she'd had for over forty years. It used to be black but had turned a soft grey. As her hair had thinned, the height had increased, and I imagined the hairdresser's arms were like Popeye's. Prue was at her best when it had just been done. By Tuesday, the edifice had started to crumble, and by Wednesday afternoon, the hairstyle, as well as her patience, teetered on the edge of collapse.

Prue drummed her fingers on the table. 'The water started flowing through the ceiling at 11.30 a.m. I know nothing of the tenant, but if Mr Klondike says there was a dead body in the bath, I for one believe him.'

Mr Klondike flashed a quick smile of gratitude. It looked like she'd acquired another devotee for her collection. Malcolm spluttered. He would have wanted to agree with Prue, but, at the same time, needed to dismiss a potential rival.

The policemen exchanged a glance. The small one brushed crumbs from his mouth. 'For your information – and we don't have to share this with you members of the public – not only was no body present, but the plug had been pulled out.'

'I may be dim, but what's the significance of the plug?' I asked. 'The person wasn't dead, or you think someone else was there? Someone pulled the plug and moved him?'

'We will investigate all possibilities,' he replied. 'But we believe the man had fallen asleep in the bath, awoke with a start, realised he was late for an appointment and rushed out.'

'What, and failed to notice there was as much water sloshing around the floor as in the bath?' I tripped over my words in scorn.

The tall one intervened. 'As my colleague said, the man was in a rush, and in his haste may not have noticed the wet floor. Furthermore, upon a brief perusal of the flat, we saw evidence of what *we* like to call a chaotic lifestyle. Most of the rooms were in some degree of disorder.'

Even The Silent Sisters' crests fell at that. Maybe, like me, they'd embraced being on the sidelines of an accidental death, suicide or even murder, so to put it down to sloppy housekeeping was a massive anti-climax.

'You members of the public jump to dramatic conclusions,' the officer continued. 'Take it from me, there's usually an obvious and ordinary explanation.'

The small policeman rubbed his hands together. 'Yes, we could spend all day telling you instances when we've been called out on these false alarms. The public panics, and we respond.'

James laughed. 'If that's your strapline, you should have it printed on your truncheons or even tattooed somewhere?'

The officer glared at James. 'Only last week we were called to a house in, where was it, Andy?'

Ah, so the tall one's Andy.

'Preston Road. Listen, you'll just love this.' He shook his head as if he couldn't believe how funny his tale was going to be. 'A neighbour reported aliens and a medium-sized spaceship – medium-sized, mind, love the detail – in next door's drive. Turned out to be the finance company repossessing the car. Two blokes in hi-vis and a flat-bed recovery vehicle.' He laughed so hard, cake erupted from his mouth and littered his jacket.

The small one guffawed in harmony. 'It just goes to show,' he said.

Goes to show what? You should keep on top of your finance payments, or aliens don't wear hi-vis jackets?

Mr Klondike raised his head. 'The body in the bath wasn't an alien.'

A loud knock on the shop door interrupted their next tale from the panic stations of suburbia. Andy took it upon himself to answer, cake in hand as if he were at home in his slippers and pants. Prue's disapproval vibrated from the other side of the room. He returned with a lone paramedic and was giving him the lowdown on the missing tenant as they entered the tea room.

Ding dong, round three. Here we go again. It was getting to be quite a party, and I rather hoped the firemen would be next.

The police made half-hearted attempts to obtain information about the tenant, but we knew nothing about him. They could see for themselves that the flat's entrance was hidden from the shop. We could only offer that the tenant had a light tread on the stairs.

'I wouldn't know him if he walked in here naked and wet,' said James.

'I would know him anywhere after today,' countered Mr Klondike.

'I keep my eyes open, and I've never seen him,' said Malcolm.

At this point, Prue rose to leave. 'I can't abide this faffing around,' she muttered under her breath. I only caught it as that was her signature statement, produced with mounting exasperation throughout the day. She signalled her departure and sailed out of the room. The sisters followed like ducklings. Malcolm's doleful eyes tracked Prue's exit, and his shoulders slumped as she disappeared through the door.

Mr Klondike emerged from his stupor and announced he would be needed at the office. 'I will contact you tomorrow, Ms Merang, regarding any necessary repairs.' He handed me his card, collected the dregs of his dignity and left. Malcolm soon followed, just in case the cad was chasing after his beloved Prue.

That left just me and James with the emergency personnel. They'd reached the competitive anecdote stage by now, and I wanted them gone. Surely they were needed elsewhere?

James must have noticed my twitching. 'Right gents, it's been a ball, and you've been amazing, but let's not keep you from your civic duties.'

They looked up with suspicious eyes, perhaps not sure how to take him. Fortunately, they must have realised it was time to leave. Andy rose to his full height and said they'd be back later to check on the tenant. And that was that. We just had cake crumbs, dirty teacups, and a wet ceiling to show for the extraordinary non-event of the week.

Drained by it all, I wanted to go home. 'James, I'm just going to clear up and go.'

'Well, do what you have to do. We'll leave together. I'll read the paper while I'm waiting.'

'That's unusually thoughtful of you – to stay behind, I mean.'

'Don't be doing your usual forensic routine with a doll's toothbrush, though, as I haven't got the time.'

'So sorry. Am I keeping you from your microwave meal for one?'

'The sooner we leave, the sooner we go take a look.' He produced a set of keys and wore that smug look of his when he knows he's one in front.

I yelped and did a bit of Silent Sister hand fluttering. 'Are those the keys to the flat above? Where did you find them?'

'No, they're the keys to my box of delights, and it's your lucky night. Course they are.' He twirled the keys around. 'I swiped them when Klondike was comatose. I mean, not composed.'

My heart thumped. 'You don't intend to go up there?'

'We certainly do.'

Anxiety rose like bile in my throat. 'But why? You heard what the police said, and they're coming back.'

'Those two wouldn't know their arses from their aliens. I believe Klondike *did* see a dead body, and more to the point, Prue believed him too.'

He had me there. Prue's judgement was seldom wrong. I wasn't scared of what we might find, but what if we were discovered by either the police or the allegedly dead tenant? In the end, key-dangling James gave his winning smile, and my curiosity clinched the deal. I just wanted to see the flat over my shop. 'Come on then. Let's go before I change my mind.'

A Dress For Any Occasion

We walked to the end of the high street. It was an easy stroll for James, but I couldn't be so carefree.

'You look furtive,' he said.

'I can't help it. People know us.' I looked from side to side and back again. 'What if we're recognised?'

'We've just walked out of the shop. Don't customers expect to see us after closing?' His voice dripped scorn. 'Do they think you curl up under the counter, and I'm a life-sized jack-in-the-box?'

I glanced up at him. 'You could be in those crazy shirts you wear.'

'Well, you dress as if you really have slept under the counter.'

'Flamboyance is your middle name.'

'Stylish isn't yours.'

I winced. James squeezed my shoulder. He'd hit a sore point; I had let myself go. Prue had already given me the 'pull yourself together' talk. She said I was too young to stop trying.

As we neared the door of the flat, I poked James in the ribs. 'Stop! Don't go any further.'

He jumped as if I'd used a cattle prod. *Not quite so cool, then.* 'What now?'

'Here, put these on.' I'd grabbed gloves as we were leaving. 'Fingerprints.'

James didn't argue. In my haste, I'd selected the novelty washing-up ones for him. Fuchsia pink and black latex with faux diamond rocks and feathers around the elbows. They'd been donated by one of our customers. The gloves were far too big for me. I slipped on a discreet black pair.

James accepted the novelty ones without comment. From the set of keys, he selected the largest for the outside door. We stepped into a musty passageway. A dim, flickering sensor light revealed an encaustic tiled floor. We stood at the foot of an imposing, wide staircase with statement banisters and a faded carpet.

I followed James up the stairs. As we reached a bend about halfway up, a subtle play of light danced down from an arched window at the top. I'd often gazed at this window from the outside, as it had a distinct and graceful shape. The evening sun filtered through its leaded panes and decorated the landing in delicate pastel squares.

When we reached the top, I peeked in at the first door on the left. 'Wow, James. Look how grand it is.' I couldn't resist walking into the centre of the enormous room. The height of the skirting boards practically reached my knees, and I had to shield my eyes against the light streaming in through the church-style windows. James approached an elegant fireplace that dominated one long wall. A scruffy armchair and a tiny side table squatted beside it. He pointed and grimaced at the badly stained surface of the table.

'James, before you say anything, we are not here to criticise the tenant's taste in soft furnishings.'

The bathroom was on the opposite side of the landing. I tiptoed into another cavernous space that had a roll-top bath and a high-level cistern. 'Oh, how I'd love to live in this flat,' I said without thinking.

James poked his head around the door. 'If you're prepared to trample over a dead body, you probably could.'

'Well, he's obviously not in here. But the floor's still wet.'

James scratched his chin. 'If he dried himself in haste before his very important appointment, surely there'd be wet towels hanging around?'

I moved along to the small kitchen next door. It was modern and functional.

James followed me in and opened a cupboard door. 'The cupboard is bare. Looks like the tenant's as interested in cooking as you are.'

Pointing to the number of empty wine bottles on the worktop, I said, 'Obviously more a drinker than a foodie. Maybe that's what the police meant by a chaotic lifestyle?'

We crossed back to the other side of the landing and entered a small spare bedroom. It contained an unmade bed and nothing else.

I stepped into the next room and shrieked. James rushed in, bumped against my back and then laughed at our multiple reflections in the large, mirrored wardrobe. Pulling myself together, I moved further in and wrinkled my nose at the stale, frowsty smell. I wanted to open the window. A double bed stood against the wall. It looked like the sheets had been hastily dragged off, and a pile of clothes dumped on top. Underpants trailed on the floor. *Yuck.*

The wardrobe held only a few items. An overflowing laundry basket stood in the corner of the room. There were no arrows on the floor pointing to a dead body. It looked like the police were correct. We were totally in the wrong, and when it boiled down to it, just a couple of snoopers.

'James, I think we should go.' He didn't argue, so he probably felt just as uncomfortable.

As we were leaving, I noticed two smaller doors in the hallway. I opened the first, and something heavy fell out and knocked me down flat. It wasn't the ironing board. I screamed but couldn't move. A heavy, naked, dead man pinned me to the floor. I twisted my head around to locate James. My so-called friend was backing away, and this had all been his idea. I bellowed at him to rescue me.

He stopped mid-backtrack, but that was possibly due to a loud rap on the door. As James's newly green face swam above mine, I clenched my body to match the hardness of the one on top, closed my eyes, and forced my mind to go blank.

As if my predicament wasn't dire enough, it looked like Arse and Alien would be joining the party. They'd promised to return. After more knocking, silence prevailed for a few seconds. I breathed a sigh of relief. Then they found the doorbell from hell. Either they didn't want to let go, or it had stuck. How had the deceased put up with that demented chime?

The bell galvanised James, and he pulled me out from under the clammy corpse. It was reluctant to let me go. That wasn't my usual experience with men.

My whole body shook as if it would never stop. 'Shall we just ignore them and hope they go away?'

'Look around, will you? We've left every single light on. Even Arse and Alien might realise someone's at home.'

What a set of amateurs. I'd brought the gloves but left my wits behind.

James moved to the exit. 'I'll let them in while you sort yourself out.'

There was a lot to sort out. In the hallway mirror, I caught sight of a drip-white face, framed by a frizz of mad curls. Rivulets of mascara had merged with red lip gloss to create a rust-spotted chin. My dress was a crumpled, damp mess. 'A dress for any occasion,' the woman at the shop had said. She was wrong.

James soon returned with the police. He must have already filled them in on the details, as they didn't look shocked when confronted by the body.

The short one dived straight in with his criticism. 'You see, this is what happens when you members of the public start interfering.'

'What, and do your job for you?' I'd had enough of men by then, dead or alive.

'Tampering with the evidence. Disturbing the scene of a crime.' He couldn't get his accusations out quickly enough.

I wasn't having that. 'Why don't you get down from your high horse and admit you've been caught short?' How dare he come out with that pompous attitude when he and his streaky mate had failed to do a proper job?

James held out his hands. 'I think we need to calm down and discuss the elephant in the room.'

The officers exchanged puzzled looks. Maybe it was our apparent obsession with large mammals, or was it James's tarty gloves that posed the conundrum?

'He means the dead body you failed to find,' I said.

The short one pulled back his shoulders. 'That's not necessarily the case. We have yet to determine the chain of events.'

'Yes, my colleague is right. Please step into the living room. Touch nothing. We need to call this in.'

'Well, here's another nice mess you've gotten me into,' I said as soon as we were alone. James didn't react, which annoyed me. 'You can take your gloves off now, Liberace. They'll be slapping the handcuffs on soon.'

Tall Andy put his head around the door. 'Just waiting for backup. You'll either be taken down to the station or escorted back to Merangs to be questioned there. Depends on what the powers above decide.'

'Thanks,' I said. The fight had left me.

James had gone into his self-containment mode – choosing not to speak. My coping mechanism was to indulge in pointless chat, so we had no middle ground.

I sat on my hands to stop them from shaking and tried to erase the memory of the walrus-like mass that had almost suffocated me.

I wasn't worried about being arrested; James wouldn't allow that. And besides, they'd soon realise it had nothing to do with us. But what if our actions reflected badly on Merangs? I might have sabotaged my own business.

I'd no idea how long we waited before blue flashing lights lit up the room. It was a relief when Andy said we wouldn't have to go to the station. Two silent officers escorted us back to the shop and stood guard outside, while we awaited interrogation.

Dempsey and Makepeace

On TV, the police make the suspects wait around so they become anxious and bored. Were we suspects? But surely they didn't think we'd murdered the tenant? I'd hold my hands up to being nosy, but that was all. Back in the tea room, I settled in my seat and prepared for a long haul.

After two large gin and tonics from emergency supplies, I didn't care and was sliding down the chair. James sat upright, reading the newspaper as if finding dead bodies was all in a day's work.

I gingerly prodded my tender ribs. 'James, I may never be able to open a cupboard again. Do you think I'll need counselling?'

He didn't look at me. 'What?'

'I'm in shock. I may suffer flashbacks.'

James rattled his newspaper. 'You're outside the cupboard alive, not dead and shoved inside. Get over yourself.'

I needed more than tough love and wanted him to acknowledge the trauma and indulge me a little. When I didn't reply, he nudged my foot and topped up my gin. That would have to do.

I was wrong about the police tactics. It wasn't long before the Dempsey and Makepeace lookalikes arrived. The woman introduced herself as Detective Sergeant Snood and her colleague as Detective Inspector Swift. Her no-nonsense tone made me straighten in my seat.

Her hair was a dirty blonde mop. Probably a similar age to me, in her early thirties, she was built like a barrel on top but with legs like spindles. Prue would describe her as unkempt.

Swift stood tall and slim with dark, curly hair. Other than that, it was difficult to say, as a paisley scarf covered most of his face. I was going to offer them a drink, but Snood didn't give me a chance. She got right down to business.

When I said my name, she smirked. 'Is that spelt as in lemon meringue?'

'No. It's spelt as in the big letters on the front of the shop.' Arsey, I know, but she'd implied I was a pie.

She pressed a pen hard against her notebook. As she turned to James, her expression softened. Familiarity had made me forget his classic good looks, and admiring glances always surprised me.

Snood requested background information about us and then moved on to our knowledge of the tenant. 'Come on, you must know something. Or was he the invisible man?' She barked out a laugh.

I wanted to snap that he was invisible to their officers, but I said, 'As we told your colleagues, we know nothing about him.'

Her dull brown eyes bored into my face. 'Yes, PC Pole said you were unhelpful and uncooperative.'

The cheek. After all that bloody cake he'd scoffed.

'Have you identified the man in the cupboard as definitely the tenant, then?' asked James.

Snood jutted out her lips. 'We do not have to share that information with you members of the public.'

Here we go again. Is this a mantra they chant before leaving the police station?

'So, how come you had the keys to the flat,' she asked, 'if you didn't know the tenant?' Without waiting for an answer, Snood added, 'In fact, how do we know you didn't regularly pop up there whenever you felt like snooping around?' She jabbed at the notebook.

'How does one prove a negative?' said James.

'Answer my question, please.' Snood pointed the pen as if she wanted to stab him between the eyes. She hadn't taken long to go off him. 'How did you come to have the keys?'

James examined his nails. 'We found them.'

'Really?' She rolled her eyes like a teenager. Not a good look on her.

'Mr Klondike, the estate agent, dropped them on his way out. He'll confirm they're missing.' James answered with more confidence than I would have shown.

'Okay, we'll go with that,' she said in a silly sing-song voice. 'So, it was, "oh look, the keys to the flat. Let's play detective"?' She resumed her normal voice. 'What did you expect to find?'

'A dead body.' James smiled as if confirming the weather was mild for the time of year.

'Why, when the investigating officers had found no trace?'

I leant towards her. 'So, are you saying, Sergeant Snood, there wasn't a dead body when they looked, but it came along later? Or, did someone take it away, after the estate agent left, before the police arrived, and then popped it back again?'

'Leave us to ascertain the chain of events. You've done more than enough for one evening. You've contaminated a crime scene, possibly destroyed vital evidence, and because I can't believe any responsible citizen would be so cavalier, I'm tempted to think this was your intention.'

My hackles rose. 'We were just trying to help.'

'Help with what, or was it about helping yourselves?' When Snood raised her voice, tiny pools of spittle formed at the sides of her mouth and ran down her chin. At that rate, she was going to end up a one-woman waterfall. 'You let yourselves in, but how did you know the tenant wasn't already in?'

I shifted in my seat. My damp dress was clinging too closely. 'Well, he *was* in. In the cupboard, as a matter of fact.'

Plum-coloured patches spread across Snood's cheeks. I hadn't meant to provoke her, but it was late, and we were going around in circles. I yawned, tried to stop and ended up choking. I stood and bent forward. James thumped my back, and four sugar cubes sprang out of my bra, tumbled over the top of my dress and landed on the table. Snood's mouth opened, and DI Swift's eyebrows rose from the depths of his scarf.

'What the ...?' exclaimed Snood.

I'd struggled to open a box of sugar earlier and thought some lumps had gone astray. My padded bra must have cushioned them during the clinch with the corpse. I snatched them up. 'It's not a party trick, and I don't pop anything out from anywhere else.' Why the hell did I say that?

Snood snorted. 'God help us.'

Was that like living in a police state where everything was deliberately misconstrued? I had a fear of answering questions from those in authority. It went back to a scary teacher at primary school. Whenever she spoke, my mind went blank.

James had inherent self-assurance. You'd think he was heir to a fortune and had attended Eton. Had he not sat next to me in class, even I'd have been fooled. He retained his hand on my back. 'Where's this going, Sergeant Snood? We've told you all we can. It's been a hard day, and we'd like to go home. We won't leave town.'

Snood closed her notebook. 'We'll need statements from you tomorrow and also your fingerprints. Here's my card, should you remember anything more helpful than the information you've provided this evening.'

She wasn't the type of woman to flounce out of a room. It was more like a charge at the door. The DI uncurled himself from the chair and followed without speaking. How rude. And what was he doing to earn his money? As he passed through the doorway, I held out the keys to the flat. He took them without a word.

I usually walked home from work, but James insisted on giving me a lift. As we entered the street, my house stood dark and reproachful. James drew up and unclipped his seat belt.

'It's okay; you don't have to see me in. I'll be fine.'

'If you're sure?' He raised his eyebrows.

Not wanting to be needy, I smiled. He pecked my cheek and drove off. As soon as he'd gone, I started to shake again and could hardly get the key in the door.

The house was cold and the cupboards bare. I'd planned to buy something on my way home. I'd got used to living alone, but sometimes it would have been nice to return to a strong pair of arms and a cooked meal. I burst into tears of self-pity, those big, wrenching sobs that come from deep down.

I gave up the idea of food and had a long, hot shower to wash away all traces of dead bodyness and then went straight to bed. My last thoughts were of the victim. Who was he? Did anybody care? How could we find out? And – just before I dropped off – why did someone move the body?

Here's Lucy

Thursday 16th April

I woke refreshed and ready to wrestle a tiger. I couldn't think why I'd got so upset last night. Being crushed by a naked dead man was not an experience I'd recommend, but these things happened. Life throws you a curveball now and again.

The sun shone brightly, and all was well until I looked in the mirror. Apart from the normal, scary, bed-head curls, my eyes had sunk into deep, dark holes. Had I been gouging them with my fists while asleep? I slapped on concealer, mascara, and extra bright lipstick to balance the eye troughs and was ready to roll.

I adored opening Merangs each morning. The first hit of the vanilla, chocolate, and coffee aroma was like a hug from a loved one. I stood for a moment, listened to the reassuring hum of the fridges and then flicked on the lights.

In planning the shop, I'd gone for looks over practicality. The glass cabinets and mirrors transformed our products into edible, glistening jewels, but they were a nightmare to maintain. It would reduce old Sisyphus himself to tears some days.

James arrived just as I'd finished wiping the glass. He didn't want to talk. His subdued mood was not reflected by his shirt choice – a turquoise, orange, and pink chequerboard. I left him to brood over his double espresso in the shop while I busied about in the tea room.

The police were due anytime to take our fingerprints and statements. Fine, as long as it wasn't Snood or the Arse-and-Alien tag team. I wondered about the identity of the tenant. If only we could pin a name on him, it might give him some dignity. It saddened me that he was just an object of inconvenience.

I heard James greeting someone in the shop. It would be Lucy, our other part-timer, who worked alternate days to Prue. A minute later, she fluttered through to the tea room.

'Morning, boss. How are you after the *goings-on* yesterday?' There was no point in my asking how she knew. In Buttersley, every *goings-on* was logged, shared, and embellished. We all did it.

Lucy tilted her heart-shaped face towards me and widened her china-blue eyes. Every time I looked at Lucy, I could see no bad in the world.

'Fine, thanks. I'll tell you the gory details later. What have you heard?'

'Well, Malcolm and Mr Klondike had a fight in the flat upstairs over a plumbing problem. They crashed through the ceiling onto The Silent Sisters, who are going to sue. Later on, the police found a strange couple up there having sex in the bathroom. The man was wearing a kinky outfit, had a heart attack and died. You were somehow injured, and the police are coming round later to arrest both you and James.'

I'd expected no less. 'All the gossip means we'll be extra busy.' I thought about asking Prue to come in, but didn't want to impose on her day off.

'Don't worry, we'll manage.' Confident words from the seventeen-year-old part-timer. While she sailed through the busiest times with an angelic smile, I became frazzled and grim. Lucy had the gift of making everyone feel special, so they all wanted a part of her. While she was held captive at each table she served, I chased around the rest and faced the disappointment of the customers who had wanted Lucy in the first place.

'You were right about one thing,' I said. 'A man, probably the tenant, has died.'

Lucy shot a delicate hand to her mouth. 'Not Vincent?'

'Vincent's the name of the tenant? How do you know?'

'I see him in Mr Choudray's when I buy my mum's lottery tickets. Vincent's a lovely man. We always have a chat.'

Her face crumpled, and tears ran down her face. James walked in and retreated when he saw the state of Lucy. I enfolded her in my arms and allowed her to wet my shoulder. It was touching that someone cared for Vincent. It took a while for the sobs to subside, but eventually, she drew away and gave a weak, apologetic smile. After all that emotion, I'd have looked like a wreck, but Lucy was all the more beguiling. Her eyes glistened Prussian blue with thick, spiky lashes.

I didn't tell her Vincent had been shoved in a cupboard; just that he'd been found dead in suspicious circumstances. I asked when she'd last seen him. Once over the shock, she wanted to talk.

'It was on Monday at the newsagents. He was arguing with Mr Choudray about money. Mr Choudray was very annoyed, but Vincent seemed to be laughing it off. Will I have to tell the police that? What if they arrest poor Mr Choudray? Oh no, he always gives me a free sherbet lemon, and his wife's so lovely.'

As she was speaking, the police arrived. Lucy scuttled into the kitchen. It was a plainclothes duo who were efficient and discreet. They processed James and me before the tea room rush. As they were about to leave, Prue popped in, and then Malcolm appeared in response to her siren call. The police took their statements, and that was it, all done and dusted, a chapter closed. An unfortunate incident that we could put behind us.

As predicted, we were extra busy, and Prue stayed on to help. All ten tables were constantly full. Punctuated by the chink of china, the tea room buzzed. The familiar, contented din was up there in my all-time favourite top-ten sounds. There was an air of expectancy and a quiver for information. Malcolm strutted around, lapping up the attention, recounting his version and covering himself in glory.

Full-on-Dora was especially attentive, but then she could enthuse over a bag of wet fish. 'Did you, Malcolm?' she gushed. 'You're such a man of steel.' She circled her fingers around his arm and pretended to swoon. If only Malcolm could see that Dora was his for the taking, but he only had eyes for Prue.

'Yes, lucky I was here,' said Malcolm, 'but Helen knows she can count on me in a crisis.'

I patted his shoulder, and his chest swelled. He moved on to impress others, and Dora flopped. She rallied when Lucy stopped for a chat, and Prue admired her hair.

Prue was willing to stay for as long as needed, so after the rush, I sent Lucy to the newsagents to chat up Mr Choudray for the low-down on Vincent. I did say the matter was closed, but I wanted to add the final full stop.

I updated James about Vincent. He shook his head and said, 'My mother told me the tenant was female.' This threw me, as Mrs Jones operated in the top tier of the local information exchange, and her intelligence was usually of the highest quality.

'Why didn't you tell me?' I said, my thoughts whirling around.

'I'm telling you now.' He tapped on the counter. 'And you've only just mentioned this Vincent character.'

'Mr Klondike didn't say the tenant was a woman.' My voice had become shrill. 'And ...' I shuddered, 'the body was definitely male.'

'That might not have been the tenant. Anyway, forget it. It's not our business.'

I seethed. How typical of James. He had a laser focus when interested but quickly became bored. 'You made it our business when you dragged me upstairs and we found a dead man. Aren't you curious?' I demanded as he yawned. 'Okay, I won't bother you with the details when Lucy gets back.' I wouldn't tell him either about my intention of visiting the estate agents to see what I could find out there.

Lucy returned with a mouth full of sherbet lemons. 'Mr Choudray has written down the details. Vincent had an account for his cigarettes and hasn't paid for months. On Monday he said he was coming into money and would settle up soon. Oh, Helen, poor Mr Choudray was devastated to hear Vincent's died. He's such a caring man. He asked if you could let him know where to send Vincent's bill?'

The note gave a full name, Vincent Newby, his address as the flat and a mobile phone number. I would think about that later. Meanwhile, while we still had Prue, I wanted to visit the estate agents to see what Mr Klondike had to say about the tenant.

The King is in His Castle

Although Mr Klondike's office faced Merangs, I'd never been inside. I pushed open the heavy door and stepped into a dismal, grey office. There was no reception; just two desks pushed together, a few chairs, and a partitioned area at the back with semi-opaque windows and panels below. The place had all the appeal of a prison waiting room.

Two women sat at the desks under a stark fluorescent strip light. The younger one wore false eyelashes, and the older one, fierce, heavy glasses. They were discussing a TV cookery show and did not break off.

I stood for a minute in the middle of the room with no acknowledgement. Prue would not put up with this, I thought. 'Excuse me.' Louder than intended, my words dropped like a grenade. The women fell silent and stared. 'Is Mr Klondike available, please?'

The older one consulted a diary and then peered at me over the top of her glasses. 'You don't have an appointment.'

'No, you're right, but he's half-expecting me.'

She sniffed. 'He's very busy today. I'll see if he can fit you in. Take a seat.'

He's hardly the President in the Oval Office, I wanted to say, but of course, I didn't and obediently sat. She didn't do anything except flick through the papers on her desk.

The younger one picked up a magazine and read out a list of celebrities who'd gone down the route of buttock enhancement. The strip light hummed like a thousand angry wasps, and the minutes ticked by on an ancient clock.

I thought of all the things I could be doing and said, 'Excuse me, I'm still waiting,' in my loud voice.

The women exchanged a look. The older one tutted and picked up her phone. An extension rang inside the partition. 'Mr Klondike, there's a woman here to see you.'

They both turned to look at the partition. Behind the frosted glass, a large head bobbed into view like a queer sort of moon. The head had no visible means of support, and it took me a second or so to realise it was attached to a body concealed by the panels. The women sniggered, and I felt sorry for Mr Klondike. From what I saw yesterday, he'd be just the sort to suffer petty humiliations by those two harpies.

Mr Klondike opened the door and beckoned me over. 'Ms Merang, come through. How are you, my dear?' He ushered me in as if we were long-lost friends.

I'd been worried he would resent my unauthorised entry into the flat, but by the warmth of his welcome, it seemed I was wrong.

The tiny office barely held his considerable frame. It had no window, and the air hung stale. Although squashed behind a desk that cut into his middle, and with no room to swing a kitten, Mr Klondike reigned in his kingdom. From his fold-up chair, he emanated benevolent good humour.

He gestured to a stool at the side of his desk. 'Don't you worry about the damage to your tea room, Ms Merang. I've been in liaison with the owner of the flat, and they've given me full *carte blanche* to authorise all necessary repairs and refurbishment.'

I put a hand to my chest and sighed as if he'd removed a ten-ton weight. 'Thank you, Mr Klondike. That's such a relief.' He smiled and patted my hand. 'Have the police been to see you?' I asked.

He chuckled into his tie. 'They have indeed. What a turn-up. To think those two idiots doubted me when I was right all along.'

'*We* believed you. That's why James and I went up later and made our unfortunate discovery.' I shuddered at the memory of that cold, heavy corpse. Do you think the body we found is the tenant?'

Mr Klondike shook his large head. 'Highly unlikely from the records I hold.'

He was so emphatic, I realised James was right, and the tenant must be a woman. 'Perhaps the tenant was sub-letting?' I forced my eyes to widen. 'Or do you think they had a lodger? Maybe the body was that of a relative or friend?'

'I really couldn't speculate, my dear, and I can't disclose any information due to data protection and *sub judice*.' He lingered on the legal term, in case his dip into the world of jurisprudence had gone unnoticed. 'What I *would* say, though, here at Klondike Estates, sub-letting is not tolerated.

We say no, no and no again.' Just in case I was unfamiliar with the word no, he vigorously shook his head and wagged a finger on each repeat.

Smothering my frustration, I smiled. It was time to poke at his professional instincts. 'Mr Klondike, I hope you don't think I'm being indelicate, but yesterday when I was in the flat, I couldn't help but notice its well-appointed features before I found the b ...' I broke off for a bit of lip-trembling. 'Anyway, I was just wondering, if it was the tenant – and now I know it wasn't, but all the same – I was thinking perhaps due to the unfortunate circumstances, you might be reletting the flat?' I knew I'd waffled and there was a bit for him to unpack, but he'd have got my drift.

Mr Klondike abruptly shifted in his chair, causing the wall to shudder. Holding his hands over the keyboard of a vintage computer, he took a deep breath and then plunged all his sausage fingers down at once. They were surprisingly nimble. It was all for show. He'd have been all over that file as soon as he left Merangs. 'Just let me see what I can find here. Yes, just as I thought, the existing lease expires at the end of the month. I can put you down as an interested party?' He pitched his voice higher with the suggestion.

'That would be great. Thanks.' *I can say I've changed my mind if necessary.* I coughed excessively. 'Sorry, I'm feeling a bit under the weather. I think it's all the trauma from yesterday and seeing that gruesome ...'

His face creased in concern. 'Oh, my dear, what must you be thinking? I've not even offered you a drink. I'll see if one of the girls can rustle something up.' He picked up his phone and jabbed at the numbers. It rang in the main office but remained unanswered. 'They must be busy with clients.' He stood, and papers toppled to the floor. Squeezing past a filing cabinet, he poked his head out the door and called, 'Elvira, Pansy,' repeating it with a hopeful rise in his voice as if calling in his cats. Judging by the attitude of those two earlier, there was more chance of a stray coming in off the street to make us a drink. 'I'll just go see what's what. Would tea be acceptable?'

'That would be lovely, Mr Klondike. Thank you very much.'

No doubt he would be making it himself, so I'd have the time to gather all the information I needed. He'd left the flat's file open, and I clicked through as many screens as I could, taking photos with my phone. By the time I heard his heavy tread, I was back in my seat – guilt-ridden but exhilarated.

'Here we are, two cups of tea, and I've even managed to locate a couple of biccies.' He'd spilt tea down his shirt but beamed with pride. My heart went out to him.

'Well, I've brought you a little gift as you were such a help yesterday.' I handed him a box of Merangs' truffles. I would have liked to add the rider that he gave none to the two cats out there.

We had a pleasant chat, and I related all the details about finding the body. Somehow, we got onto the subject of his late mother.

'We were everything to each other, Ms Merang. I do miss her so, but at least I have my work.' He swept his arm around and brushed a wall with the back of his hand.

I searched for something to divert him from his grief. 'You've got quite a set-up here, Mr Klondike.'

'Thank you, my dear. It keeps me out of mischief.' He chuckled. 'Of course, I have Elvira, my office manager. She keeps me on the straight and narrow.'

'And Pansy, what does she do?'

He pressed a finger to his lips. 'She, er, she helps Elvira.'

I rose to leave and told him that Prue had said to pass on her regards. His eyes lit up. I added that he would be very welcome anytime at Merangs. I'd make sure we made a fuss of him, as I doubted he got much of that in his life. He accompanied me to the door. The two desks were empty. Did Pansy and Elvira come and go as they pleased? Mr Klondike didn't comment on their absence.

I hurried back to Merangs, guilty at being away for so long. The shop lights shone like beacons. As I crossed the road, I took a quick peek at the name of the tenant, a Mrs Claudia Easby. I knew that name, but where from? It rang a faint bell from somewhere back in the past.

All in a Day's Twerk

I wanted to march up to James, stick out my tongue and taunt him with, 'You don't know what I know.' But he would only feign indifference, and then I'd be bursting to tell him and blurt it out anyway. I'd felt like a real detective, employing my diversionary tactics to find out the tenant's name, but during the short walk back to the shop, I thought, so what? James was probably right. It wasn't our business.

Back at Merangs, they'd hardly noticed I'd gone. James was filling up the truffle cabinet, and Prue and Lucy were cleaning the tea room. Malcolm held a mop, waiting for an order.

I decided to keep the information I'd discovered to myself, to be discreet and not rush into anything. 'Mr Klondike sends his best regards to you, Prue.'

Malcolm slammed the mop into its bucket.

Prue raised her head from the sink. 'So, young lady, what did your sharp little nose dig up over there?'

'Oh Prue, I love it when you call me young lady.'

Lucy giggled.

Prue wagged a finger at her. 'Be quiet, child.'

I joined Prue at the sink. 'I just went over to discuss the repairs.'

She looked me straight in the eye. 'My hairnet you did.'

James wandered into the tea room for his last espresso of the day. 'Steady on, Prue, you'll be getting Malcolm all worked up again.'

Prue flared her nostrils, Malcolm gripped his mop, and Lucy tried not to laugh.

'Does the name Claudia Easby mean anything to anyone?' My discretion had just flown out the window.

'Wasn't there a girl at school with that surname?' James asked. 'Why do you want to know?'

I toyed with not telling him, but said, 'She's the official tenant of the murder flat.'

'That means absolutely nothing to me,' said Prue, 'and I don't know why you're being so silly over this business. A man has been killed, and the police will find the perpetrator in due course. It's nothing whatsoever to do with us.' She removed her rubber gloves. 'I'm leaving now. I need to buy a zip.'

'Indeed, what could be more important than that?' called James as she hurried away. I would have to phone her later with my thanks for helping out on her day off.

Lucy turned to Malcolm, 'Have *you* heard the name?' She gazed at him as if her life depended on his response. Bless her for trying to take the sting out of Prue's departure. How could he resist Lucy's full-beam attention?

Malcolm narrowed his eyes, sucked at his teeth, and with finger and thumb pressed against his forehead, gave the impression of rummaging through vast receptacles in his mind. 'It does sound vaguely familiar, but I wouldn't swear to anything,' he finally pronounced.

I patted him on the back. 'It might come to you later, Malcolm, when you're not thinking about it. When you're at home, watching the telly.' Like a mother at a party, I wrapped some cake for him and sent him on his way.

'Just a bit more cleaning and then we're done, Helen,' said Lucy as James retreated into the shop.

I enjoyed hard work, but cleaning the same area night after night was dispiriting and wearisome. To alleviate the boredom, Lucy and I pretended we were in a girl band when wiping the tables. She was showing me how to twerk when James stuck his head around the door.

'Come and join us, James. I'm channelling my inner goddess.'

He averted his eyes. 'Doesn't look like that from where I'm standing. Just to let you know, I've invited us round to my mother's for tea this evening, so you can tap into her knowledge of Claudia Easby. I've checked and she recognises the name.'

'Brilliant, James. Thanks. You're not as bad as everyone says.' The evening was looking up. Not only would Mrs Jones have details about Claudia, but she was also a wonderful cook. 'We'll be finished in twenty minutes.'

Lucy stood in front of me, hands on hips, shouting her instructions. 'Helen, you need to squat down further. That's it. Stick your bum out more: in out, in out.' I grunted with the effort. My thighs burned. 'Look like you're enjoying it. Smile confidently as if you know how sexy you are.' I tried. 'Oh Helen, that's not what I meant.' Lucy giggled. 'Start again. Look over your shoulder and show some attitude. Keep it low and pulse those thighs.'

Muffled voices in the shop undercut her instructions. *Strange, I thought we were closed.*

'Just go through. She's expecting you,' said James's distant voice.

The door opened. Lucy squealed, and I found myself leering over my shoulder at Sergeant Snood and Inspector Swift. Under the circumstances, it took a moment to register they'd both had a makeover. Snood wore a smart suit, make-up, and nearly looked nice. Swift, also in a suit, was carrying a briefcase. Was I always destined to humiliate myself in front of those two? My face sizzled, and I gulped. Don't apologise, don't explain, someone famous said – or was it, don't complain or explain? Whichever, it was the optimum time to refrain from either.

'Please take a seat.' I smoothed down my skirt. 'I'll be with you in a moment. My colleague will bring refreshments.' I showed them to a table as if they were special guests at the queen's garden party.

'Lay it on thick,' I whispered to Lucy, as I dashed to the toilet. For the second time that day, I confronted the mirror monster. A few strands of hair clung to my forehead, but the rest was a nebula, light-years away. I carried out emergency repairs until my complexion had reduced to an enthusiastic glow, and the hair had regrouped. I still burned with embarrassment.

Snood and Swift were deep in conversation when I returned. Lucy had served a large cafetiere, teapot, hot and cold milk, cream, soft drinks, mineral water and a tasting platter of cakes.

DI Swift looked up and smiled. 'Sorry to intrude on your ...' he cleared his throat, 'on, er, your routine, Ms Merang, but we thought to update you on the case and clear up a little matter with Mr Jones while we're here.'

What could they want with James? I called him in. We both squeezed in at their table as if out on a double date. Lucy had already melted away.

'First of all, I must apologise for yesterday evening,' continued the DI. 'I'd just had emergency dental work and wasn't quite with it.' Swift flashed a smile that was right up there in the dazzle league. He could certainly give James a run for his money. 'Also, there's been a change in personnel,' he said. 'The department's extremely short-staffed, and I'm now Acting Chief Inspector, as from twenty minutes ago. I've come straight from the briefing, actually.' He grinned like a boy who'd won at conkers.

Should we offer our congratulations? Perhaps I could twerk?

'More pertinent to this case, and also to yourselves, let me introduce Acting Inspector Snood, who's now in charge of the day-to-day operations on the murder case.'

Cancel that twerk.

James smiled at Snood. 'It could not have happened to a nicer person.'

Snood's upper lip twitched, and a tiny leak started in the lower right corner.

Swift loosened his tie, sat back in his seat, and started on the cakes and coffee. 'Thanks for the lavish refreshments. Excuse me if I wolf it all down. I've just realised I've not eaten all day.' Prue would have clucked at this and rushed off for more.

So far, Snood hadn't spoken. She sipped a glass of water. I looked towards her. 'We should be offering you champagne, Acting Inspector.'

She put down her water as if it were laced with arsenic. 'I don't drink alcohol.'

Swift's mobile buzzed. He glanced at the screen and, with a wistful look at the table, said he had to leave. I repeated my mother-at-a-party act and sent him away with his briefcase full of cake.

No sooner had he left, Snood started. 'Just to let you know, there's a PC waiting in the shop, should I need him.' Was that her idea of an icebreaker? She leant towards James. 'We see you're known to the police, Mr Jones, and not just in this country.'

I'd have been less shocked if she'd slapped me. James had been my best friend for twenty-odd years since we first sat together at primary school. I'd no idea he was an international criminal. Did his mother know? The only time we lost contact was after university when he lived abroad for two years. When I saw him again, he had a minor limp, and I had a husband.

James raised his brow. 'I hardly see that's relevant, Acting Inspector.'

Snood stood her ground. 'In a murder case, everything is relevant.'

Fair Point.

She raised her voice. 'You've used violence in the past.'

It gets worse. I didn't know he had it in him. The worst I could say of James – he was a merciless and creative tormentor. At school, he used to stick paper and sweet wrappers to my curls and give me paperclip extensions. I was an avant-garde installation before I was six years old.

'Arrest me then.' James held out his hands with his wrists together.

'You can't arrest him. We're going to his mother's for tea.'

Snood flicked her eyes at me as if I were a buzzing fly. I wanted to rewind and assert with simple dignity that James was not a violent man.

She focused back on James. 'Don't be ridiculous. I've not come to arrest you, but there are questions for you to answer.'

'Acting Inspector Snood, I'm all yours. What do you want to know?'

Feasting With Panthers

Snood placed her elbows on the table, jutted out her jaw and stared at James. 'Do you still maintain the tenant was unknown to you, Mr Jones?'

'Not totally unknown.'

Snood gave a sly, knowing smile and moved in closer. If she wasn't careful, she'd end up in his lap. 'Would you say you were intimately connected?'

Not as much as you will be, love, if you don't back off. My eyes followed them as in a riveting game of tennis.

James curled his lip. 'I wouldn't put it quite like that.'

'So what exactly was the nature of your relationship with the tenant?'

I jumped right in. 'He didn't know him.'

Snood continued to focus on James and ignored me.

'Claudia Easby was an acquaintance of my mother's, many years ago.' James offered a candid, open smile. Snood snorted and folded her arms. 'I'm not sure if Vincent Newby was in this circle of friends,' James continued. 'I could ask my mother for you.'

'It's your circles I'm concerned with, not your mother's.'

'All these circles are making me dizzy,' I said. 'Do you know, by the way, Acting Inspector, what Vincent was doing in Claudia's flat?'

Snood's eyes flicked towards me, and she relieved her irritation with another snort. 'Mr Jones, I won't beat about the bush. How intimate were you with Vincent Newby? You were unaware of his existence yesterday, but now you confess to knowing his full name.'

James nodded. 'Yes, I must confess to that.'

'I confess also,' I said in solidarity.

'And the rest, Mr Jones.' Snood had a gleam in her eyes and a voice thick with saliva.

James and Vincent intimate? What sort of information did they have on him? Would Snood accuse me next of crushing on her? I shuddered.

James placed his hands on the table and brought his face up to Snood. 'Are you insinuating that Vincent and I were lovers, had a tiff, and I nipped upstairs to murder him because I'm a violent criminal and that's what I do?'

She didn't flinch. 'That's not unfeasible.'

I wanted to get in on the act. 'He doesn't have a lunch hour.' Pretty weak, but it's all I could manage with a mind reeling in shock.

James stood and pushed the table away. 'I may have enjoyed some ripe altercations in my salad days, but that doesn't mean I feast with panthers, nor does it make me a murderer.'

Snood opened her mouth, held up a finger, but didn't speak or even snort. The salad-eating panthers must have confused her as much as they'd thrown me. A natural pugilist, she'd marched straight in, fists flying. The promotion must have gone to her head. James, apart from being my friend, was technically my employee, and she'd hurled all sorts of accusations at him. Riveting as it was, she should have done all that in private. I rose and stood beside James.

'Acting Snood, you are harassing my employee on some flimsy, tenuous nonsense. Neither of us has any connection with Vincent Newby, other than finding his dead body for you. As for discovering his name, mobile number, and the real tenant's details, that was easy, but you seem to take it as an admission of guilt.'

Snood leapt from her seat. 'I will remind you, this is a murder enquiry, and we don't have time to massage your precious egos ...' She stopped as if her thoughts had caught up. 'What are you doing with his mobile number? Give it to me, so I can see if it ...' she grasped for words, 'matches our records.'

Match their records, my arse. 'I don't know what I've done with it.' I looked around as if I were ninety, and had mislaid my glasses for the umpteenth time. 'Oh dear, where did I put it?'

Snood raised a hand to her temple. 'Can you really be that feeble-minded?'

'Yes, she can,' said James, back in helpful mode. 'Don't you have it anyway? Did you not find his mobile phone in the flat?'

'I'm not at liberty to disclose that information to—'

'You members of the public.' We joined in the chorus.

Snood clenched her fists. 'You've not yet told me where you got the number from, and if you would hurry up and find it ... in fact, as soon as you do, I'll be on my way.' A note of anxiety had crept into her voice.

I felt mean. She was, no doubt, under all sorts of pressure and was probably hoping to prove herself on this case. 'Oh, look,' I said. 'I've stored it in the contacts on my phone. I'll text it to you. As for how we got it – if you've lived in Buttersley for any length of time – do you really need to ask?' I sent her the number, which I'd rung several times. It had always gone straight to voicemail.

Snood checked her phone. 'I'm not satisfied with your explanations, and I'm warning you now, I'll be keeping an eye on you both.'

'Fabulous,' said James, like he'd won a tacky prize at the fair. 'We'll sleep safely in our beds. Feel free to drop in for a glass of water any time.'

Snood barged at the connecting door, and I accompanied her through to the main shop, where a constable snapped to attention. Her actions puzzled me. Surely, she couldn't have much on James when she'd let it go so easily?

When I returned to the tea room, James was flicking through a magazine.

'What did you make of that?' I asked. I couldn't bring myself to mention Snood's accusations; it would be like asking your parents if they enjoyed an active sex life. I'd leave it to the appropriate, drink-fuelled moment to uncover his secret past.

James shrugged as if it were all too much of a bore. If he was going to play it like that, I would overcome my reticence and poke a big stick. I repeated my question.

'It merely shows they've made no progress with the case.' He returned his head to the magazine.

I wanted to shake him. 'Aren't you bothered Snood's accused you of being Interpol's Most Wanted, with a penchant for middle-aged men?'

'Sticks and stones and all that. Who cares what Snood says?' It would have been easier to prise open a clam. James placed the magazine on the table and folded his arms. 'Put another record on.'

I smiled at his use of a phrase from our youth. 'Okay, what sort of day have you had?'

'I got trapped by a regular. Do I look like I'm interested in the storage of biscuits? Mrs McKenna spent an hour telling me she has three separate biscuit tins with a detailed description of each. Could I guess what she puts in them? Could be her husband's scrotum for all I care.' He groaned. 'God, how boring.'

I knew what he meant. Merangs could drain us all. Those in the market for sugar-based products often had need of a sympathetic ear. James didn't have the patience, but, according to Prue, he was hoisted with his own petard. Beguiled by his professional charm, the loquacious and lonely seized the opportunity to confide.

'How *does* she organise her biscuits, then?' I asked to get my own back for his reticence. 'I'm interested.'

'I can't share that information with you members of the public,' he said in a fair imitation of Snood's gruff tones. We both laughed, and the slight awkwardness between us dissipated. But the daily banalities took their toll. James was due for a meltdown anytime soon.

As I finished the cleaning, I pondered further over James and his ways. He'd never been short of admirers. In high school, the girls formed a queue, and he went through them like skittles. Some pretended to be my friend. I was never jealous, as I knew they meant nothing to him. It would be different perhaps if he embarked on a serious relationship, but there was no point dwelling on that. Anyway, according to Snood, he'd broadened his horizons, but I found that impossible to believe.

I put on my coat. 'James, do you still want to go round to your mother's?'

'Of course. She's expecting us.'

'Come on then, let's get going before the bounty hunters ride into town.'

At Home With the Jones'

We drove in comfortable silence, with the evening news a soothing background noise. James had a fancy car, the make of which eluded me, but I appreciated the luxurious leather seats.

I must have nodded off as I awoke with a jolt when we stopped in the old, familiar street. Mr and Mrs Jones had lived in the same pebble-dashed house forever. Having spent much of my childhood exploiting their hospitality, my heart swelled at coming home.

Mrs Jones threw open the door and held out welcoming arms. 'Helen, love, it's lovely to see you. Come in, come in. You're looking as pretty as ever. Here, put these slippers on. I've been saving them for you. You'll be wanting a cup of tea. I know I do. Henry, kettle, please. What about a drop of sherry? Jimmy, what are you doing? Shut the door. You're letting in all the cold. We can't afford to heat the whole street. That boy has no common sense.' She stopped to draw breath.

It had been too long since I'd last seen Mrs Jones. The smile on her wide, jowly face was as warm as ever. Her big, solid hug lifted me off the floor.

'Sorry to turn up at such short notice,' I said as she put me down.

'We're delighted to have you. Looks like you need a good meal inside you. You're much too thin and scrawny. Henry, look, doesn't she need some meat on those bones? Just look at those sparrow legs.'

Mr Jones waved a cheery, calloused hand from the business end of the kitchen-cum-dining room.

'I'm here too, Mother,' said James as he pecked her cheek.

'Sit down, Helen, love. Sit down. You've been on your feet all day.'

'Not to mention those sparrow legs of yours,' said James.

I sank into my favourite armchair and looked around the familiar, cluttered room. The furniture had shrunk and Mrs Jones along with it. She was still a well-made woman, but her shoulders were now a little hunched and her own legs thinner. James's dad, a small, wiry man, had hardly changed. He was perhaps more wizened and redder in the face.

Mrs Jones tapped James's shoulder as he perched on the chair arm. 'Jimmy, love, why don't you set the table while Helen and me have a nice chat. Henry, is our tea ready yet? Have you found the sherry?'

He placed the china on the sideboard along with a decanter and four delicate glasses. His wife beamed at him as if her favourite pupil had got straight As.

She drew up a chair and, with a worried expression, said, 'Now, love, tell me all about it. How are you? I still don't know what that husband of yours was thinking, leaving a lovely girl like you.'

Mrs Jones had always been one to arrive at her point early. I'd nothing to hide. She knew my life story. While James tripped around the world and embarked on his alleged criminal career, I married Zack, his friend from university. We spent a blissful two years in London messing around. Then James returned, and we all got jobs in the City and earned crazy money. With excellent timing, we piled it into property. Six years later, the party was over. Zack announced he no longer wanted to be trapped in a relationship. He also wanted to travel.

I'd heard nothing from Zack since. At first, I kept a miniature globe on my bedside table. Each morning, I'd give it a spin and wonder where he might be. Last New Year's Eve, I dumped it in the bin.

When I returned to Buttersley, James came too. He'd done clever things with his money and made even more, which is why he could spend his time primping cakes for me.

Mrs Jones patted my hand, and I realised she was waiting for me to speak. I took a sip of sherry. 'Well, it's been nearly two years now, and I love the shop. It keeps me busy, so I don't have time to think, but I'd still prefer to be happily married.' I'd not said that out loud before and reached down to my bag to hide my face.

'I'm sure you would, love, because you're loyal and stick to your promises. These days there's too much of this personal happiness, personal space and all that self-regarding nonsense of, "I owe it to myself to be happy".'

James called over from the table, 'So, Mother, should everyone be miserable?'

She tutted. 'Jimmy, love, Helen and me are talking. Have you asked your dad about his new garden furniture?' We chatted a while longer before she heaved herself out of the chair to check on the food. 'I hope you're not expecting anything special. It's just what I had in.'

'Mother, you always say that just before serving up a *cordon bleu* masterpiece.'

'Silly boy. What do you know about cooking?' She ruffled his hair and pushed him out of her way.

Glen Miller played on the stereo as we tucked into scallops with a chorizo and lemon mini risotto. Mrs Jones wanted to hear all about the *goings-on* at the shop over the last two days.

'Shocking.' She put a hand to her chest. 'In broad daylight, too. Can you believe it?'

I introduced the subject of Claudia Easby once we'd started on the main course of duck breast on kale with blackberry sauce, while pretending that celeriac rosti was nothing new to me. 'Apparently, she was the official tenant of the flat above the shop.' I looked at Mrs Jones. 'James said you might know her?' I tried to keep my voice casual.

Mrs Jones put down her knife and fork. 'Yes, we were acquaintances, you might say. We first met at the school gate when she was waiting for her daughter, Ruth, and I was waiting for little Jimmibobs. Always the last to come out, he was, daydreaming as usual.' She smiled across the table at him, and Jimmibobs grinned back.

'Was her daughter in our class?' I asked.

'Yes, she was. Poor, little Ruth. When I say little, I mean big. So tall for her age. Do you remember her? She had long, dark hair.'

I could hardly recall anyone except James and the scary teacher. I shook my head and looked at James, who shrugged.

'Ruth didn't go to your high school because they'd moved away by then.'

'Thomas Easby was a very clever man,' said Mr Jones as he cleared away the plates.

'Claudia's husband, yes, that's right. He was an inventor, and he invented, oh, what was it now? It was ...' Mrs Jones clicked her fingers and looked at the ceiling for inspiration.

'The wheel?' suggested James.

'No, Jimmy, better than that. It was a thingy-me-bob, and it made him a fortune.'

Mr Jones placed the stack of plates back down on the table. 'Yes, I don't know the correct name, but it was a vital component of a machine used in the plastics industry. Easby was wise enough to get it patented. He invented a lot more stuff and then went on to invest in the stock market.'

'Where did they move to?' I asked.

'Well, it was all a bit of a scandal. It kept the tongues around here wagging for months.' Mrs Jones checked over her shoulder as if scared of being overheard. 'Claudia had an affair with a married man, and they ran off together. She left Ruth with her father for a few weeks, and then all of a sudden, Ruth herself disappeared.'

James glanced at me. 'What do you mean "disappeared", Mother?'

'Some folk around here wanted to make something of it, but nothing came to the attention of the authorities. I think Claudia simply sent for Ruth, once she was settled.'

'What about Mr Easby?' I asked.

'He was a very quiet man. Kept himself to himself. He stayed for another year, and then the house went up for sale, and he was off. Nobody knew where.'

'Do you know the name of the man Claudia ran off with? What happened to *his* wife, and did they have any children?' A tingle of excitement ran through me, and I couldn't get my questions out quickly enough.

'Sorry, can't remember his name.' She threw a questioning glance at her husband. 'I can still see what he looked like, though. Thought he was God's gift to women, he did. The way he used to strut around and expect women to fall at his feet.' Mrs Jones pursed her lips and folded her arms tightly under her chest. 'Some of the silly ones did, of course. Claudia wasn't the first, and I doubt she was the last.'

James winked at his mother. 'Perhaps she just wanted a bit of excitement in her life?'

'Excitement?' Mrs Jones flapped her hands. 'Who needs that? Me and your father have been happily married for nearly forty years and haven't bothered with any of that.' She looked across at her husband. 'Have we, Henry?' He bent to retrieve something he'd dropped, and his answer was lost under the table.

'Sorry,' continued Mrs Jones. 'Can't remember his wife. Nobody knew much about her. Someone said they had a young son. I heard the fling with Claudia didn't last, but too late; his wife had already died. Tragic for their son.' Mrs

Jones dabbed at her mouth with a napkin. 'As far as I know, Claudia never set foot back in Buttersley. I can't think why she'd be renting a flat.' Crinkling her brow, she added. 'I'd have thought she might have mentioned it to me.'

I sat up straight. 'Did you keep in touch?'

'We used to exchange Christmas cards.'

'So, would you still have her address?' My excitement bubbled. It seemed as if we were getting somewhere. I'd failed to find that detail in Mr Klondike's records.

'Yes, love. It's in my address book, but it won't do you much good. Claudia died two months ago.'

As my elation sank like a soufflé, Mrs Jones explained the vicar at her church knew someone who knew Claudia and had passed on the sad news. She'd been ill for some time, and the death had been expected.

I had to console myself with two servings of Eton mess. Stuffed, tired and deflated, I vented my frustration at James as we drove home. 'What do you make of it all?' I demanded.

He didn't speak until we stopped at a red light. 'The information is probably all there. You just need to join up the dots.'

'What do you mean?'

He shrugged and turned on the radio. 'Put another record on.'

I could have screamed.

The Wheels Fall off Merangs

Monday 20th April

The Monday morning after tea at the Jones', I stood at the counter thinking about the murder. After the literal dead end of Claudia, I'd run out of ideas.

The door flew open, and Shakira stormed in with her cake trays held high. 'I'm not having it.' Strands of blonde hair had whipped around her face, and she blew them out of her mouth. As she slammed the trays onto the counter, the edge of one caught the cup in my hand.

'Morning.' I dabbed at my cappuccino-spotted top. 'Don't worry, it's a new blouse, but I'm sure the stains will come out.'

Shakira continued her tirade. 'She's a fat, sneaky slag. It's above the butcher's. It would have been perfect for me. It's massive but cheap. Smells of meat, but I don't mind. Plenty of sausages, he said, and the kids would have a bedroom each.'

'Sounds nice. Is this a new flat you're after?'

Shakira smacked the counter. 'She went behind my back, chatted up the butcher, and now *she's* moving in.'

'Are you talking about Candice?'

'Who else but my vile sister would stab me in the back like that?' Shakira glared as if it were my fault. 'I could report her for benefit fraud, you know. I won't, but you'll have to sack her.'

I'd never sacked anyone in my life. Candice deep-cleaned Merangs once a month. 'If I did sack her, could you cl—'

'Don't even think about it. I'm the creative. She's the scrubber.'

As Shakira ranted, I surveyed the delivery. Her fondants were even more wonky than normal. Although her baking *tasted* divine, it wasn't so hot on looks. James had to perform miracles and turn her rough-cut gems into jewels. *He won't be happy with this lot.*

Shakira insulted Candice all the way to the door and nearly collided with Lucy, who'd just arrived.

I waited until Shakira was safely outside. 'Here, Luce, look at these. Quick, before James gets here.' I pointed at the delivery. 'What do you think?'

Lucy didn't even look. 'Yeah, whatever.' She dropped her handbag and burst into tears.

I gathered her into my arms. 'Hey, Lucy, sweet, Shakira's cakes aren't that bad.'

'My life is over. Kane's broken up with me.'

I spouted soothing platitudes until James arrived. Leading her into the tea room, I mouthed, 'boyfriend trouble' over my shoulder. James ignored me. He was peering at the delivery and scowling.

It continued like that for the rest of the week. Shakira's standards plummeted, Lucy moped about, and James brewed up a storm.

On the Friday, James snapped. 'I can make a silk purse out of a sow's ear but not dainties out of a pig's doo-dahs.' He walked out.

There was no point in chasing after him. So, as in any crisis, I turned to Prue.

'Leave him to stew.' She flicked through her ancient address book. 'I'll see if my friend Betty is free.'

In the afternoon, Prue outlined her recovery plan. 'As Lucy's useless and miserable at the moment, tell her to take time off, and I'll cover the hours.' She held up her hand as I started to protest. 'Tell her you'll still pay her wage.'

I gulped. 'But ...'

Prue insisted she'd work for nothing. 'I'll take time off when we're quiet.' She compressed her lips into a firm line. 'As for Shakira, leave that Jezebel to me. She's become far too big for her ridiculous shoes. Her sister will continue to clean. Don't you worry.'

'What about James?'

'Oh, his lordship won't stay away for long. At least we'll have a bit of peace and quiet around here for a change.'

Overcome with relief, I wrapped my arms around her and squeezed tight. 'What would I do without you?'

She pushed me away but failed to hide her smile. 'Get off. You're like a big, soft dog. Someone has to sort it when you let them walk all over you.'

Shakira's baking only slightly improved, and as I was now in charge of the presentation, it meant a ridiculously early start. It took hours for me to achieve what James did in minutes. Betty looked after the shop, and Malcolm did the tea room shopping.

As I slogged away, I fulminated against James. Although I didn't have the time right then, I was all the more determined to find Vincent's murderer. I'd show that so-called friend of mine what I could achieve without him.

One afternoon, the second week into the crisis, I was dog-tired and could hardly face the customers. My heart sank when Full-on Dora, one of our regulars, arrived with a friend. Dora had a soft spot for Malcolm, and I cursed that he wasn't there to divert them. The women wore raincoats buttoned up to the neck. Dora sashayed up to me and giggled. 'We're trying out our costumes for the show. They're a bit naughty. I wouldn't want Malcolm to see. Is he here?' Her eyes raked the room.

'He'll be back soon. Take a seat. He'd hate to have missed you.'

'This is my co-star, Gwyneth Paletoe. Yes, people always look like that when they hear her name. It's uncanny, isn't it? Two actresses with practically the same name.'

I turned to the skeletal woman with walnut features and hard, black hair. 'How do you do, Gwyneth?' She brushed my hand with ice-cold fingertips but didn't reply.

'We open in two weeks.' Dora handed me a flyer. 'There's so much still to do, but the show's hilarious, isn't it, Gwyneth?' Perhaps Gwyneth would convey the mirth through mime, as she'd yet to speak. Dora placed her hands on her hips and pouted. 'We're the two belles, providing the glamour. You can have a peek if you want. Just don't tell anyone what I'm nearly wearing, especially Malcolm.'

Returning with their drinks, I found the actresses in an awkward situation. The Silent Sisters stood over them, staring fixedly down. That had stemmed even Dora's flow. I'd forgotten it was the sisters' table. 'Dora, I'll put your order over here. There's a spare seat for me, and I want to hear all about *Carry-on up the Sauce.*'

Fortunately, we weren't busy, so I could afford to sit for a while. With half an ear to Dora, I thought about tracking down Claudia Easby's daughter, Ruth, when I got the time. She might have information about Vincent. Mr Klondike would surely have her details? I could ask Prue to sweet-talk him.

Dora got so carried away with backstage gossip, she failed to notice Malcolm walk in. He stopped and did a quick about-turn. At the same time, a glamorous, young woman entered on the arm of a man I vaguely recognised. He sat with his back to me, and I realised it was DCI Swift. I'd not thought him the type to be cavorting with girls nearly half his age. I suddenly felt older than my years, jaded and inexplicably let down. When Prue attended, he turned around and waved at me. I pretended not to see.

It was a revolving door for the police. No sooner had Swift departed with his arm around the girl's shoulders, than in marched the small one of the Arse-and-Alien police combo. He was all smiles and *bonhomie*. He'd left his attitude at home along with the uniform. 'I'm off duty. Call me Daz.'

He presented his fiancée, Sadie, who was shorter than him but twice as wide. She had a smiley face and held a bag decorated with butterflies.

'Ms Merang, I was telling Sadie all about your amazing place and wonderful cakes, and she was desperate to come.' He flashed a nervous smile.

Maybe he thought I'd be hostile, but he'd not yet seen me in customer service mode. 'It's Helen, please. Lovely to see you both. Would you like a tasting platter of everything? It's on the house.' *Take me out and shoot me. I've gone too far.*

Sadie swooned. 'I've never dared come in here before. I thought it was too posh.'

Daz's chest swelled. 'You can rely on me, my love, to show you all the best places.'

The day trundled on. Prue and Betty left early, but Dora, minus her friend, stayed until the bitter end. When she'd gone, I stood for a moment's rest. My eyes must have closed for only a minute, as when I looked up, James was standing before me. He wore a petrol blue suit.

'You look like a loan shark,' I said.

He grinned. 'You look like crap.'

'That's because someone dropped me in it.'

'I have my standards.'

'But no loyalty.' I banged both fists on the counter. 'If you're not here to seize the reins of your cake stand right now, you can just go and ... trot off.' Exhausted and full of self-pity, I couldn't have cared less about my lame retort.

James's easy laugh irritated me. 'Since when did I become a horse?'

'You say horse, I say arse.'

'Hey, calm down. I've come to take you for a drink and tell you the latest. I've done a deal with Klondike. Told him it's for your benefit. Shakira will soon ...'

I was too incensed to listen. 'I'd rather do my VAT return than go out with you.' How dare he waltz in and think he could put it right just like that? James raised an eyebrow but didn't reply. As soon as he'd gone, I regretted my petulance and nearly ran after him.

I was turning the lights off when Shakira bounced in. 'Just who are those two sarky women at the estate agents? Who do they think they are, snobby cows? But lovely Mr Klondike has offered me the flat.' She did a happy little dance and punched the air.

'The butcher's flat?'

'Nah, keep up. The one above here. It's not yet back on the market, but Mr Klondike's pulled some strings.' He must have pulled them hard, as there was no way Shakira could have afforded it. 'He said my micro-business is the powerhouse behind Merangs, which is a community asset. So, as long as I'm flogging cakes to you, I can live above the shop at a special rate.'

The petrol-suited puppeteer had flashed his cash. James had mentioned doing a deal, and I now regretted being mean to him. 'That's wonderful, Shakira. You deserve a break.'

'I'm going to bake Mr Klondike the best cake he's ever had, and while I'm at it, I'll whip up a few specials for Merangs. Lucy's gone all Gloria Gaynor, by the way, so expect her back anytime soon. Gotta go and buy cushions and stuff.'

So, it was looking like things would soon get back to normal. I could afford to be diverted by the murder again. Daz had said the coroner had released Vincent Newby's body, and the funeral was going to take place next Thursday. I intended to go on my own.

The Funeral

Thursday 14th May

I stuck to my decision not to tell James about the funeral. Although he'd redeemed himself over the Shakira business, I'd still not completely forgiven him for leaving me in the lurch.

Lucy, her effervescence restored, said she'd cover my shift. The funeral wasn't until two, but I'd taken the day off and enjoyed a blissful lie-in. I spent time getting ready, so I looked half decent in a tight black skirt, fitted jacket, and nude-coloured heels. Even my hair had got the message. I'd no idea why I'd gone to so much effort – possibly as a mark of respect? More like my social life was so poor; I saw it as a rare occasion to dress up.

As I searched for a bag, my eyes filled with unexpected tears. Despite my best efforts, I failed to suppress the memories of the only other funeral I'd attended. My mother died when I was fourteen. At the funeral, I'd clung to Prue, sheltering under her black cape to avoid the pitying looks and well-intentioned remarks. Wiping away the tears, I told myself that was years ago, and to stop dwelling on the past.

I reached the church early and stood on my own, wondering if I'd got the right date. With relief, I spotted Snood and Swift, but that created fresh anguish. Would I be trapped in conversation? Snood stared through me, but Swift was just about to speak when James popped up between us.

Already sick of going it alone, I'd never been more pleased to see him. I forgot we'd fallen out and bestowed a joyful smile. Recovering my composure, I said, 'It's not fancy dress, you know.' He looked armed and dangerous in a precision-cut suit and sheer white shirt. His shoes had lethal, sharp points.

James eyed me up and down and whistled. '*You've* scrubbed up well for a change.'

Malcolm and Mr Klondike – an unexpected pairing – arrived five minutes later. Mr Klondike, the size of a mattress, wore his usual grey suit. Malcolm had opted for a navy blazer and brown checked trousers. He'd coated his comb-over with Brylcreem, and the green shirt was new.

Mr Klondike beamed. 'We *had* to attend, seeing as we were instrumental on the day, as you might say.' His smile dropped as he looked over my shoulder. 'Oh, I say, I didn't expect Elvira and Pansy. Oh dear, they must have closed the office.'

Any excuse for those two, I would have thought. As they passed me, the older one, whom I assumed to be Elvira, said, 'I wonder if *she'll* turn up. The church is practically on her doorstep.'

'You'd think so,' said the other. 'She's his wife, after all.'

Elvira flashed warning eyes. 'Be quiet.' She nodded towards Mr Klondike. 'He'll hear you.'

Was Mr Klondike married? In that case, he should back off from Prue.

The Silent Sisters appeared next, and then Shakira and Candice. I should have realised the funeral would be a Buttersley event. They were arriving in pairs like a dystopian Noah's Ark.

Shakira and Candice tottered past in their knock-off Jimmy Choos and dolled-up faces. Shakira dug a candy-pink nail into my shoulder. 'Turns out there's no such thing as a free sausage for our Candice,' she whispered. 'The butcher's flat's off.' She pushed her sister towards Mr Klondike. 'C'mon, you. Let's try and fix you up with another flat. Ignore his bitches.'

We all hushed as the cortège approached. A single limousine followed the hearse. A good-looking man and a woman about my age stepped out. They stood side by side and stared at the ground. The undertakers removed the unadorned coffin and heaved it onto their shoulders. After a brief kerfuffle, they were ready to go, and we all shuffled into the church. Seconds before the service started, the door crashed open, and Dora and Gwyneth piled in, gasping for breath but no doubt satisfied with their dramatic entrance. The ark would not have been the same without them.

The Reverend Peter Buckle began with a biography of the deceased. 'Vincent Newby was known as a tall man in Buttersley. He was often seen in the town going about his business, and he always had the time of day for those he should meet.' It was evident that The Reverend Buckle had never laid eyes on Vincent Newby, nor been given much to go on by his nearest and dearest. 'Born here, lived here and died here. Buttersley was very dear to Vincent's heart.'

A loud sob rang out from the back of the church. Who was that? I had to stop myself from swivelling around.

'Vincent leaves behind his only child, Charles. While not living here in Buttersley, Charles also holds Buttersley very dear to his heart.'

The vicar glanced at a man in the front row, the one who'd arrived in the limousine with the woman. I could just about see them both if I balanced on tiptoes when we sang a hymn. He stood tall and erect. She matched him in height but was more solidly built. From behind, you'd almost take her for a man, except for the long, dark hair cascading down her back. They stood a little too far apart. She turned to glance at him, but he didn't respond.

The vicar closed his Bible and scanned the congregation. 'Those of you who wish to stay for the committal will be more than welcome.' I didn't think many would have an appetite for that, especially as he'd not mentioned a funeral tea. There would be bitter disappointment all round if that wasn't in the deal. 'The family have nominated a local charity and there's a collection plate at the door as you leave,' he continued.

Well, good luck with that. I half expected Mr Choudray to be hanging about looking for the settlement of his debt.

There was the usual hold-up at the door for everyone to offer their thanks to the vicar and condolences to Charles. The Reverend Buckle was a touch too jolly, but it was probably his relief at having managed a tricky send-off. The woman at the side of Charles didn't speak, but Charles was taking the time to talk to everyone.

He equalled James in his smooth good looks and possessed an easy, affable charm. He was no slouch in the expensive suit department either.

Shakira, standing in line behind me, announced to the back of my head, 'He can lick out my mixing bowl anytime he wants.'

This caused me to greet the vicar with a crazed grin. He returned it with gusto as if he'd found a kindred spirit.

I shook his hand. 'The service was so sincere and meaningful.'

He replaced the grin with a mournful expression. 'Were you a close friend or relative of the deceased?'

'They were virtually inseparable at the end,' cut in James before I'd time to answer. I offered a sad smile and followed James down the line.

James now stood opposite Charles. They only needed Swift to join them, and it would be a boy-band reunion ten years on – a band who'd been light on the drugs, booze and tattoos. They faced each other like stags and exchanged a few formal words.

James moved on to greet the woman as if they were long-lost friends, which to some extent they were. 'Ruth, I'd have known you anywhere.' He clasped her hand.

Of course, she was Ruth Easby, daughter of Claudia. I was so caught up with that and then wondering if she and Charles were together as a couple, I hardly registered him speaking to me.

'You must be Helen. I'm so glad you could come.'

Soft brown eyes gazed into mine. Why should he be glad? How did he even know who I was? Not knowing how to answer, I jumped right in. 'If you've time after the ... you know, afterwards, why don't you come back to Merangs for a drink? I'm thinking of asking the others.' So, I did well there. Tongue-tied, I'd landed us with the catering.

His eyes widened and he took my hand. 'That would be amazing. I've been out of the country and not had the time, and obviously, it all came as a shock.'

'If you and Ruth could make it, you'd be most welcome.' I gently withdrew my hand and smiled at Ruth. She managed a faint one in return. If she and Charles were an item, that would possibly explain why Vincent had been living in Claudia's flat.

I asked Malcolm to rush back to Merangs to alert and help Prue. He shot off down the path like his pants were on fire. 'Got my skates on,' he shouted over his shoulder. 'I'll be there in no time.'

I set about inviting everyone who still hung around, including a rackety group of smokers loitering at the church gate. I could have been welcoming the murderer for all I knew.

'Mr Klondike,' I said. 'You've got to come. You were a key figure on the day.' The mattress swelled, but then deflated when I added, 'You could bring your wife.'

He puckered his brow in puzzlement. 'Wife? I'm not married, my dear. I've not yet found that special lady to do me the honour.' He stared into the distance as if one might materialise.

I flushed at my error, but Elvira and Pansy had mentioned a mystery wife as if she were significant. I crossed Mr Klondike off the list. Could they have meant Vincent's wife?

'Sorry, got my wires crossed, but a man in his prime like you will be snapped up in no time.' Of all the patronising things to say, I could usually nail it. I added hastily, 'It wouldn't be the same without you.'

James turned away from Ruth and dragged me to one side. 'You start off wanting to be all alone at this funeral and then end up hosting the wake.'

'Well, it's a shame to leave everyone hanging about with nowhere to go, and we have the facilities.'

'Count me out.'

I placed my hand on his arm. 'James, pretty please. It's our opportunity to discover more about Vincent. It's the only way we'll find out who killed him.'

Our eyes locked, and James lifted an eyebrow. 'Is that our game, then? Since when?'

'You can't escape us being involved. We've been there from the start. It's personal, almost. If you won't help, I'll go it alone.' I tossed my curls and raised my chin.

'Calm down, Boadicea.' James looked towards the hill – the one we used to race down as kids. 'I've got somewhere else to be. I'll see you later.'

'Fine.' He didn't fool me with his nonchalance. He was on board all right. I turned my back on him and went to round up my flock.

The Wake

We had catered for funerals before at Merangs, so we knew what to expect. Prue and Lucy stood sentry-like at the tea room door, holding trays of sherry. Dora, first in the queue, was throwing down her third before most guests had even arrived.

Mr Klondike's gaze followed Prue as he stood in the middle of the room with his coven of two. Elvira was knocking back the sherry, and Pansy tapped at her phone.

I greeted everyone and pranced around with the sandwiches Prue had hastily prepared.

The Silent Sisters sat primly at their usual table, on the horns of a sherry dilemma. Their glasses remained untouched. Although it was free, alcohol was akin to hemlock. Dora would probably confirm their worst suspicions later by keeling over. They pounced on the sandwiches; they'd no qualms there. I signalled to Prue for more.

I scanned the room for any new guests. Snood and DCI Swift sat at a table away from the sherry crowd. I was surprised they'd come, but most likely they saw it as an opportunity to find out more about Vincent. Leaning into her boss, Snood talked earnestly. It can't have been riveting, as DCI Swift had half turned away. His gaze caught mine, and he raised a glass.

Twenty minutes later, Charles and Ruth walked into a full-blown party. James had arrived moments before with three cases of wine. They both accepted a large glass. Shakira and Candice pounced on Charles, leaving Ruth on her own.

Emboldened by alcohol, I rushed over. 'Sorry, I didn't remember you from school, Ruth, but I've got a terrible memory for faces and names.'

She smiled. 'I couldn't forget you and James. The things he did to your hair, and poor you always got the blame. It's lovely you're still friends.' She sighed and looked down at her glass. 'Mother and I moved a few times, so I didn't have time to make proper friends.' Ruth had a childlike voice with a faint lisp. It didn't match her imposing physique.

James joined us and topped up our glasses. Ruth said she lived in Essex and was in the process of selling her mother's house. Did we know her mother had recently died?

James made all the right noises, and I plunged in with the burning question. 'So, Ruth, how do you know Charles and Vincent?'

Her answers were brief. She'd first met Charles at her mother's funeral. He'd accompanied Vincent. They'd become friends, and she had wanted to support him at Vincent's funeral. Charles glanced over several times as we talked. I left James with Ruth as the sandwiches needed replenishing again.

DCI Swift rose to leave when Dora proposed a sing-along. 'You certainly know how to throw a good wake, Ms Merang.'

'Thanks, I'll put you on the waiting list.'

He smiled. 'Let me get back to you on that.'

'Here's one for the road.' I gave him a large slab of chocolate truffle cake. Then I recalled his penchant for much younger women and wanted to snatch it back.

Snood made a few phone calls and then marched past Prue and me without speaking. Prue bristled with annoyance. 'She's no manners, that one. And she needs a good haircut. Have you made the effort to talk to Charles yet, Helen? He seems a very nice young man, or at least not an egocentric, selfish show-off, like some I could name.'

James sidled up and placed his hands on her shoulders. 'I hope you're not referring to me, Prue. It's only our pleasant exchanges that stop you from going to seed.'

Prue pushed him away, and he wandered off to top up the glasses again. As instructed, I went over to Charles.

He raised his glass and smiled. His dark eyes danced. 'I've wanted to talk to you all afternoon. Thanks for giving my father a proper send-off.'

Brushing off his thanks, I grabbed the opportunity to discover more about Vincent. 'So, were you and your father close?'

'We didn't see much of each other. I travel abroad a lot on business. I was in Brazil when he was ... I mean, when he died.' He raised his eyebrows slightly as if perhaps encouraging me to ask more about his work. I wasn't having that.

'So, did you and Vincent not get on?'

Charles embarked on an automatic reply, but the intensity of my sherry-induced stare made him blink and start again. 'No, not a bit, and now it's too late.' He cast down his eyes, and the lashes almost touched his sharp cheekbones. 'Why do we think time's infinite, always a tomorrow, or that people will change?'

Philosophical debate wasn't my forte. If he continued like that, I'd have to call for backup. 'What went wrong?'

He grinned. 'Helen, you're so direct. I like it. Okay, I'll give you the low-down. My father was a gambler and an alcoholic womaniser who broke my mother's heart. He sent her to an early grave, and I had no respect for the man.'

I filed that away and said, 'Did he remarry?'

Charles shrugged. 'Not that I know. Father dangled several women at once. He could easily have remarried and not told me. I wouldn't put it past him.' My penetrating gaze must have made him think again. 'Wait a minute.' Charles touched my arm. 'Is there something I should know?'

I played it down and filled up his glass. 'Tell me about your job. It sounds fascinating.'

I listened with half an ear while admiring the view. He had an easy charm, and I lost track of both the time and the occasion until Prue tugged at my arm. 'Helen, we need to wind this up. It's all getting out of hand.' I'd not realised the volume had cranked up. Prue had to shout, which accentuated the lines around her mouth. 'Just look at that ridiculous woman.' She threw a weary hand in the direction of Dora, who was standing on a table, belting out 'Amazing Grace'. The Silent Sisters, with roses in their cheeks, clapped along like children at a pantomime.

'I'll sort it,' I said. 'Leave it to me.' Short of setting off the fire alarm, though, I'd no idea what to do.

Catching James's eye on the other side of the tea room, I performed an elaborate mime. He mimicked my actions and laughed. I glared and beckoned him over.

He sauntered across. 'Sorry, I thought you were acting out the dying swan in competition with Dora.'

'Just get her down and send her home,' I said through clenched teeth.

He bowed. 'As you wish, Madame Pavlova.'

I left him to it and approached the Klondike party. Earlier, I'd seen Elvira clutching Lucy's arm, but now she was sobbing into her plate as Pansy and Mr Klondike exchanged embarrassed looks.

I tapped Elvira on the shoulder. 'Can I do anything for you?' I used my most caring voice.

Elvira lifted her head. 'Who are you? Leave me alone.' The remnants of a sandwich had stuck to her face. 'She stood between us. She wouldn't set him free, and now it's too late.'

Who did she mean? 'Do you want to talk about it?' I said, trying to keep the eagerness out of my voice.

'Can't you see my mum's upset?' said Pansy. 'Leave her alone.' She pushed me away. 'Don't interfere.'

I turned and bumped into Shakira. She leant into me. 'Gotta-go-before-I-throw-hash-bag, I mean tag.' Her face had suffered a landslide; the heavy-duty make-up was miles from where it had started.

'Where's Candice?'

Shakira collapsed into a chair. 'She's got her head down your toilet. She's a disgrace, my sister.'

'I'll ask James to run her home.' That would please him and his pristine car.

I dispatched a grumbling James on his errand. Prue helped me to round up the undesirables, and Lucy and Malcolm cleared up most of the mess. Prue must have been exhausted as she nodded when Malcolm offered to escort her home.

That left Charles and Ruth. They stood at opposite ends of the tea room. Ruth was twiddling her glass, and Charles was examining the display shelves. The distance between them, along with their closed body language, puzzled me.

'So, what are your plans?' I addressed an imaginary line down the middle of the room.

Charles said he'd booked a hotel nearby, but Ruth muttered something about driving home to Essex. She'd quaffed at least four large glasses of wine.

'Ruth, there's no way you can drive home,' I said.

Charles stepped towards the door. 'I could see if there's a room in my hotel, but I'm sure I got the last one.' With his hand on the doorknob, he added, 'I think there's a conference in town. All the hotels might be full.'

Ruth made an odd sound between a hiccup and a sob. She placed a hand over her mouth.

'It's fine,' I said. 'Ruth, stay with me if you like? I've got a spare room.'

She gripped me in a steel-like hug. 'Really, can I? That's so kind of you, Helen. So, so kind. I'd love to, thank you.'

I pulled away while I could still breathe. 'No problem. Nice to have some company for a change.'

We said our farewells to Charles outside the shop. He rushed off in one direction; Ruth and I staggered in the other. The thought that I'd never see him again gave me a slight pang.

Ruth leant heavily against me, and I didn't have the strength to support her, not for long, anyway. As she steered us both towards a wall, Ruth said, 'I'm so sorry about this. What must you think? I don't normally drink, but what with Mother dying so recently, and my coming back to Buttersley for the very first time in years, it's brought back memories and made me think about ... things.'

I dragged on her arm to avoid the wall. 'Don't worry, Ruth. We've all been there from too much drink. It sneaks up unawares.'

She pulled up sharply, and I banged into her side. 'It didn't sneak up on Vincent,' she shouted at a lamppost. 'He grabbed it by the hand and gave it a good shake.' Ruth steadied herself. 'Sorry, I shouldn't speak ill of the dead.'

'Charles mentioned Vincent liked a drink.'

Ruth gave an unladylike snort, which morphed into a guffaw and ended in a cough. I patted her back. It felt like a rock. She shook her head from side to side like a horse. 'Sorry, I don't know where all that came from. What was I saying? Oh, yes. Charles may not have known what his father was truly like. Vincent seduced my mother, and she remained besotted with him right to the end.' Ruth paused and hiccuped. 'She supported him financially, you know?

She took that flat on for him – he couldn't provide a reference – and then paid the rent. She even left him all her ... oh no, I shouldn't go on like this. What must you think?'

I sensed that if I asked questions, she'd clam up. *Best to let her talk while she's on a roll.* Ruth grasped my hand. 'It doesn't matter to me about the money. Dad was so scr ... scrupulous.' She struggled with this ambitious word choice. 'He set up a trust fund, so I've more money than I know what to do with, but what would he think of her?' She wrung my hand and began to cry. Her body and my strength gave way, and she crumpled against a fence.

I'd no choice but to ring James. He groaned but arrived within ten minutes. By then, Ruth had fallen asleep. I gently shook her shoulder, and it took both of us to help her into the car.

James protested that she might be sick on his leather seats. 'Thanks to you, I've already had one journey from hell this evening.'

I panted to catch my breath. 'There's more to life than clean upholstery.' He didn't answer but switched on the radio.

Once home, I put Ruth to bed and left a pint of water and a bucket at her side. She whispered, 'Thanks,' from under the duvet.

Downstairs, James was unpacking a hamper of cheese and gin. 'I was on my way over when you called.'

I realised I'd not eaten at the wake, and I reached out for the cheese.

James rapped my knuckles with a knife. 'Get some plates and glasses.'

I did as told, and he poured me a pink gin.

'We've got a lot to discuss on this murder business,' I said. 'It's all jumbled up in my head. I need to draw a diagram or a chart or something.'

James handed me a plate of cheese and crackers. 'I agree on a logical approach, but do we actually know anything?'

I nearly dropped the plate. 'James, where have you been? I've discovered so much today, my head's spinning.'

'Well then, you'll need a cool, analytical mind, and since Prue's probably polishing her Formica right now, it will have to be mine. So, what have you got for me?'

Don't Drink and Dial

We didn't speak about the murder until after we'd eaten our cheese and biscuits. I tried to arrange the information in my head first, to appear efficient, but soon gave up. Let James, with his so-called superior mind, untangle it all. He faffed around with his gin bottles, trying not to look too expectant, but I could tell his interest was piqued.

I took a quick slug of gin. 'Vincent died a rich man, as Claudia left him all her money.'

'How much?'

'I don't know. Don't ask questions until I've finished.' I gulped at my glass. 'He was carrying on with Elvira – that's my take on it anyway – and she indicated he'd possibly remarried. Charles is not aware that Vincent had, but he didn't rule it out.' I paused for breath.

'How do ...'

'James, *will* you shut up when I'm on a roll. Charles blamed Vincent for the death of his mother. Ruth said he'd exploited her mother, Claudia, and according to both, he was an alcoholic, a womaniser and also a gambler.'

James raised a single eyebrow. 'Can I speak now? Is that all?'

The cheek of the man. I wanted to ram his head onto the cheeseboard, but settled for banging my glass on the table. 'Okay, hotshot, what information have *you* brought to the party?'

He smiled. 'Calm yourself, woman. I merely meant is that the extent of your findings, or is there more?'

'What more do you want?' I picked up my glass and downed the lot.

James tipped his head to one side. 'Did you expect a pat on the back, and for me to say how clever you've been?'

'You look like a giant budgie with your head like that. Who's a pretty boy then?'

James poured us both another gin. 'Cheers, mate.' He stretched out his legs and ran a finger around the rim of his glass.

'So, what do you think?' I couldn't disguise my eager tone. I was so like a dog desperate to please.

'What were Elvira's exact words to indicate Vincent had a wife?'

I related the exchange between Elvira and Pansy about the church being on the mystery woman's doorstep. 'Why do you ask?'

James sipped at his drink and poured in more tonic. 'This is a long shot, but what if Vincent's alleged wife lived in one of Klondike's rentals and that's how they knew of her whereabouts?'

I sat up straight. 'James, you could be onto something. Mr Klondike would have the details.' I pictured myself breaking into the agency, hacking into Mr Klondike's computer and solving the murder before breakfast.

James held up his palm. I knew he was about to rain on my parade. 'But Vincent could have invented this wife. After all, she wasn't there at the funeral.'

I slopped gin on my hand. 'Why the hell would he do that?'

James smirked. 'To stop Elvira getting ideas, of course.'

'No, I won't have it.' I thumped a cushion. 'There *is* a wife, I know it. Elvira looks like she's been around the block and not the type to be easily fooled.'

James held up both hands. 'Okay, then. We'll go with the secret wife theory.'

I fetched a notepad to write everything down. Under the heading *Action,* I wrote, Elvira: Interview about a wife. I then added the heading, *Motive.*

James laughed. 'It's like watching a child on their first day at school.'

'Shut up, boy, and top up the gin.' I pushed my glass forward. 'So, money would be the obvious motive due to the inheritance. What else?'

'Revenge, jealousy, overdue cigarette bill, random act, no motive.' He ticked them off on his fingers.

I chewed on the pen. 'Take this seriously, James. Who do we have as suspects?'

'Under money, assuming Claudia *did* leave Vincent a fortune, there's the mystery wife, as she would probably inherit. Charles, if he was unaware of the mystery wife. In fact, Charles, even if he knew, could have had the motive of being pretty miffed. Stick him under revenge as well.'

I didn't want to think of Charles being a chief suspect. He had such soft brown eyes and lovely, straight teeth.

James leant in to look at the notepad. 'Ruth should come under the money motive and the pretty miffed subheading, too. She might have hated Vincent for taking all her mother's money.'

I didn't like that idea any better. Ruth seemed too lost and lonely, and besides, she was in my spare bedroom.

As usual, James was trying to take over. I moved the notepad away from him. 'The mystery wife's our best bet. She could have had any of the motives, including jealousy. Also, there's Elvira; I don't like her.'

James laughed. 'You can't suspect people just because they're unpleasant. Elvira may have been a woman scorned, though. Pop her under jealousy and revenge. Vincent may have rejected her when he realised he'd inherited Claudia's money.'

I checked to see if I'd noted everything down. 'One thing's puzzled me all along. Why did the murderer move the body? It would have been classed as an accident or even suicide otherwise.'

James cut us both more cheese. I needed it to soak up the alcohol. He was taking his time to answer. He'd probably no idea why the body had been moved.

'I can think of two reasons.'

Trust him and his big brain.

'Number one: pure panic. Klondike's hysteria would have affected even the coolest murderer. Number two: he or she wanted it to look like murder. If they'd not been interrupted, they might have staged the scene for that to be more obvious.'

James's face had become fuzzy around the edges. His lips moved, words came out, but I couldn't make sense of them. 'Write that down in my book, please.' I hiccuped and rested my head on the couch. Gin was the number one of my all-time favourite top-ten drinks, and my best friend was an obsessive connoisseur and collector. How lucky was that? Through half-closed eyes, I watched him pack the bottles away like they were the Crown jewels.

Suddenly overwhelmed by the good fortune of having James in my life, I wanted to throw my arms around him and plant a big kiss on his cheek.

James looked up. 'You've got that gleam in your eye. Back off. Any sloppy display of affection, I'll lock up the gin.'

'James, you're such a pom-pom, I mean, pompous cold fish.'

'You're well on your way to being pickled. If you become incapable, I'll put you in bed next to Ruth. How would that play out for you in the morning?'

I couldn't stop giggling. All thoughts of the investigation had drifted out of my head. 'Where were we?'

James drummed his fingers on the table and stared at the ceiling. He moved my glass out of reach. 'Irrespective of the attempted concealment of the body, we can't discount it being a random attack by a mentally deranged stranger, unlikely as that sounds.'

I nodded as if I'd understood his every word. I tried to focus. 'Or it might be a serial killer, and Vincent could be the first victim?'

'True, but someone known to the victim is still the most likely. I suggest we start there and eliminate each one. The most important thing is to find the mystery wife.'

I was glad James had accepted there might be a wife kicking around. It made her existence more real. 'I think you should sweet-talk Elvira. Make her reveal all she knows. She's more likely to respond to your silky charms.'

'Okay, I'll tackle Elvira, but we should tell the police our suspicions about the wife, first.'

I wanted to disagree, but he had a point. We didn't need Snood unleashing her bulldog again. Prue always said, 'Don't put off until tomorrow what you can do today'. I dug out my phone and jumped up from the couch. 'I'm going to ring Snood right now.'

James tried to snatch the phone from my hand. 'Wait until you're sober. We have to be careful. We don't want Snood interviewing Elvira before I've had a chance to speak to her.'

I danced out of his way and held on to the phone. Why did he always think he knew best? 'I'm not drunk. We need to seize The Snood by the horns. Don't worry, I won't infiltrate Elvira.'

James shook his head. 'Don't implicate her either while you're at it.'

'Implicate, that's what I said, big boy. It's gone straight to voicemail. I'll leave a message.'

James attempted another ambush on my phone. 'Don't. You'll regret it in the morning.'

At the back of my befuddled mind, I knew he was right. Even when sober, I tied myself in knots leaving a message, but I couldn't turn back.

'Ssshhh, be quiet. Sergeant Snood. I know you're not there right now, and it wasn't you I was telling to be quiet. It's Helen Merang. I mean, Inspector, you're Inspector Snood now, sorry, and I'm still Helen Merang.' I held the phone away and gulped for air.

'Just say, you'll ring her tomorrow,' whispered James.

I can do this. I cleared my throat. 'Just wanted to give you some information, Acting Inspector. Nothing urgent. We've not found another dead body, not yet anyway, ha-ha. I think – we both think – James, what are you doing?'

James stood with his feet apart, holding an imaginary sword in both hands and swishing it from side to side, dangerously close to my head. 'Ring off now,' he urged.

I turned my back. 'Sorry, where was I? Oh yes, married. We think Vincent was married to a woman living near the church, as I overheard someone, definitely don't know who, saying about a wife arriving from her doorstep. So that's what we think, and you said you wanted information, so that's something for you to act on. If I can be of any more assistance, please let me know. Bye, bye, bye.'

James had abandoned the swordplay and sunk to his knees. He remained on the floor with his head buried in his hands. His voice came out muffled. 'That went well.' He stared up at me with bloodshot eyes. 'Why can't you think and talk at the same time? You've made complete fools of us both.'

I was too gin-soaked to care. He was obviously exaggerating. I yawned. Our brainstorming had ended, and I could hardly keep my eyes open. James cleared away his stuff in silence and then left in a taxi. I crawled into bed. My own bed.

I woke with a heavy head and nausea. *Must have eaten too much cheese.* If I remained still, the queasiness might subside. Through the open curtains, the sunlight hit the back of my eyes. As a door on the landing opened, I shot up. Wincing at the sharp pain in my head, I remembered my guest.

I gingerly stepped out of bed and stubbed a toe on the discarded notebook. As I flicked through the pages of my terrible handwriting, I recalled the mystery wife. Despite the throbbing head, a surge of confidence rose in me. James was on board, and he'd always been good at Hide and Seek.

We're coming to get you, Mrs Newby the Second, ready or not.

Snood Snaps Back

Friday 15th May

I dragged myself downstairs to find Ruth sitting at the kitchen table. Her hair hung limp around her sallow, puffy face. She looked as rough as I felt.

'Good morning.' My hostess-style voice rang out loud and false.

Ruth froze like a startled deer. After a couple of seconds, she rose from her seat. 'Helen, I need to apologise for my disgraceful behaviour yesterday.'

'There's nothing to apologise for.' I rubbed my hands together. 'Let's have breakfast.' I'd switched to hale and hearty.

'Just a cup of tea for me, thanks.'

Thank God for that.

Ruth placed her hand on my arm. 'Tell me honestly, did I say anything inappropriate?'

'No, not at all, but ...' My stomach sank. '*I* did. I left a message on the inspector's voicemail. New information about the murder, but I'd had a few gins, and it came out all wrong.'

'New information? That sounds interesting.' Ruth listened intently as I gave her the details. 'You know, you could be right. Not long after Mother and Vincent eloped

– as she called it – Vincent's wife died. Mother wanted to marry him, but couldn't face a divorce. Then, after Dad died, she used to say, "If only my poor love were free". Maybe she meant Vincent had married again?' Ruth looked down at the table, avoiding my eyes as if not used to conversing one-to-one.

I suggested we should walk to Merangs when we'd finished our tea. The fresh air would clear our heads. I chose my favourite route. We ambled through the cherry blossom-filled park and paused to watch the ducks squabbling on the lake. I asked how well she knew Charles.

Ruth's thick hair concealed her face. 'We knew *of* each other but, as I said, we met for the first time at my mother's funeral. We kept in touch, and I offered to come to Vincent's funeral in turn. It seemed the right thing to do.' She pitched the last sentence almost as a question, as if seeking approval.

'What are your plans?' Conscious of the time, I set off walking again. 'And I don't mean for today.'

Ruth swept back her hair and smiled. 'Just the rest of my life? I haven't any. I've spent the last few years looking after Mother, and ... after a few glasses of wine, everything seemed more hopeful and I almost felt like I ... this sounds stupid, maybe I shouldn't say?'

'Say what you want to me, Ruth. I'm the princess of stupidity.' My voice had assumed a silly sing-song quality all of its own.

She sighed. 'That's what I mean. You're all so warm and welcoming. I was happy here. I just need to sort myself out.'

I'd assumed Ruth would come into Merangs, but on the doorstep, she said, 'I'm enjoying the walk so much, I'll continue to my car. You've put up with me for long enough, and thank you again for everything. I'm so glad to have met you all, and I hope to come back soon.'

'Make sure you do. You know where to find us.' I sounded like a supermarket slogan. I gave her my card. 'There's always a bed for you at mine.' I was probably over-egging it there, but she was unlikely to take me up on the offer.

Prue had arrived early to clear up properly after the wake. I was making us both a cup of tea when a door banged overhead, followed by a clomping down the staircase. I put an extra cup out for Shakira.

She barrelled in with her cake trays. Setting them down on the counter, she prodded me in the chest. 'Fab do, Helen. If he's still in town, I'm in there.'

I reeled back. 'Knock knock, who's there?'

'She's referring to Charles,' said Prue with a sniff. 'Shakira, there's more to life than chasing men.'

'What do you mean?' Shakira smoothed down her tight skirt. 'I've never chased a man in my life. Did you notice he was talking to me most of the afternoon? Candice was well-jel. Not my fault, she's got a face like a spud. It's like our parents poured all the good genes into me and she ended up with the scraps.'

Prue moved away, muttering, 'In my day,' and something about breeding.

'Anyway, if he's gone,' Shakira continued, 'there's always that police bod, the one in charge. He's hot, and they like a bit of action, policemen.' She winked. 'I could take it all down for him.'

I was only half-listening, wondering if James had called into the agency to see Elvira. If she knew about the wife, James would wheedle it out of her. A surge of excitement ran through me.

Shakira pounced on him as soon as he arrived. 'Jameykins, I've got an idea for a new naked sponge. Let's grab a drink, and I'll show you the pics.'

I had to stop myself from pushing her out of the way.

'Be with you in a minute, Shakira. I've got to speak to Helen first.' His lack of swagger said it all. 'Elvira and Pansy haven't turned up for work,' he said. 'Klondike's no idea why.'

I wanted to smack my head on the counter. How more frustrating could it get? Before I could process this properly, the shop phone rang. Prue answered.

'Merangs' Confectionery and Tea Room. Prudence Mayflower speaking. Can you repeat that, please?' Prue frowned and hardened her voice. 'I cannot converse with someone who has bad manners and no concept of English grammar. Well, if you are the police, then you should know better. Please wait a moment, Inspector Snood. I'll see if she's free.'

'Hold the naked sponge, Shakira,' said James. 'Helen's going to get the full barrels backlash.'

My hand slightly shook as I took the phone. 'Inspector Snood, how can I help?'

She honked out a false laugh. 'That's just it, you can't. Your ridiculous call gave some light-hearted relief to the hard-working officers on the investigation, but little else.'

'What do you mean?'

'I broadcast your message on loudspeaker so we could all tune into your words of wisdom.'

My face burned. I hadn't a clue what I'd said, but I could recall James's reaction. 'You said to call with any relevant information.'

'I didn't say I wanted muddle-headed tittle-tattle or unfounded speculation.' Snood snorted. 'Stick to making tea and coffee, Ms Merang, and leave the rest to the professionals.'

That got my goat, so I said in a firmer voice. 'You don't think there could be a wife, then?'

'What the public fails to realise is, the police follow numerous leads which cover not only the most obvious but also the areas that someone such as you would never think of in a million years.'

She'd probably written that down to read aloud. 'So, is that a no?'

She sighed as if her life was expiring. 'That's not a line of investigation we will be pursuing while we have more significant leads.'

'Is that what DCI Swift thinks?'

She raised her voice. 'I'm the senior officer on this case. *I* make all the decisions. I have not yet apprised him of your information. I will play him your message at the first opportunity.'

'No, don't.' The phone nearly fell from my sweaty grasp. 'Please don't.'

'I'll make sure he hears it. I wouldn't want to deprive him of your in-depth knowledge and insight. Goodbye.'

I'd bowed my head during the conversation. I looked up into the concerned faces of Prue and James. Shakira was picking at her nail varnish.

'What was all that about?' demanded Prue as I put the phone down.

James gave a précis of our ideas about the missing wife, and that I'd left Snood a message while tired and emotional.

'Hey, Hels,' said Shakira. 'I've done a lot worse when plastered. I remember when I lost my—'

Prue interrupted. 'That policewoman is insufferable. She has no sense of decorum, cannot manage her hairstyle, and yet is in charge of a murder investigation.'

'Well, she's put me in my place and dismissed our idea.' I felt like I'd been robbed on Christmas morning. 'They've got all the facts, so they know best.'

Prue steadied her hair, which had listed in her anger. 'Nonsense. It's highly likely you're right. Even if this Elvira is indisposed, I will find out the details from Mr Klondike later today.' She bustled into the kitchen and banged about in the cutlery drawer.

'Jeez Louise,' said Shakira. 'Not so long ago, she told you off for interfering with the police investigation.'

'That's before Snood rattled her Mother Goose cage,' said James. He gave my arm a quick squeeze. 'Don't let Snood get to you. Come on, Shakira, let's get naked. Two coffees in the shop, Hels, soon as you can. Thanks.'

I smarted all day at Snood's words. I spent the first hour cooking up lines I should have fired back, but derived no satisfaction, and my mood sank further.

Late afternoon, Prue hung up her pinny, patted her hair and applied two spots of lipstick to the centre of her lips. 'I'm going to see Mr Klondike. I won't be long.'

No sooner had she left, than Malcolm arrived. As usual, his eyes searched for Prue.

'She'll be back soon,' I said.

He touched my arm. 'I need to tell you something urgent before Mrs Mayflower returns. I need your advice.' He pulled at the lining of his ancient cap.

I didn't want to hear. I'd used up my sympathy quota on Ruth. My headache had returned, and my nerves were all over the place. If Prue didn't deliver the goods, I'd give up this ridiculous notion of solving the murder. Just who did I think I was? A joke to the police, that's what. My face burned all over again.

Malcolm's normally ruddy face had turned grey at the gills, and his little eyes had lost their sparkle. It would have been cruel not to help. 'I'll make you a cup of tea, Malcolm, and you can tell me all about it.'

As we sat at a table, he produced his mobile phone – a cumbersome object, the size of a brick. I'd never seen him use it, but he lugged it around, 'just in case.' 'That Dora woman's been ringing me all day. How did she get my number? Look, it says she's sent me twenty-seven messages. Not that I know how to get them.' He banged his phone on the table, making the teacups jitter and bounce.

'What's set her off?'

Malcolm plopped three sugar lumps into his tea, stirred it forever and then dropped the spoon. 'Promise not to tell Mrs Mayflower?' Avoiding my eye, he embarked on a rambling tale. After seeing Prue home, he'd found Dora dancing in the street. He led her back to her house. At the door, Dora fumbled with her key. When Malcolm tried to help, she pulled him into the house, locked the door, popped the key down her cleavage and pounced.

'She kissed me and then she ...' He wiped his face with a serviette. 'I can't tell you the rest. You'd be shocked.'

'I know Dora comes on too strong, but what's so wrong with her? She's attractive and vivacious. She can't sing, but you can't have everything. She could make you happy.'

Malcolm straightened his back. 'There will only ever be one woman for me, and if she can't bring herself to like me in *that* way, then I'll accept any crumbs she throws. I won't settle for second best.'

Selfishly, I thought of my own situation. Had Zack settled for second best with me, and when he could stand it no longer, he'd taken off?

Despite his comb-over, mismatched clothes and pot belly, Malcolm's solemn dignity pierced my heart.

I thought for one wild moment Prue could do a lot worse; then I pulled myself together.

I took Malcolm's hand. 'You know, Prue wants to remain faithful to the memory of her husband?'

'I know that, Helen, love. Can't do anything about it, and that's that. I'm here to be of service.' He dropped my hand and frowned. 'But what am I to do about that pest of a woman?'

I'd had an idea and was about to reply when Prue entered the tea room. I jumped from my seat and ran towards her. Her face gave nothing away.

'Prue, have you found out about …?' I stopped and stared, open-mouthed. Charles had walked in behind her, carrying an enormous bunch of flowers.

'These are for you,' he said, as he thrust them towards me.

The Three Musketeers

Prue took Malcolm's arm and steered him into the shop. 'There are some light bulbs that need replacing if ...'

I wanted to chase after her to hear about the mystery wife, but as I took the white roses from Charles, he held my hand and locked his eyes on mine.

'Thanks for organising the impromptu wake for Vincent. I should have sorted it myself, but my schedule's so hectic and I've been abroad on business. I'm due to fly back tonight.'

The ferns around the roses tickled my nose, and I fought back a sneeze. Had I asked what he did for a living? I couldn't enquire now when he probably thought I knew. Too busy thinking about that, I missed his next line.

He smiled and raised his eyebrows as if waiting for an answer. 'If you could, that would be awesome,' he prompted.

If I could what? Remember my name in a crisis? Probably not. I gave an enigmatic smile and hoped he'd repeat himself.

'Sorry.' He hesitated. 'Have I been too forward under the circs?'

'No, not at all,' I replied with enthusiasm. He could have asked me to streak across Vincent's grave at the next full moon for all I knew.

'Don't feel you have to.' His soft brown eyes searched my face.

Oh hell, I'll have to come clean. 'I'm sorry, Charles, but I missed the important bit. I get so distracted at work. What was it you asked?'

He released my hand, and his eyes flicked towards the door. He was probably thinking, *Should I get the hell out while I can?* 'I asked if you'd like to have dinner with me one evening when I get back.'

'That would be nice.' I reclaimed his hand, meaning to jazz up my lukewarm response with a subtle squeeze. In my flustered state, I pumped out a vigorous handshake as if closing a deal.

'Acesome,' he said.

What?

He withdrew his hand and flexed his fingers. 'Sorry, got to shoot, but I'll call you next week.'

Acesome? Shoot? Oh, no. His vocabulary set my teeth on edge. Yes, he was possibly a murder suspect, but it was the little things that could put you off.

No sooner had he left the tea room than James and Shakira rushed in. Prue followed at a more sedate pace with Malcolm at her heels. 'So, has that nice boy asked you for a date?' she asked.

'He might have done.' I couldn't wipe the smile off my face. 'But don't go booking the bridesmaids yet. He's going abroad for a few days, and he'll probably forget all about it.'

'And, *you* are still married to Zack,' said James.

My smile probably dropped off. 'Yes, James, to your best friend who ran out on his marriage.'

Prue moved into the space between us. 'I don't condone infidelity, but Zack doesn't deserve Helen's loyalty. She's still a young woman in her prime.'

'Prue, you're right as always,' said James. 'So, moving on, why don't you tell our Miss Jean Brodie your news?'

'Yes, please. I'm dying to hear.'

James laughed. 'Prue's compromised her integrity.'

She lifted her head. 'I did employ a certain amount of guile, but if the police will not be led to water, then the end justifies the means.'

'Come on, Prue. Tell me, or I'll faint with the suspense.' I really did feel light-headed.

'I merely expanded upon a truth. I told Mr Klondike I was on flower duty at the church, had mislaid my keys, and Mrs Newby, who lives near the church, might have a set. I said I couldn't remember her exact address and would he be so kind?' She patted her hair and smiled.

'How could he resist his favourite damsel in distress?' said James.

Prue stepped backwards in her kitten heels. 'Sorry, James, was that your foot? There is indeed a Mrs Eileen Newby who lives near the church in one of Mr Klondike's rental properties.'

She produced the address with a flourish, and I planted a kiss on her papery pink cheek. 'Prue, you're a whizz.'

'According to Mr Klondike,' continued Prue, 'Elvira's rung in sick. Couldn't say when she'd be back, and he's no idea where Pansy's got to. The poor man is at all sixes and sevens.'

'Nah, he's better off without 'em,' said Shakira. 'Hey, Helen, what you gonna do with that address? That Snood's a cow, yeah? But if you're gonna go see the top cop, I'm in.'

Prue pursed her lips. 'Shakira, is this to do with you chasing men, again?'

'I'm just being flexible, seeing as Hel's nabbed my number one target.'

I clapped a hand over my mouth. 'Sorry, Shak, I completely forgot you liked Charles. I'll say I've changed my mind if he calls.'

'Nah, you're all right. I'm not bothered.' She stuck out her chest. 'He must like the skinny birds, and that'll never be me in a million years. Anyway, I'd already decided he loves himself too much.'

'Couldn't agree more,' said James. 'I won't even mention that Charles is our chief suspect for the murder.'

I wanted to slap that jeering expression right off his face.

Prue put a hand to her forehead. 'Shakira's right on one thing. You should take this information to that nice tall policeman, but no doubt you'll ignore my advice.'

'Got it in one,' said James. 'We'll be visiting Mrs Newby as soon as we shut the shop.'

Prue turned away, and her shoulders slumped. The art of deception must have taken its toll, and by that time of day, she'd usually had enough of us all anyway.

'Thanks for everything, Prue,' I said. 'Why don't you leave the cleaning to me? James might help.'

'Him?' She prodded James in the chest. 'Help? And I might catch a helicopter home.'

James laughed. 'You can't go wrong with a big chopper, Prue. Watch out for the blades, they'll mess with your hair.'

'Take care, Mrs Mayflower,' said Malcolm. He waved goodbye to her retreating back. 'Have a pleasant weekend. I'll help Helen.' His face fell when she didn't bother to reply.

I tapped his shoulder. 'Thanks, Malcolm. Come on, I'll tell you how we're going to sort out your problems with Dora. I've got plans to distract her, but in the meantime, if you give me your phone, I'll swap it for my old one.'

He fumbled in his pocket. 'Thanks, but I don't quite get you.' He held on to his phone as if it were his most treasured possession.

'With my phone, Malcolm, you'll have my old number, one that Dora won't know. *And*, it's more up-to-date than yours. I'll bring it in tomorrow and get Lucy to show you how to use it.'

His face lit up. 'That'll do the trick, Helen, love. And, what did you say about distracting Dora?'

'I've heard she's looking for a job, and I know the very man who needs her, in more ways than one.'

Although we cleaned up in no time, Malcolm was in no hurry to leave, and it dawned on me he was hoping to be in on the Newby action. 'Malcolm, if you can spare the time, come with us to see Mrs Newby. We may need your advice.' Fingers crossed, James – wrapped up in *The Times* crossword – hadn't heard that.

Malcolm's chest inflated. 'Of course, Helen, love, you know you can count on me.'

'What would we do without you?'

'We're like the Three Musketeers,' said Malcolm as he climbed into the back of James's car.

I gave a silly, nervous giggle. James drummed the steering wheel. His lips compressed into a tight line when he saw Malcolm was in the gang.

I'd not given much thought to how we'd tackle Mrs Newby. We couldn't force her to talk. It would probably work best if the woman-magnet asked the questions – James, not Malcolm. I suggested that, and James agreed with a curt yes.

'Acesome,' I said.

'What?' He turned to look at me.

'Just saying.'

'That's even worse than awesome. Have you witnessed an act of God or a stunning feat of human endeavour I somehow missed?'

I fidgeted with the seat belt. 'No.'

'Well then?'

'Oh, just …'

'What?'

'Oh, shut up, you fuss-arse. You need to get out more and let some air into your drawers.'

Malcolm was leaning in from the back, a hand on each headrest, his head following the exchange. 'Do you think we need to do a stakeout?' We both ignored him.

Mrs Newby lived at the end of a terrace, and her neighbours must have been praying for the day she would move. Their well-maintained houses had seasonal window boxes and Farrow and Ball front doors. Mrs Newby's had peeling purple paint, grimy windows, an overflowing dustbin, and a wayward gate. Mr Klondike needed to know about that.

As we parked outside the weed-filled strip of garden, a sudden movement at the house made me grip James's arm. A mangy, thin white cat emerged through the cat flap. It sniffed the air and crouched on the step as if it didn't have the strength to move. I nearly shot through the windscreen when it started up a crazy, primeval yowl.

As we approached the gate, the cat stared and then bolted back through the flap, continuing to screech. The noise reverberated through the house. Despite the warmth of the evening sun, I shivered. I wanted to run for the hills and forget all about Mrs Newby.

I tugged at James's sleeve. 'Perhaps we should come ...'

Too late. He'd already knocked on the door.

The Cat Told Me

The house appeared to be sleeping. The uneven curtains were haphazardly drawn but revealed no chinks of light. I strained to hear the cheerful murmur of a TV or radio, but only the mournful echoes of the cat rang out.

James gave another resounding knock that rattled the terrace. Nothing changed.

Malcolm tried around the back but soon returned, shaking his head. 'Perhaps she's gone away?'

'What, and left her cat?' I said.

He shrugged. 'It might not be hers. Maybe it's a stray that comes and goes?'

'Malcolm may be right,' said James. 'Look at all that junk mail sticking out of the letter box.' He pushed it through and bent to have a look. Then he shot straight back as if someone had fired a water pistol into his eye.

I laughed until I noticed his face had turned white. 'What's wrong?'

'Something bad has happened in there. The smell is indescribable.'

'It'll be fried food and stale tobacco,' said Malcolm. 'My pal's house smells of that.'

James stepped away and spoke as if reciting lines on stage. 'It's the smell of putrefaction. There's a dead body in there.'

Talk about shocked. I'd no idea Malcolm had pals, smelly or otherwise. As for James's announcement, it wasn't a total bombshell. The cat had sort of given it away, and I was getting used to this dead body business. 'We need to call the police.' My calm, steady voice surprised me.

'I'll do it,' said Malcolm. 'I did it last time. They know me.' He patted down his body with increasing urgency. 'Damn and blast, where's my phone?' I reminded him he'd left it at the shop due to Dora's nuisance calls. 'That blasted woman. Look what she's done now.'

I tapped in the number and gave him mine. He moved a distance away, and we watched him pace up and down and shout at the phone. He strode back with his hands in his pockets. 'They said to wait in the car and they'll send someone immediately.'

Malcolm had hardly finished speaking when sirens wailed in the distance. They were taking us seriously the second time around. Within minutes, two police cars arrived from opposite directions. I covered my eyes, expecting them to crash head-on.

'Sit tight for an episode of the Keystone Kops,' said James as policemen piled out of the cars and jostled at the gate.

After peering through the letterbox, one of the crews charged at the door with a battering ram. It immediately gave way. Then, the other lot stole the show by running in past them, only to ping straight back as if tied to elastic. One officer threw up outside the door. The other crew smirked, drew back their shoulders and entered the den.

All the buzz I'd expected the first time was soon there in spades. We watched in silence as they cordoned off part of the street, got to business with the police tape and donned white suits. Snood and DCI Swift arrived together.

After a lot of pointing, conferring, and directing officers, Swift wandered over to our car with Snood hot on his tail. He folded his body into an easy crouch at my passenger window. 'You seem to be keeping us in business, Ms Merang.' Despite the circumstances, he seemed relaxed. 'Did you just happen to be driving by?'

'No, obviously not. As I told Inspector Snood, we suspected—'

Snood captured my attention by staging a coughing fit. She held her hands over her mouth, so only her eyes were visible, but they blinked like semaphores. She shook her head vigorously from side to side.

Despite her previous hostility, I'd no desire to land her in trouble with the boss. If I helped her out, she might soften her attitude. *Yeah, and pigs might fly.* She'd obviously not played him my message, so I'd been spared that embarrassment at least.

'We're out on one of our team-building exercises,' I said. Weak, but the best I could do.

Swift's mouth twitched at one corner. I didn't look at Snood as she exhaled.

'I reported it.' Malcolm leaned forward and thrust his head out of my window at the DCI. 'Do you want me to bring you up to speed?'

'That will be helpful later, sir. We'll need to take your statements. Thanks for your input. If you could all remain here for now, please.' Snood and Swift returned to the action.

Malcolm sat back with a contented sigh. He could not have looked prouder than if he'd saved Gotham City on Batman's day off.

We waited for over an hour. Trapped in a confined space with the two most irritating men of Buttersley was not my idea of a good night out. Malcolm was pulling at my headrest and clicking his teeth. As for James, I'd tried to discuss this latest development, but he was doing his clam impression again. Time to summon my new best friend. I sent a text, and Snood appeared ten minutes later.

'Yes, you lot can go now. Call in at the station first thing tomorrow to give your statements.' She addressed her remarks to the car roof.

'So, what have you found in there?' James asked.

'I can't share that with you memb—'

'Before you start,' James raised his voice, 'let's just reflect on how we arrived at this position.'

Snood sighed. 'We've discovered a badly decomposed body.'

'I'm no detective,' said James, 'but I knew that.'

'How?' She shot down to our eye level. 'Did you enter the property?'

James stared straight ahead. 'The cat told me.'

'How is the cat?' I asked.

Surprisingly, Snood answered in detail and said it had perked up after devouring two tins of food. 'I'm going to get a vet friend of mine to check the poor thing over.'

These unexpected friends were popping up all over the place. First Malcolm and now Snood.

Just before we left, I spotted Arse and Alien. I couldn't imagine what I'd seen in that tall Andy. He wasn't a patch on Charles. I let down the window and asked Daz when he was bringing Sadie back to Merangs. I probably overdid the cordiality and implied my life would be nothing without them, but hopefully, he'd taken the bait. I would pump him for news on the case.

James drove us back and said he'd pick us both up early the next morning. I must have looked even more vacant than usual.

'Statements,' he said. 'Best get it over with before we open the shop.'

'Aye aye, Captain. I'll be ready,' said Malcolm.

James gritted his teeth.

We continued in silence after that. The initial excitement had worn off, and the men were probably as tired and deflated as me. I was relieved to get home and shut out the world.

Ravenous, I rustled up an omelette but then pushed it away. Thoughts of Mrs Newby and her cat removed my appetite. After a quick shower, I went to bed. I'd wanted to be alone, but now I shivered, all lonely and vulnerable. Is that how Mrs Newby had felt? What if she'd ended her days in fear? Yes, it could have been natural causes, but even so, how long had she lain there with no one to care about her whereabouts?

Too exhausted to consider the implications of Mrs Newby's death, I pushed it away to deal with later. I couldn't get warm. My cosy bed had developed wrinkles and bumps. I wriggled, turned over and then turned back again.

Thumping the pillows, my thoughts drifted to Charles. I smiled in the dark at how his chocolate brown eyes had gazed into mine. But settling back down to think nice things, I shot up again.

His father had been murdered. I knew that when I accepted the date. But now, maybe his stepmother had been murdered, too? A stepmother, he'd reckoned to not even know about. I'd only gone and agreed to date a possible serial killer.

Death Lets Ltd

Saturday 16th May

There was no getting to sleep after my morbid speculation about Charles. I flung myself from one scene to another. Charles was either a pantomime villain coated in blood or a wronged hero in need of support. I willed myself to stop those crazy thoughts. After all, he'd only said he'd call me. I might never hear from him again. But if I did, all the more reason to find the real killer. It surely couldn't be him?

Perhaps I dozed off after the birds started their racket at dawn. The next thing, someone was pounding on the front door. I leant out of the bedroom window to meet James's upturned face. 'Sorry, I've overslept. I'll let you in.'

He scowled. 'Hurry up, Medusa. I haven't got all day.'

I flattened down my curls as I flew down the stairs. James stood on the doorstep in a new grey suit and a piercing pink shirt. He held two takeaway coffees.

Glancing at the clock, I realised he was ridiculously early. We'd agreed on a much later time to go and give our statements. Another one who couldn't sleep? The shadows under his eyes suggested that.

'My God, have you got a licence to wear that shirt?'

James looked me up and down. 'Rough night?' He handed me one of the cups. 'Did you sleep in a bush?'

I scooted upstairs to sort myself out. James called after me. 'Bring something decent to change into. We'll go for a drink after work. We need to discuss the rising body count.'

On the way to the police station, I worried about our statements. 'It's tricky,' I said. 'We alerted Snood about a Mrs Newby, and then I told Swift, we just happened to be driving by.' I picked away at my thumbnail. 'I know, let's say we saw a distressed cat disappear through the cat flap and, being animal lovers, we knocked on the door.'

'Whatever.' James yawned. 'I really couldn't care less what they think.'

We picked up Malcolm, and I drilled him on the story. He soon got it when I said Prue would be in trouble, otherwise. As it turned out, we were in and out of the station in twenty minutes. I could have been dictating my shopping list, for all the officer cared. Fortunately, neither Snood nor Swift was around.

We arrived early at the shop, but customers were already queuing outside. The rumour mill must have been at it all night.

Malcolm didn't disappoint. In the tea room, he stopped at each table to recount the events, embellishing his role by the minute. 'I had to liaise with the police, you know.' He patted my old phone, stowed in the top pocket of his blazer. Instructions from Lucy were taped on the back. 'Directed initial operations, I did.' Somehow, he'd activated the phone's torch function, and it shone out like a miniature lighthouse.

That reminded me: I had to ring Dora about my job creation scheme.

Mid-morning, I escaped and visited Mr Klondike. The desk phone was ringing, but he sat immobile, staring at the wall. As I approached, he let out a groan, slumped, and his head fell onto the desk.

I rushed towards him. 'Mr Klondike, are you ill?'

He looked up with tears in his eyes. 'Every time the phone rings, it's a tenant giving notice, or a landlord withdrawing their property.'

I'd not considered the implications for Mr Klondike. On reflection, dead bodies found in two of his properties would never bode well in Buttersley. I placed my hand on his arm. 'Is it really that bad?'

'My whole business may crumble. I've spent years building it up to what you see before you.' His voice quivered. 'Have you heard? They're calling it Death Lets?'

'People have short memories. They'll pick on something else next week.' I patted his shoulder. 'Don't worry, it'll soon die down.' I could have worded that better.

'Is it a personal vendetta? Is the murderer after me?' His voice had risen to a fine falsetto.

'No, of course not. Don't be so paranoid.' Harsh, but did he actually think a killer was going all around the houses just to get to him?

He produced an enormous off-white hankie and wiped his nose. 'The police came here first thing this morning and demanded a list of all the properties. I gave them full *carte blanche*. I've got nothing to hide.' He gripped my hand. 'What am I to do? Even Elvira and Pansy have deserted me.'

I put on my good news voice. 'You've got friends at Merangs, and I'm going to send a special someone to help you get through all this.'

Mr Klondike's face lit up. 'Not Mrs Mayflower?'

'No, but it's a very lovely lady with a big heart and an even bigger smile.' I sounded like I was introducing a music hall act. Maybe I was.

Dora had said she'd be willing when I'd asked, and was contrite about her harassment of Malcolm. She reckoned she had secretarial skills and couldn't wait to get started on Mr Klondike.

I was hoping to kill three birds with one stone. Mr Klondike needed a firm female grip. But it would also divert Dora away from Malcolm, and best of all, I would have a mole at Death Lets Ltd. I invited Mr Klondike to take afternoon tea with Dora.

'I'd be delighted, my dear. I'll pop round when I close the office.'

Back at the shop, James's parents had turned up. Mr Jones was reading a newspaper, and his wife was holding court. 'I knew Eileen Newby as well as anyone, and I don't like to speak ill of the dead, but she wasn't one you could take to. Kept herself to herself, and look where that's got her.' Mrs Jones nodded in triumph, as if privacy were a capital crime.

'You didn't know she was married to Vincent, did you, Mother?' James said in a quiet voice at her side.

She flicked him away like a speck of dust. 'I can tell you this, though: she was at one time a wealthy woman but in the last few years had fallen on hard times.'

James hadn't stopped to listen and returned to his post in the shop.

Other customers chipped in with snippets of information, but Mrs Jones cut them off. She even disputed that a neighbour had seen Mrs Newby in the post office six weeks ago.

The audience gradually melted away and eventually, Mrs Jones rose and looked around as if she'd mislaid something.

Lucy appeared at her side. 'Mr Jones said to tell you he'll be in the hardware shop. He left about an hour ago.'

The tea room fell quiet after Mrs Jones left, and I was wondering if Daz, my pocket policeman, would ever turn up. But he didn't let me down and strutted in near closing time. Sadie hung on his arm. He announced he'd been on frontline duty all night at the murder scene and was fit to drop.

'Keeping us safe in our beds at night, he is.' Sadie's eyes shone with pride.

Malcolm, the terrier, was on him at once. 'Did you see the dead body, and was it Mrs Newby?'

'Don't be so ghoulish and nosy, Malcolm,' I said, but he was bang on. *Come on, Daz, tell us. I know you want to.*

'I had more of an external role. One of security and safekeeping, which is vital in a case like this, but what I can tell you is …' He paused for a gulp of tea. 'Smashing sponge as always, Helen.'

'Thanks, you were saying?'

'Female. Definitely not natural causes.' He pushed away his plate and folded his arms. 'And, I'm saying no more.'

'Daz, let me get you more cake. Don't feel obliged to tell us anything. I'm just glad you can relax and offload some of the stress you must be under from such an important investigation.'

Daz accepted this with a nod. 'Bludgeoned to death, she was.' He ran a hand over his mouth. 'What a mess.'

My stomach dropped. Poor Mrs Newby.

Sadie gasped. 'The things he has to deal with.'

Daz turned his head to see who was listening. 'I've got a piece of information which is not yet common knowledge, but will probably be of interest to you, seeing as you were in on the Vincent murder, so to speak.'

Though my stomach churned from the details of Mrs Newby's death, my ears pricked up. 'Daz, don't tell us anything that might compromise your position.' *Spit it out now, man.*

'Well, I don't think I'm totally out of order here to disclose that two independent witnesses saw a man in work clothes, a high-viz jacket and a peaked cap, coming away from Vincent's flat, on the day of his murder. One witness said a tall man. The other said medium, but that's what you get with the untrained eyes of the general public.'

Daz's trained eyes had wandered over my shoulder. I turned to see Dora making her entrance. She tottered towards us in needlepoint stilettos. Her lower half was encased in a black pencil skirt, slit up one thigh. A tiny white blouse and corset belt hoisted her boobs dangerously high.

She pouted her crimson lips. 'Where's the poor darling? I'm ready to apply my succour.'

Was that Daz behind me, spluttering out his tea? Malcolm had scarpered.

I ushered Dora to a table. 'I see you've made an effort.'

With difficulty, she lowered herself into a chair. 'Sweet of you to say, darling. I gave it a lot of thought, but when you've been in the acting profession as long as I have, dressing for a job is second nature.' She took out a notebook and pen from her bag and perched heavy-rimmed glasses on her head. 'And, if I'm confident I look the part, then I can play it to perfection.'

I sat for a moment beside her. 'I don't know how much paperwork you'll have to do. You may just have to hold Mr Klondike's hand to steer him through the crisis.'

'Leave it to me, darling. I'll sort him out.' She held up her hand and wiggled her fingers. 'Here he comes. Oh, what a big boy.' She shooed me away. 'Mr Klondike, how lovely to meet you.'

While I was preparing their afternoon tea, the shop phone rang.

The voice on the other end cackled a throaty laugh. 'Found any juicy dead bodies today?'

'Shakira, I'm busy. Did you just ring for the gossip?'

The line went silent for a beat. 'Well, Miss Hoity-toity, I did have some information for you from my loser sister, but I might not bother now.'

'Sorry, Shak. Go on. I'm all ears.'

'Yeah, okay. You know Candice works for a cleaning agency, yeah? Well, guess who worked on her shift?'

'Not Mrs Newby?'

'Bingo. Only thing, she's not turned up in the last six weeks, so they've sacked her.'

'That won't be too much of a blow. Six weeks confirms something I heard earlier. Thanks a lot, Shakira.' My God, what sort of state would that body have been in?

Serving afternoon tea to Dora and Mr Klondike, I could have been invisible. As she recounted a tale through tears of laughter, he rocked backwards and forwards in glee. I made a note to check the chair for damage later.

Daz and Sadie didn't stay long. Daz could hardly keep his eyes open, even though they'd remained fixed on Dora. When only she and Mr Klondike lingered, I told Lucy to go early and then broke my own rule of not starting to clean while we still had customers. But those two were so engrossed I could have turned a fireman's hose on the place and they would not have flinched.

We'd been officially closed for ten minutes when James plonked himself between them. 'Is this a private party or can anyone join in?'

'Gerald and I were just discussing his needs.' Dora threw out a coquettish smile. 'Business-wise, I mean.'

Mr Klondike's face turned red, and he coughed.

'However pressing Mr Klondike's needs are, could you continue elsewhere?' said James. 'You've been so involved, you may not have noticed we've closed.'

They both jumped up. 'Of course, you'll be wanting to get home,' said Dora.

'We're going to Bangles for cocktails,' I said, hoping to plant a seed for them to cement their newfound connection.

Dora put a finger to her mouth. 'Oh, Gerald, doesn't that sound deliciously decadent?'

'Perhaps we might see you there?' I said, thinking Mr Klondike might need a push. 'It's two for one until seven,' I added, in case he was tight with his cash.

He smiled at Dora. 'We could perhaps amble over there, my dear? It's an establishment I've not yet patronised.'

'I promise to be good.' Dora giggled like a girl. She almost carried it off.

Mr Klondike offered Dora his arm, and they stepped out as the perfect couple.

Bangles

I loved Bar Bangles. *The Bright Young Things* who worked there knew how to shake a cocktail and stocked all the best gins. Charles would say the food was acesome and, best of all, it was close to Merangs.

I wasn't so keen on the high circular tables. The choice was either to stand – not an option after a full day at the shop – or take a flying leap at one of the high, narrow stools. The Buttersley custom was then to shoot daggers at the show-offs who'd bagged a booth.

When we arrived, Bangles was full enough for there to be an atmosphere, but not overly busy. I spotted DCI Swift in a corner with his young floozy. He looked more rugged with dark stubble on his chin. They sat at a table next to Mr Klondike and Dora. I willed myself not to stare.

After we'd chucked back the champagne shots of our Porn Star Martinis, James wanted to hear the latest.

I admitted I'd not discovered much, and Mrs Newby remained an elusive and friendless character. 'We don't even know for certain she was married to Vincent.'

'We'll assume she was.' James swirled the passion fruit around in his glass. 'Let's concentrate on what we know. Not necessarily proven facts, but good enough for us.'

I sort of knew what he meant. 'Okay, she was violently killed.' We both pulled a face. 'And she was last seen six weeks ago.'

'So, she died around the end of March, which makes it about two weeks before Vincent's murder.'

As usual, James's analytical mind was stealing the show. I wanted to get a date in of my own. 'Both were killed after the death of Claudia. She died mid-February. The deaths must be linked, surely? And, is it significant Mrs Newby died first, even though Vincent was found before her?'

James shrugged. 'Are you ready for another Porn Star?'

I drained my glass. 'When am I not?'

James went to the bar. Relaxed and mellow, I glanced around with a big, goofy grin and caught the eye of DCI Swift. He raised a glass and smiled. His young, Bambi-eyed friend turned around and stared until Swift tapped her shoulder, and she turned back to face him.

'Where were we?' James handed me cocktail number two – the maximum I could handle before hitting the gin.

'Filing the deaths in date order.'

'Okay, so Claudia's the catalyst for both our deaths. Who benefits from both?'

'That means you think the same person killed ...' At a commotion in the corner, I swivelled on the stool. Both Mr Klondike and DCI Swift were hauling Dora up from the floor, while Swift's young date looked like she wanted to disappear. James rushed over.

Dora brushed herself down. 'Gerald made me laugh, and I tipped backwards on this ridiculously high stool.' She gave Mr Klondike a playful push. 'It's his fault for being so entertaining.'

'As long as you're still in one piece, my dear.'

Everyone resumed their places. 'One, two, three,' I shouted, a little too loudly, and James and I knocked back our shots.

'What were we saying?' James asked.

'Wondering if the same person killed them both. Or, I've just thought, Vincent could have killed Mrs Newby, and then someone knocked him off in revenge.'

James snorted. 'What? Avenge the death of your loved one, but leave their body to rot down like a pile of manure? I'd expect a bit more from my nearest and dearest.'

'Oh, I didn't think of that.' I went back to my drink.

'One thing puzzling me,' said James. 'Did the killer anticipate it would take so long to find Mrs Newby's body? Did it matter to him?'

'That's what I meant earlier.' My head was gently swimming. 'About Mrs Newby dying before Vincent.'

James puffed out his cheeks. 'Even with two deaths, we can't be certain the murderer intended Vincent's death to look like murder. He may just have panicked and shoved him in the cupboard, giving him more time to escape from a sticky situation. I'm just using male pronouns for convenience, by the way.'

'I know, I know. I'm not totally thick, by the way.'

'Touchy but not thick.' James smiled. 'Let's call our murderer, M. If that's okay with *The Brains Trust?*' He clinked my glass.

'Nearly forgot to say, but according to policeman Daz, witnesses had seen a workman walking away from Vincent's flat on the day of his murder. That could have been M?'

James nodded. 'Could have been. Anyway, M drowns Vincent in the bath but doesn't realise the water has leaked down below. Presumably, Vincent put up a struggle, thrashed around, and he was a big bloke.'

I shuddered at the memory of his corpse on top of me. 'You don't need to tell me that.'

James squeezed my hand. 'Anyway, M was unaware he'd drawn attention to his crime. Then Klondike came pounding up the stairs.'

I thumped the table. 'Honestly, you can't even get away with murder these days without some busybody sticking their nose in.'

James laughed. 'Helen, calm down. You're too excitable when you drink. And consider the irony of what you've just said.'

'Oh, yeah.' I thwacked my forehead. 'So, M had time to hide with the noise Mr Klondike makes.'

We both looked to the corner. Mr Klondike and Dora had interlocked their arms and were drinking from each other's glass. The DCI and his date were not so loved-up. As I stared, she stuck one finger in front of his face, jumped down from the stool, and pushed her way to the exit.

DCI Swift shrugged and picked up his phone. Why had he not rushed after her? How callous. He was probably scrolling through his contacts to find his next victim.

'What's the fascination? Look away now,' said James. 'We were saying, M drowns Vincent, hears a buffalo charging up the stairs, so he hides somewhere in the flat. Klondike sees the body, has the screaming abdabs and crashes out. M hides the body and scarpers, knowing, at some point, the body will be found and classed as murder, and that may or may not have suited his plans.'

We didn't seem to be getting anywhere. My phone buzzed, and I glanced at it when James went to the bar. A text from Charles, wanting to know if I was free on Tuesday evening, as he was so looking forward to seeing me.

Wow. I wanted to broadcast that to Bangles. I gazed around with my big, dopey grin and caught the eye of DCI Swift. He was fiddling with his empty glass, and in my euphoria, I felt sorry for him. He gave a brief nod, picked up his phone and left the bar.

James placed two pink gins and a packet of my favourite cheese and onion crisps on the table. 'The more I think about it, I can't understand why they've not arrested that creep.'

'Which creep?'

'Charles, of course. He's the only person who benefits from all three deaths.'

'In money terms only.' A fragment of poetry popped into my head. Something about treading softly on my dreams? James had just run a bus over mine. 'There could be another motive and more suspects we don't even know about. And what about Elvira?'

James folded his arms. 'It all points to Charles.'

That wasn't the debut onto the dating scene I'd anticipated. 'The police don't seem to think Charles is involved.'

My statement hung in the air as James jerked backwards and spilt gin down his fancy pink shirt. Dora had attacked from behind and was dragging him into her arms. 'We're leaving now, my darlings.'

I grabbed James's legs to stop him from doing a backflip. At the same time, I was hugged by a bear.

'Ms Merang, Helen, I can't thank you enough for introducing me to this captivating lady.' Mr Klondike released me and took Dora's arm. 'Come, my dear. Your carriage awaits.'

She clasped both his hands. 'Oh, my knight in shining armour.'

James muttered something about how that would take a lot of metal, but I felt all warm and fuzzy at their delight in each other. Selfishly, I wondered if *I* would ever experience that joy again.

After our friends departed, I steered the conversation away from the murders. The subject had become too hot for me. 'James, I'm starving.'

He looked around. 'Too late for food here. They've stopped serving.'

'Let's go for a curry. Bombs Away will still be open.'

Meet Maureen

Monday 18th May

At the start of another week, I enjoyed my brisk walk to work in the cool morning air. Then, once I opened the shop door, the sparkling glass cabinets and hug of vanilla thrilled me as always.

James had already arrived. He stood at the counter in a shirt of metallic blue and orange stripes.

'Have you been shopping in London again?' I said. 'They wouldn't shift many of those around here.'

'What's up with you? Still hungover? I bet you spent yesterday in bed.'

I shook my head. 'Not at all. I had to get up early as my new best friend came around with a surprise.'

James yawned. 'I can't pretend to be intrigued until I've downed an espresso.'

He rolled up his sleeves, carefully washed his hands and began to restock the truffle cabinet. I went to make our morning coffee. The best one of the day, before the customers arrived.

I made three drinks, as Shakira would soon be down with the delivery. She clattered in as I was handing James his cup. I nearly threw it over him when I saw the state of her face. Not only was she make-up free, her complexion was also bloated, blotchy and raw.

I thought carefully before I spoke. 'Shakira, you're not looking yourself.'

James looked up from his truffles. 'My God, it's the monster from the deep. Do you come in peace?'

'Shut up, James,' we shouted together.

Shakira wiped a tear from her swollen eye. 'I swear Candice did it on purpose, the cow. You know how jealous she is of my looks.'

James snorted and turned away.

'My God, what has she done?' I asked.

'She's doing beauty treatments. She should stick to scrubbing floors, not making face scrubs.'

'Looks like she's scrubbed a floor with your face,' said James as he moved in for a closer look.

Shakira dug her elbow into his ribs. 'Candice has turned her kitchen into a health spa. She wanted me to trial the experience before the paying punters. I told her to remove the deep fat fryer first.'

I glanced at the clock. We were late in opening, and I was anxious to do so before Prue arrived. 'Back in a mo.' I ran to the door. As I turned the sign, Prue was marching up the street with her Mary Poppins umbrella.

Here she comes. Jump to it. Spit spot.

I rushed back to the counter to hear Shakira telling James, 'It was supposed to be a relaxing experience to get me over the disappointing date.'

He groaned, but I wanted to know. 'Why was it disappointing?'

Shakira sniffed. 'Turns out he was a twitcher.'

'A what?'

'A twitcher is an extreme bird watcher,' James said.

Ah, so he is interested.

Prue hung up her coat. 'What a lot of nonsense. Shakira, you know your cake trays shouldn't be in the shop when we're open. Please take them through to the tea room.'

Shakira picked up a tray. 'I will, Mrs Mayflower. I'm just a bit upset today.'

'You're always in some state of high emotion, dear.'

Shakira placed her tray back down. 'I bought a new dress, and he turned up in a dirty anorak with binoculars around his neck. "You won't need those to spot my assets", I joked. You know like, to put him at his ease. Guess what he said?'

James laughed. 'It won't have been, is that the lesser spotted tit.'

'James!' shouted Prue. 'You go too far.'

Shakira tried to smile, but her bee-stung lips wouldn't go there. 'He literally said nowt. I couldn't get a word out of the rabbit. So I went to powder my nose. Came back to a note under my BGB.'

She'd lost me there. 'What's a BGB?'

'A big girl's blouse?' James suggested.

'Don't be ridiculous,' said Prue. 'And what is that garment *you* are wearing, by the way?' She prodded his chest. 'You look like a clown.'

I joined the attack. 'I thought clowns were meant to be funny.'

Shakira sighed. 'Don't you lot get out? BGB is brandy, Guinness, and Babycham. You don't need many.'

'What did the note say?' I persisted. As usual, we'd gone off track.

Shakira touched her cheek and winced. 'He'd had a tip-off, a short-toed eagle had been spotted in Surrey, and he had to leave. He put a kiss at the end of the note, so I think he liked me.'

'How could he not?' I said and then tossed in one of my clichés. 'It's his loss. Come on, we'll take these trays through together.' Prue would start tutting if we didn't move soon.

One of our regulars, Don't-Mess-with Maureen, muscled past us. Built like a battleship, but with wispy grey hair, she scared me witless. One of the few people I disliked, and I suspected it was mutual. Maureen started the week with early-morning gym classes and popped in afterwards for a mint tea. Shakira dumped her trays and ran.

Maureen headed for her usual table and whacked the seat cushion into submission. 'Some people think Lycra's a licence to act like a Nazi.'

'Has someone upset you, Maureen?' Did I sound like I cared?

'The idiot boy leading the spin class dared to say I wasn't keeping up. I told him I was spinning when he was just a sperm. And, it was my opinion he'd not progressed much since.'

Nice. Maureen never required much of a response. I fetched the *Morning Post* so she could rant at the news.

'Where are The Silent Sisters when you need them?' I whispered to Prue. They acted as sponges when Maureen got going.

After we'd served Maureen, Prue and I had a moment together. Our conversation was punctuated by Maureen's exclamations. Aimed at no one in particular, they hung in the air like puffs of poison gas.

Maureen stabbed the newspaper with her finger. 'They should make 'em shovel up dog-mess all day long.'

We both ignored her. Prue put down her cup. 'What has silly Shakira done to her face?'

I explained, hoping she might know of a soothing remedy. She didn't comment and turned to the cup shelf. But I hadn't finished and wanted to share my news. 'Prue, I've got a cat. Mrs Newby's cat. It needed a home.'

Prue still had her back to me. 'You can't even remember to feed yourself.'

'Freeloaders. They should line 'em up and shoot 'em. If I had a gun, I'd do it myself,' offered Maureen.

I didn't give Prue the details, but yesterday I'd contacted Snood. I needed to know if Charles was a suspect. As an icebreaker, I enquired about the cat. Next thing, Snood arrived on my doorstep, and Snowy was mine. The three of us bonded over a saucer of milk. Snood revealed that Charles had a rock-solid alibi for the day Vincent was murdered. And, though early days as regards Mrs Newby, she confirmed they weren't interested in him.

I took Prue's hand. 'Owning a cat will make me more responsible. I'm nearly thirty-two, and I think I can handle it.'

Prue's lips twitched. 'You should be starting a family.'

I wished she wouldn't go on about that. 'I thought you'd be pleased about the cat.'

Prue sighed. 'I just want to see you settled.'

'I know, Prue, I know.' I patted her hand. Should I tell her I was meeting Charles tomorrow? But there was no point in raising false hopes.

'It's all a load of codswallop, and that's my final word,' said Maureen.

We should be so lucky.

It was a quiet day, and in the afternoon, I popped out to see the lovebirds. Mr Klondike and Dora were sitting side by side at the front desks. They looked like game show contestants who'd won the jackpot.

'Hello sweetie. How lovely to see you,' said Dora.

'Ms Merang, Helen, I mean.' Mr Klondike beamed. 'Thank you so much for finding me this treasure. She's the very interface I was seeking.'

Dora perched her glasses on her head. 'I'm contacting all the clients and reassuring them of our best service at all times. It's all about communication, and as you know, that's where my talents lie.'

Mr Klondike's smile widened, and I surmised he'd uncovered her other talents by then.

'That's wonderful. I knew you'd work your magic, Dora. Have you heard from Elvira or Pansy, Mr Klondike?'

He looked to the ceiling like he needed to think and then said, 'Not a dicky-bird. I wondered—'

Dora interrupted, 'I'm so glad you called in, Helen. I wanted to give you these. Tickets for the show. We open on Wednesday. Ta-da.' She finished with jazz hands. Mr Klondike joined in, waggling his thick, meaty sausages with gusto.

'Fantastic, thanks. I'll be there. Can't wait.'

Dora then launched into a monologue about her role, which apparently was the pivot of the entire production. After ten minutes, my eye started to twitch.

I was saved by Shakira, who'd come to pay her rent. 'I'm going to get my face sorted later. Prue has fixed me up with her beautician and said to put it on her account.'

I smiled. 'Prue's got a heart of gold.'

'That's what James said, and then he spoilt it by saying, "Pity you have to hack through a forest and scale the fortress to find it".'

That reminded me I'd been too long away from the shop. I threw out a quick goodbye and dashed out. In my haste, I collided with a woman outside Merangs. I was horrified when she fell to the ground, but then realised two things: it was Pansy and she'd fainted.

A Crime of Passion

I'd always known that first aid course would come in handy. I placed my jacket under Pansy's head and raised her legs high. She moaned, and her eyelids fluttered. I reached across to push open the shop door and yelled for help.

James ran out and then ran straight back in again. 'I'll fetch Prue.'

Seconds later, Prue emerged with a chair. 'Get a glass of water and you'll find smelling salts in my bag.' She pushed me out of the way. 'Now. Quick. Move.'

Keep your hair on, Matron. I've managed pretty well so far.

Pansy was soon restored, but tearful. 'I've just come out of hospital and found out what's happened. It's a nightmare. I feel so alone. I need to contact the police.'

I looked at Prue and James over the top of her head. Did they have any idea what she was talking about? James raised his eyebrows and shook his head.

'Pansy dear,' said Prue. 'Do you think you could manage to walk into the tea room?'

Pansy nodded and allowed Prue to guide her through.

'Hot, sweet tea is what you need, Pansy,' I said, feeling Prue had hijacked my medical role. 'I'll see to it now.'

Minutes later, we gathered around Pansy as she sipped her tea. Without the false eyelashes, painted eyebrows and orange foundation, her dull eyes had sunk like rain holes in the snow.

'Pansy, dear, do you need to go back to hospital?' Prue asked. 'You're very pale.'

Let's get down to the nitty-gritty. Why does she want to contact the police?

'No. I'm not ill. I'm pregnant. I couldn't stop being sick and got dehydrated. They put me on a drip and have given me tablets.'

Prue poured more tea into Pansy's cup. 'How dreadful for you, dear. Have some caramel flapjack. It will put the roses back into your cheeks.'

After Pansy had taken a couple of bites, my patience snapped. 'Why do you need to contact the police?'

'Mum's missing and Aunty's dead.' Pansy's tone suggested she wanted to tag 'you brainless idiot' onto the end.

A light bulb flashed. 'Oh, I see. Elvira's your mother, and Mrs Newby is, I mean was, your aunt?' *So, Elvira was having an affair with her sister's husband.* 'Sorry for your loss,' I hastily added.

Pansy looked through me and continued her narrative. 'Mum was upset at the funeral. Dave, my husband, picked us up. We took her home. I wanted to stay with her, but he wouldn't let me. They don't get on. That's the last I saw of her.'

Prue patted Pansy's hand. 'When did you go into hospital, dear?'

'Friday morning.' She started on her second piece of flapjack. 'I felt ill at the funeral. Was sick all night. Dave took me, and they kept me in.'

'Did Dave tell Elvira you were there?' I asked.

'I suppose so, but I don't know if he spoke to her.' She glared at me as if I were the most annoying child in class. 'I phoned her myself when I started feeling better, but got no answer. She's not rung back or texted or anything. It's been four days since I've seen her. I called at her house. She wasn't there. Where is she?' Pansy's eyes darted around the room with suspicion.

While Prue trotted out the platitudes and held Pansy's hand, I kicked James's foot and swivelled my eyes like a madwoman. I was hoping he might ask a relevant question.

He furrowed his brow and said, 'Sorry to hear about your aunt, Pansy. It must have been a terrible shock. How did you find out?'

She flicked her eyes at him. 'Mum's neighbour told me.'

I tried to find my caring voice. 'Maybe your mum was in shock and so affected by the deaths, she went to stay with a friend?'

Pansy glanced back at James as if he'd spoken again. 'She's not got any friends. We've not seen Aunty Eileen for months. They fell out over Vincent.'

I could see how stealing your sister's husband might take the fun out of family occasions.

The shop bell sounded, and James bounded off.

Pansy placed her hands flat on the table and pushed herself up. 'I need to go home. I was on my way to see Mr Klondike, but can't be bothered now.'

'Let me take you home,' I said. 'I'll call a taxi.'

Prue pursed her lips and tapped her watch. The afternoon tea crowd would be in soon, and it was impossible to cope single-handedly.

'Sorry, Prue, but this is practically an emergency, and Lucy said she'd call in after college. She'll give you a hand.'

I'd only finished speaking when James threw open the tea room door and announced, 'Here's Lucy.'

Lucy giggled. 'Oh, James, you *are* silly. Why do you always do that?' She stood in the doorway, radiant and fresh in a white sleeveless dress.

Mollified, Prue fussed around Pansy while I called a taxi. It turned out Pansy lived close to the shop, and despite my ingenious efforts to elicit information, she remained tight-lipped for the journey.

When we pulled up outside a modern townhouse, I gave her my card. 'Don't hesitate to ring if you need anything,' I urged. 'And let us know when you hear from Elvira.'

'Yeah, right.' She tossed the card into her bag without even looking and climbed out of the taxi. At her front door, she threw a quick thanks over her shoulder.

'Pansy, wait a moment.' I chased after her.

She turned. 'What?'

'You left your belt in the taxi.' I held it out, and she snatched it without a word.

Through the open door, I peered into the hallway. 'Looks like you're well prepared for the baby.' There was enough stuff piled up to furnish a crèche.

'Mum bought it for me.' Pansy slammed the door and shot the bolt. She was probably erecting the barricade as I walked down the path.

Prue's voice rang in my ear. 'Why do you want everyone to like you?'

I decided to walk back. By the time I reached the high street, I'd solved the case. It was a classic crime of passion. Elvira murdered Eileen Newby, the sister who stood between her and lover-boy Vincent. But then, having gone to all that trouble, the sleazeball rejected her. So, in for a penny, in for a pound, she thought and topped him off too. He had it coming. She was on the run.

I barged into Merangs, breathless but exhilarated. 'James, I know exactly what happened. Elvira did it.' He folded his arms and heard me out. 'Find a hole in that if you can.'

'There *is* another angle to consider, of course.' James paused and looked at me as if I could supply it.

'And that is?'

'Elvira could be the third victim.' He laughed. 'You look like you've been slapped. Forget about that for a moment. Someone is waiting for you in the tea room.'

I flung open the door to find Ruth deep in conversation with Shakira. Ruth looked up and gave a warm smile.

'Lovely to see you, Ruth. Has Shakira been looking after you?'

'We've found out we have much in common,' she said.

'Yeah, we're both fashionistas,' said Shakira. 'Ruth knows all the labels.'

Ruth shrugged. 'I've always had an interest in fashion. I wanted to study it, but my mo ... I mean, circumstances prevented me.'

'Look at these beauties.' Shakira pulled out a pair of shoes from her bag and placed them on the table. 'Just got 'em off eBay.'

'Armani,' Ruth pronounced. 'They're ... erm, stunning.'

They looked like any other stilettos to me. 'Let's hope they've stuck the heels on better than that other designer did.'

Ruth and Shakira exchanged a puzzled look.

'I've forgotten the brand,' I said. 'You know, the heel snapped off when you tripped over that dog?'

'Louboutin,' said Ruth.

Prue swooped in like a buzzard. 'Take those shoes off the table, now.'

Shakira scooped them up and said it was time for her to leave. 'Bye, Ruth. Hope to see you again?'

'Without a doubt. I've enjoyed our chat. I'm here for a week.'

Ruth said she was staying at The Cavendish, our town's grandest hotel and known as The Butterdish. 'I was wondering, Helen, if you'd like to join me there for dinner tomorrow evening? My treat.'

Her shoulders slumped when I said I was already booked. Typical, I spent most evenings alone, counting the peas on my plate for excitement. Any other night, I would have bitten her hand off. I thought it best not to mention Charles.

'Let's make it another night, Ruth. If you're free on Wednesday, we're all going to the local amateur production and would love you to join us.'

Her shoulders rose. 'That sounds like fun. Count me in.'

Ruth went on to talk about her cousins she was meeting later. Apart from Claudia's funeral, she'd not seen them in years. Her eyes shone as she showed me photos they'd sent.

Call me shallow, but as she prattled on about people I'd never meet, my mind wandered. There was so much to do for my upcoming date with Charles. I'd nothing to wear, having rejected every single item in my wardrobe. He'd liked me in my funeral outfit, but I could hardly wear that. The main job was to get my hair sorted. My lion tamer was double-booked but said she'd try to fit me in. Otherwise, it would have to be Prue's Popeye stylist or a wig.

'Have you heard from Charles?' Ruth asked.

'Charles, hmmm.' I hoped I hadn't blushed. 'Oh yes, he's coming here for a few days to tie up Vincent's affairs.' I couldn't meet her eye.

'I would imagine he's a few debts to pay.'

I told Ruth about poor Mr Choudray and Vincent's cigarette debt. 'It's not extortionate, but it means a lot to him.'

Ruth switched back to her cousins, and I thought about my outfit again. It depended on the venue. Charles had left the choice up to me, and I couldn't decide on that either.

Prue and James approached the table to chat with Ruth. I told them both to sit down while I did some work.

'Hallelujah,' said Prue, and James feigned a collapse. Ruth laughed loudly.

Loading the dishwasher, I thought about Pansy and whether I should mention Elvira's disappearance to Snood. I took out my phone and found Snood's number, but my finger hovered over the call button. It wasn't my business. The phone pinged with a text from Charles:

Pick you up at 7.30. Can't wait.

Me neither. I was a bag of excited nerves.

A Meaty Date

The doorbell rang. My God, Charles had arrived, and I was standing ankle-deep in the detritus of my wardrobe. I pulled on the little black dress, which had been my first choice. Not a showstopper, but it clinched in all the right places. I grabbed my bag, patted Snowy's head and ran down the stairs.

My hands shook as I opened the door.

'Wow,' exclaimed Charles. He whistled. 'I'm blown away.'

He leant against the door jamb in a black leather jacket, narrow jeans, and a crisp, pale shirt. He smelt divine – a blend of citrus and musk. I could hardly believe my luck.

'You look, er ... very nice too.'

He grabbed my hand. 'Let's go, hun.'

Hopefully, he didn't notice Malcolm hiding behind a bush at the end of the garden. At the last minute, I'd told James and Prue about my date. While I had it on good authority that Charles wasn't a serial killer – always a bonus – he *was* still a stranger. Prue must have alerted Malcolm, so it looked like there would be three of us on the date.

We hit Bangles first, and bingo, we got a booth. Malcolm stood with his back to us, squinting through a mirror on the wall.

Charles cupped my chin. 'Do you come here often?'

'So original. Not corny at all. I like your style.'

'Speaking of style, hun, you've got it all going on. Your hair is ... er, A-one.'

I peered into Malcolm's mirror and saw a giant frizz-ball perched on my head. Why did it have to be such a damp evening?

'My lion tamer had other fish to fry and the wig shop was shut.'

Charles opened his mouth and then closed it. A tiny frown appeared on his smooth forehead. Why had I said such a stupid thing? At least I'd not dragged Popeye into the equation.

I encouraged Charles to talk about his job. He rattled on about a consortium involving projects and properties abroad.

I gazed at his classical features and velvet eyes. 'You sound like you really enjoy your work.'

'I love the buzz of making an acesome deal.' He raised his fist, and I thought about calling Malcolm over so they could do a high five. I settled for an echoing acesome.

Charles went to the bar, and Malcolm scooted to the other end. I had a quick look around, and who should be there but DCI Swift. This time, he was seated with a much older woman. Her hair was elegantly styled, and her clothes expensive. Swift looked tired and weary. What was it with him? Was he some sort of extreme dater? She had wrapped her hands around his.

Charles returned, and Malcolm resumed his post. 'Sorry, I've been gassing about myself, but you're such a good listener.'

Years of practice in the tea room, mate. It's automatic.

He leant towards me. 'So, where are you taking me next, Ms Merang? Deal-making is hungry work. I'm famished.'

'Cheeky Chops.'

'Is that an endearment, already?'

I'd just gulped my gin, and the unexpected quip made me snort it through my nose. 'Sorry about that,' I said, groping in my bag for a tissue. Charles handed me a pristine white hankie. 'Cheeky Chops is Buttersley's new restaurant.' Tears streamed down my face and turned the hankie black. 'It's run by a local farming family.' Charles's face remained blank. 'It's quirky for Buttersley,' I ploughed on. 'They just serve chops, salad, cheese, and home-baked bread.'

'Cool.'

'And these are a few of my favourite things.' I sang in a loud falsetto. That did get a reaction, and not just from Charles. He froze like a rabbit in the road, while DCI Swift stood and applauded. The mother figure pulled him down.

Ration the alcohol, please.

'Have you finished?' I hoped Charles meant my drink and not the singing. 'Shall we go?' He held the door open and, once outside, held my hand. I liked it.

In the short walk down the high street, I watched Malcolm's reflection as he darted in and out of shop doorways. He probably thought he was doing a good job.

'I think we've arrived,' I said as we approached a door featuring a giant moose head with flashing, rotating eyes. We entered the restaurant under a portal of antlers.

'Howdy,' said a smiling cowgirl. 'Please take a seat in the byre while I find you a table.'

I thought she'd mispronounced the word 'bar' until I found myself crouched on a milking stool in a pretend cowshed. I wriggled my dress back down my thighs. 'Well, this is different,' I said, giggling at the thought of what James would make of the place.

'When you travel as much as I do, you get used to the wacky and bizarre.' Charles brushed straw off his jeans. 'I remember a tea ceremony in Japan ...'

I'm ashamed to say I missed the rest, as I was surreptitiously searching for Malcolm. I eventually located his leg sticking out from behind a hay bale.

Our cowgirl returned, ringing a bell. 'Follow me, partners.' She gave a little skip and a jump, and I had to stop myself from copying her.

The restaurant was bright and cheerful. Thankfully, they'd exhausted the gimmicks, and the decor was restrained to showcase the food. A long table dominated one side of the room. It held a mountain of bread. A crusty, cheesy, herb-filled slice of heaven. Salad islands were dotted around the room, and the staff weaved in and out of the tables with platters of grilled meat. My nostrils twitched at the smoky, rich aroma.

'The concept is simple,' said our cowgirl. 'Help yourselves to anything on the salad and bread tables. When you require meat, press this red button here.'

She remained unruffled when Charles said he was vegan. 'And I'm also wheat intolerant,' he added.

'We have provision for that,' she said, although her smile had faded.

'I eat everything else.'

What else could there be?

Charles gave a charming smile. 'Except nuts.'

'I'll just go see.' She hurried away, looking thoughtful. Perhaps she needed to put the kitchen on red alert so they could activate some emergency procedure?

I fidgeted with the cutlery. 'Charles, I'm so sorry. I should have checked with you first.'

He took my hand. 'Hey, no biggie. It happens all the time. Eating in some of the far-flung parts of the world can be tricky. Last time I went to ...'

'A corner of the moon,' he might have said, as my thoughts had drifted to Snowy. We were too recent a couple for me to have left her alone all evening.

The tables were full of determined diners, desperate to get their money's worth. Some had their fingers stuck on the red buttons, and the place was as noisy as a farmyard. I spotted Malcolm at a table by the gents, hiding behind the wine list.

The waitress returned with satellite-dish plates and a board of fake bread for Charles. 'Chef is looking for the Quorn, but please help yourself to everything else, except the nut butter on the bread table, or the bread, of course, or anything else on that table. The salads are lovely.'

Maybe I should have shown solidarity and stuck to salad, but I'd been saving myself for a feast all day. I pressed the button, and an ear-splitting cock-a-doodle-do erupted from our table. I grimaced at Charles, but he didn't break off from his tale.

A waiter arrived in seconds and piled a heap of meat onto my plate. At least I wouldn't need to activate the cockerel anytime soon. I hid the cutlets under the salad and positioned bread over the steak, so as not to offend Charles.

As Charles talked more about his business interests, I concentrated on my food. The meat fell off the bone. The citrus salad zinged, and the crusty bread was the freshest I'd ever tasted.

In a gap in Charles's monologue, I introduced the subject of the murders. Charles disclosed he'd been interrogated by the police. 'Fortunately, I was able to supply solid proof I was abroad when my father was murdered.' He ran a hand through his sleek hair. 'Otherwise, I might have been suspect numero-uno.'

'What about Vincent's wife?'

'I was shocked to hear about the wife. Poor woman. I honestly didn't know he'd remarried. It's a lot to take in.'

He sounded sincere. Detective James was barking up the wrong tree.

Charles said he would be staying in Buttersley for a few days, and I asked if that would be sufficient time to tie up Vincent's affairs.

'I may stay longer. It depends.' His deep brown eyes devoured mine. 'Here, let me top up your wine.'

I told him about Mr Choudray's unpaid bill and added, 'There may be others. Minor debts possibly, but a fortune to some.'

The more I drank the heavy red wine, the more my appetite increased. While Charles nibbled at leaves, I tore at the meat like a wolf. In front of a vegan, too, how could I? With my lips and fingers smeared in grease, I couldn't stop apologising for being such a carnivore and dragging him to a chop joint in the first place.

'Chill, hun. We're cool. No biggie,' he said, possibly expecting me to howl at the moon, once outside.

I asked where he lived.

'I'm in the process of buying a flat in London. Then, the next project is a penthouse apartment on the coast.'

'A-one,' I said, being a quick learner.

Charles did all the talking. He didn't need any prompts. I was happy to listen and nod while stuffing my face. He described his early life in Buttersley and the trauma of his parents' break-up. He had to care for his mother, and he'd vowed to be a better man than Vincent.

I raised my glass. 'You're a better man than I am, Gunga Din!'

Charles looked over his shoulder. 'Say what?'

'Sorry, couldn't resist. Don't you know the poem?'

'Helen, you crack me up. Anyway, I've succeeded so far, career-wise at least. And I don't think I've broken too many hearts along the way.' He gave a disarming smile and winked.

I was tempted to wink back, but full of food and wine, I'd probably have fallen asleep. Also, I tended to over-engage my mouth when winking. It wasn't pretty.

Charles walked me home, and our gumshoe came too. Malcolm had been no great shakes when sober, but after his binge at Cheeky's, the wheels from his wagon were rolling down the road.

Speaking of roads, what had happened to ours? It used to be straight. I lurched from left to right, even though Charles held me tight.

'First thing tomorrow,' I said, 'I'll be firing off an email to the council. This footpath's a disgrace.' Charles laughed. He'd probably spotted Malcolm. 'I'd invite you in for coffee, but I've only got two cups, and we couldn't leave Malcolm out. You have to bring spies in out of the cold, you know.' *My God. What nonsense am I spouting?*

'I didn't know it was compulsory,' said Charles.

My dating book says men like women who laugh at their jokes, so I cackled like a crone. 'Hope you don't mind about the coffee,' I said, 'but I need to—'

'Another time.' Charles squeezed my hand.' I'm hoping there *will* be another time?'

I'm glad he'd interrupted, as I was about to say, 'get out of this dress.' It had shrunk two sizes in the course of the evening.

At my front door, Charles planted a kiss on my lips, which was quite nice. He said he'd had some A-thingy time in my company and finished with, *'Ciao bella.'*

Once inside, I leant against the door and waited to feel like Scarlett O'Hara. Maybe the passion would come later when I wasn't feeling so bilious?

'Where's my little darling?' I shouted. Snowy poked her head out from the banister at the top of the stairs. I bounded up, and she skipped down to meet me. I wanted to cry with joy.

Snowy and I were just getting into bed when James rang. 'How was it for you?'

'I'm in bed asleep. What do you want?'

'Just had a distress call from Prue. Sounds like her hair net's on fire. Malcolm's in the dog house. She couldn't decipher his gibberish and suspects he's been drinking.'

'Why didn't she call me, herself?'

'She thought you might be *in flagrante*.'

'As if. Tell her I had a nice night and all is well.'

I slept like the dead until dawn and awoke to a gentle tapping on my eyelids. I pushed one open to meet the magnified eye of a cat.

My phone was flashing. A text from Charles, already. He'd had an amazing evening, and he was captivated by my story. What? He knew nothing about me. If we were to enter the TV show *Facts about Each Other*, it would be the work of seconds for him. I could run to a series. That was perhaps unfair. I'd encouraged Charles to talk, so it was my fault, or 'my bad', as he would say.

He wanted to meet up again soon and wouldn't take no for an answer. It was thrilling to be wanted, especially by one so desirable. I should have been jumping out of my skin with excitement, but I felt not the slightest tingle. What was wrong with me?

My mind raced back to when I first met Zack. I couldn't peel my eyes away from his face. I'd sat on my hands so I wouldn't reach out and touch his lips. It was fireworks at first sight for me. Zack said he felt it too, but probably lied. He made the world all shiny, and I loved not only him, but the couple we became.

Maybe you were allotted a once-in-a-lifetime connection, and if you messed that up, then it was hard cheese for the rest of your days. I shook my head; it was time to get real. Zack and I met as teenagers with swirling hormones and raging acne. Everything was more intense back then. As a mature woman, I should expect a slower burn. Charles deserved another whirl.

Funky Town

Wednesday 20th May

After feeding Snowy, I fell back asleep and awoke with the sort of headache you'd expect from drinking wine by the bucketful.

I peered in the mirror. A face as white as Snowy's stared back. A few more years, I'd have the whiskers to match. Bloodshot eyes and livid freckles added nothing to the picture. I couldn't even begin to describe my hair.

A long, hot shower and a cup of tea refreshed me slightly, and by the time I was out of the door, I almost knew my name.

Fortunately, I wouldn't have to face Prue's disapproval. She'd swapped shifts with Lucy, having her hair done a day early for Dora's show. Yesterday, we'd taken bets on whose appointment she'd nabbed. Popeye's clientele demanded that their hair appointments were set in stone at the same time every week. In much of Buttersley, tea was on the table at five and dogs walked at six.

As I approached the shop, Lucy waved. She was standing at the door with a girl I vaguely recognised.

Lucy grasped my arm. 'You look poorly. Is it flu?'

'Nothing heavy-duty coffee won't shift.'

'Helen, this is Emily. We take some classes together at college. You know her brother.'

Do I? 'Sorry, can't quite place ...'

'Tom. Tom Swift. He's in charge of the murder investigation,' said Emily.

'Of course. You were at Bangles with him on Saturday night.' I curled my toes in shame at the conclusions I'd reached. Hanging my head was not an option in my current condition. 'Come in for a drink, Emily.'

Despite the hangover, I prepped the shop in minutes. The girls soon had milkshakes, and I clung to a four-shot cappuccino.

Emily stirred her milkshake. 'Tom's my half-brother, actually. Same dad, but my mother's his evil step.'

'I think I might have seen her with him last night.' I held a hand against my throbbing temple and hastily added, 'Not that she looked evil.'

Emily tinkled a dainty laugh. 'Mutton dressed as lamb, more like. No, that's harsh, but she sort of tries too hard, if you know what I mean?'

'*Were* they out together?'

'Possibly. He's our go-between.'

My face burned in shame. I'd done the DCI wrong twice over.

'Mother's so strict, it's ruining my life. I'm a joke at college. I have to be in by eleven. Won't let me get a taxi. Insists she picks me up like I'm still at school.' Emily pouted her coral-pink lips and ran a dove-shaped hand through sleek blonde hair. 'It's so like embarrassing. I'm nearly eighteen.'

'It must be hard for you.' Weak, but the best I could do.

'Sorry to go on, but Lucy said you were a good listener. Oh, look, Tom's here already.' Emily's pout transformed into a sunny smile. 'My hero. He's giving me a lift to college.'

I hailed DCI Swift like we were long-lost friends. He whipped around as if someone else was standing behind him and then turned back with wary eyes. He was probably gauging the extent of my personality disorder.

'Good morning, Ms Merang. Did you enjoy the rest of your evening?'

'It got meaty and messy.'

'Whoa.' Swift held out his hands like he was stopping traffic. What did he think I was going to do? Jump on his back? 'Too much information for me, Ms Merang.'

I blushed. 'Cheeky Chops, the new restaurant, I mean. Haven't you been? Can't move for meat. Not the place for a vegan.'

'Oh, I see.' He grinned. 'I think.' Both girls laughed.

Emily rose from her seat. 'Thanks for the best milkshake ever, Helen, and for listening.' She linked her arm in the DCI's. 'C'mon, cheeky chops, we gotta go, or I'll be late again.'

'Oh, isn't he lovely, Helen?' Lucy's eyes shone like a summer's day. 'He's so kind and thoughtful. I wish I had a brother like that. Don't you?'

With my assumptions blasted out of the water, I didn't know what to think. 'He does seem the strong, dependable sort.'

'And some.' Lucy sighed. 'Speaking of strong men, how did your date with Charles go?'

There was no point in asking how she knew about the date; it would be all around town by now. 'Great, thanks. He wants to meet again this evening. I thought about inviting him to Dora's show. What d'you think?'

'Go for it. Why not? Oh, I nearly forgot. I called at Mr Choudray's shop this morning. He said to thank you for getting Vincent's bill settled.'

That was quick work by Charles. It looked like you suddenly couldn't move for strong, dependable men.

I hugged myself with that thought until another one came from nowhere. It must have been the mention of Mr Choudray that led me back to Vincent's murder. Someone had said something recently that couldn't possibly be right. Something that didn't fit. What was it? The more I tried to grasp it, the more elusive and insubstantial the fragment became. I shook my head like a dog. If I didn't try too hard, it might come back again.

I phoned Charles to thank him for last night and for paying Mr Choudray.

'Hey, no biggie. So what about tonight?'

'I'm sorry, but it's the opening night of Dora's am-dram show. I've got to go to it.' There was silence at the other end. 'Hey, are you still there?'

'Yeah, I'm still here.'

'Would you like to come? I've got a spare ticket. I just need to warn you, everyone's coming. It's drinks at the shop first, on to the show and then a curry at The Bay of Bombay. Steel yourself for anything and anyone.'

Charles laughed. 'As long as you're there to hold my hand.'

I was distracted by Shakira barging into the tea room, wearing a dressing gown and Scooby-Doo slippers.

'Sorry, a strange woman's just walked in. I'll call you later.'

I looked Shakira up and down. 'Did I forget it's look-stupid-at-work-and-raise-money-for-charity day?'

'Helen, no one could accuse *you* of forgetting that,' said James, who'd followed Shakira in.

She yawned. 'Yeah, sorry about that. Slept in and didn't want to be late with your delivery. Where's Prue?'

'Having her hair rebuilt a day earlier than usual, James said, as he hung up his coat.

'Are you and Candice coming tonight?' I asked Shakira. 'Ravi wants me to confirm the numbers.'

'Count me in, but not sure about her. She needs to get her haystack sorted. Can't get in with her hairdresser. "Candice", I said, "does it matter? Who's going to be looking at you"?'

I gasped. 'Shakira, that's an awful thing to say.'

'Nah, she says worse to me. Besides, she needs all that hair to cover her ugly mush.'

'Book for both The Beverley Sisters,' said James. 'Candice won't miss out on a free meal and endless champagne.'

Shakira slapped his back. 'You're so right, Jamie-boy. That's my free-loading sis, all right. Anyway, forget about her. What do you think of this marmalade-infused pain au chocolat as a breakfast line?'

James and Shakira started one of their cake discussions, and I didn't have the strength to tell her to leave in her unsuitable attire.

Customers started trickling into the tea room, so Lucy and I got down to business. We were busy all morning, and the adrenaline must have cancelled the hangover. At noon, I realised it had gone.

Still hazy on numbers, I rang the restaurant. 'Sorry that I can't be more exact, Ravi.'

'It's always unpredictable when you and your friends dine at The Bay of Bombay, Miss Merang.'

I outlined Charles's dietary requirements. 'And Ravi, one last thing – please could you make a fuss of Dora and treat her like a star.'

'Of course, Miss Merang. The Bay of Bombay does not disappoint.'

The afternoon dragged, despite a steady stream of customers. All the ones you wouldn't want in the same week, never mind the same day, came in. While Mrs Crab spoke for thirty minutes on the pros and cons of buying a new umbrella, I reflected on what Charles had said about striving to be a better man than his father. Vincent had given a gaggle of women the runaround and extracted money from Claudia and possibly his wife. All three of them were now dead, and where the hell was Elvira? I resolved to contact Pansy tomorrow.

I closed the tea room early and made a mad dash home. Important things first, I fed my hungry cat. Snowy ate her food while I had a quick shower, and then she sat on the bed watching my slapdash routine.

I pulled clothes on without drying myself properly first, so my tights were all in a twist. I jittered with nerves and fretted about how Charles would fit in with everyone. My hair would not behave, so I dumped the hairdryer and compensated with too much make-up. I applied eyeliner like I was tarmacking the road and then sneezed before it had dried.

Snowy stretched out a pure white paw and touched my arm. I took deep breaths, calmed down and pulled on my new red dress. A daring design for me, which had been too much for a first date. Risking a glimpse in the mirror, I decided it would do.

I raced back to the shop to set out the canapés and champagne flutes. Prue arrived first, wearing her little black dress that had forty years on the clock.

'Prue, you look so swish, and your hair's immaculate.'

She patted the skyrocket and permitted a smile. 'Why don't I finish off, dear, so you can sort *your* hair out? You've probably not had the time.'

James arrived with the champagne. He'd ditched the Savile Row for cashmere, soft, dark trousers and Chelsea boots. Malcolm followed soon after. His outfit a jumble, but his shoes shone, and he'd combed his strands of hair. He stood next to Prue, but she turned away. She'd possibly not forgiven his drunken antics of the previous night.

Lucy and Shakira arrived together. Lucy twinkled in a pale pink gossamer number, while Shakira had gone for the 1980s disco diva meets cheerleader theme. She'd squeezed her assets into a sequinned boob tube and mini ra-ra skirt.

James held out a glass of champagne and yelled across the room. 'Hey, Shakie, won't you take me to *Funkytown?*'

She sashayed towards him in her silver platforms. 'In your dreams, big boy.'

I drifted towards the door, on the lookout for Charles. He was waiting outside and enfolded me into his arms like we were insatiable lovers. He planted a lingering kiss and, in a hoarse whisper at my neck, said, 'I've been longing for you all day.'

His level of intimacy overwhelmed me, and I could just about manage a feeble, 'That's nice.'

He retained an arm around my waist as we joined the others. James raised an eyebrow and smirked. He dropped the smirk when he noticed Charles was wearing the same style of boots.

Lucy called across. 'Hey, James, why don't *you* try skinny black jeans for a change?' He was about to reply when the door opened again.

'Hello hello hello,' said policeman Daz as he marched in with a smiling Sadie on his arm. He sported a red dicky bow and white trousers. She wore a prom-style dress and had squashed her feet into narrow sandals with thin, biting straps. A sociable couple, they soon got the hang of the champagne.

The popping of corks and Big Band music jollied us along. Everyone was mixing. I even heard Prue laugh out loud. I resolved to drink only one glass of champagne.

When I next looked up, Ruth stood hesitantly in the doorway. There was a break in the chat, and all heads turned. She towered above us in shiny gold stilettos. A white column dress exposed bare shoulders and muscular arms. Despite the strength, she exuded fragility. Her pale, unblemished skin shimmered under the lights and looked as soft as down.

James was the first to greet her. 'Hail Juno, our warrior goddess. Have you come to lead us into battle?'

She gave a tentative smile and smoothed down her dress. 'It's not too over-the-top, is it?' Her little girl's voice took me by surprise again.

'Hell no,' I said. 'You look magnificent.'

Shakira mobbed her. 'Omigod, Ruth, those shoes are the real deal – not fakes. And a Bottega clutch. Can I touch it?'

Ruth smiled and held out the bag. 'How could I deny a true connoisseur?'

Charles said in a terse voice and only to me. 'I didn't know *she* was coming.'

Ruth looked over at that moment. The smile for Shakira lingered, but the warmth had left her face. She walked towards us and held out a hand. 'Charles, so unexpected but how nice to see you.' Her voice had a catch.

Charles didn't respond. I seized her hand. 'Ruth, delighted you could make it. You look stunning. Doesn't she, Charles?'

'Yes. Very nice,' he said, with the level of enthusiasm you'd find at a grave.

James intercepted with a drink for Ruth, and we were joined by Daz and Sadie.

'Thanks for the tickets, Helen. The boss and Snood are coming and some of the lads.'

I smiled automatically while I considered the undercurrents between Charles and Ruth. Puzzled, I'd thought they were friends. I would have to tell Ruth about my date with Charles before she heard it elsewhere.

James clapped his hands. 'Showtime, everyone. Time to go.' He started to herd us out. 'See you at Bombs,' he whispered to me.

'What? Aren't you coming to the show?'

'I can't sit through that trash.'

'That's so mean of you.'

'Dora won't know if I'm there or not.'

There was no point in trying to persuade him. He closed the door.

The others had walked up the street, with Shakira in the middle of Charles and Ruth. My mobile rang – a local number which I didn't recognise. I ignored it and turned the phone to silent.

Showtime

In the packed auditorium, the noise was almost unbearable. People were yelling at friends they probably met every day and might have just seen in the bar.

Dora had reserved the whole front row. Mr Klondike sat slap-bang in the middle, dabbing his face with an enormous grey hankie. 'I've just left Dora. She's not a bit nervous.' He glanced over his shoulder and shuddered. 'All these people.'

Exactly on time, the band struck up, the lights went down, and the coughing started. The air rippled with anticipation.

Actors ran onto the stage, and the action began. I had no idea of the story, but it romped along with plenty of laughs. Performances varied, from Gwyneth Paletoe – more wooden than the stage – to Dora, who ripped up the boards and set them on fire.

At one farcical scene, I turned to Charles, but he was checking his phone. Ruth nudged my arm, nodded to the stage and stuck up both thumbs.

Further down the line, Shakira and Candice were honking like seals. Lucy was giggling, Prue smiling, and Malcolm was a helpless case. Mr Klondike beamed up at the stage.

As we stood at the bar in the interval, Charles kissed my cheek and said he had to go make a call. I seized the opportunity for a word with Ruth. 'Sorry, I didn't tell you Charles would be here, but it was all last-minute.'

Ruth smiled. 'I was surprised to see him, but it's not a problem.'

'Also, I should mention ...' I picked at the label on my bottle of water as my nerves twanged. 'Charles and I, we've been out on a date.' There, it was done, but I felt no relief. Ruth had taken a sip of wine. Her grasp tightened on the glass. She turned to place it on the bar, so I couldn't see her expression. 'Just the one,' I added to break the silence.

She didn't respond. Then Shakira and Candice rushed up to talk about the show, and we were soon back in our seats.

The second half of the show made the first look restrained. Dora squeezed the pips out of the script and received the loudest cheers. At the end, Mr Klondike threw red roses at her feet. I bet she'd told him to do that.

The house lights going up was one of my all-time top-ten dislikes. And all that undignified shuffling out – it totally killed the magic for me.

'Onwards and upwards,' said Malcolm at the exit. 'Mrs Mayflower, will you take my arm?'

Prue must have mellowed during the show, as she accepted with grace.

I needed to talk to Ruth, so I'd primed Shakira to distract Charles on the way to the restaurant. He looked anxiously over his shoulder as she and Candice whisked him away. I mimed a 'Sorry, what can I do about that?' and linked arms with Lucy and Ruth.

'The show was totes a scream,' said Lucy.

'The funniest thing I've seen in years,' agreed Ruth. 'My insides are hurting with all that laughing, but I don't think it was Charles's sort of thing.'

Glad she'd brought his name up, I said, 'You know him best.' Was that tactful or tactless?

Lucy's phone rang. 'Sorry, do you mind if I answer this? It's Emily.'

She hung back, which created an ideal opportunity to make it all fine and dandy with Ruth, but I couldn't. Sudden lockjaw struck me down.

Ruth placed a hand on my shoulder. 'Helen, I can see you feel awkward about the situation, but I've no problem with you dating Charles.'

'I should have ... I mean, it's not—'

'Charles and I are nothing to each other,' Ruth interrupted. 'After Mother died, we went out for a couple of meals, and that was it. End of. I'm not his type.'

The blood rushed to my head. 'I don't know if *I* am either.'

Ruth squeezed my arm. 'I don't want this to spoil our friendship.'

I squeezed her arm in turn. It felt like iron. 'Absolutely not.'

'Just be careful.'

I would have liked her to expand on that, but Lucy caught up, and we soon hit the bright lights of Bombay.

Charles reclaimed me as soon as I stepped through the door. Moving as one, we joined the others at the bar where Ravi held court. A whirling dervish of a host, he knew everyone's name and all of their business.

As we drew close, he held his arms out wide. 'Here she is, Miss Merang with her Mr Vegan.' Ravi landed a smacker on my cheek. I don't know how he'd managed to insert himself between Charles and me. It would have been easier to separate two plates of glass.

'Nice to meet you,' said Charles in his graveside tone. He tightened his grip on my waist.

Ravi spun around. 'And, you must be Miss Ruth. How delighted I am to meet you. My good friend, Choudray, tells me you've been settling debts on behalf of another.'

Hang on a minute. I thought Charles had paid?

Before Ruth could answer, Ravi turned again and captured Shakira and Candice. 'My two favourite sisters in the whole of Buttersley.'

I was just wondering about Dora and Mr Klondike when Ravi clapped his hands and gestured to the waiters. They formed a line to the door. Each held a gong, and as Dora walked in, they bonged away like there was no tomorrow. Through the cacophony, Ravi led Dora and her consort to a central table. He beamed as he pulled out two throne-like chairs, which he'd mounted on a platform.

'What a wonderfully clever man you are,' said Dora.

The rest of us took our seats around the elevated pair. Ravi, though, had not thought it through. They had to reach down to the table, and Mr Klondike's groin nestled near my face.

The noise at our table crushed my ears, and the diners who'd paled at the gongs were reaching for their coats. Ravi had tried twice to take our order, but only Prue had opened a menu.

As Ravi patiently waited, Prue stood, banged on the table and shouted. 'I'm going to order for everyone.' Under her breath, she added, 'Or else we'll never get out of here.'

I'd pre-ordered a vegan meal to share with Charles, and Malcolm requested fried egg and chips. Good luck to the rest of them, as according to Prue, there was no point in a curry if it wasn't as hot as hell.

'Not for me, thanks,' I said as James came around with the wine. After the excesses of last night, I couldn't face alcohol. James wasn't drinking, either. As it turned out, I was glad we were sober.

I tried to concentrate on Charles, feeling guilty for plunging him into that frenetic soup. 'I'm sorry, but I did warn you.'

He grabbed my hand and brought it to his lips. He winked, but his eyes didn't focus. James had perhaps topped him up a glass too far.

Lucy leant across the table. 'Look behind you, but don't make it obvious.' The rider came too late. I jerked my head around to lock eyes with DCI Swift.

'Good evening, Ms Merang.' He was sitting at a table with Snood and Emily. 'Thanks for the tickets. The show was, er ...' He chewed at his lip. 'Exhilarating.' He raised his glass. 'Dora, you're under arrest for stealing the show.'

She blew him a kiss.

'Why don't you join us?' I said without thinking.

Emily kissed Swift on the cheek, jumped up and sat beside Lucy. 'They're talking shop, and I'm bored.'

'We are discussing important police business,' said Snood.

Who wanted you anyway?

And that would have been that, except when I rose to propose a toast, I dislodged a waiter's tray and delivered a Bombay Special into the DCI's lap. Compounding the calamity, I seized a napkin and pounced right in. It took a full minute to realise I was dabbing away where I'd no business to be. I looked up to find everyone staring.

I escaped to the cloakroom to headbutt the mirror but settled for resting my face against the cold glass. Time to go home. Fishing in my bag for a comb, I picked up my mobile. Still on silent, it showed ten missed calls and six voicemails, all from Pansy.

The first one said, 'The worst has happened. Ring me back.' The last one, 'You're a bloody hypocrite. You pretend to care. Selfish bitch. Don't bother ringing. I won't speak to you.'

I rang and she answered. 'I'm so upset. Talk to Dave.' There was a kerfuffle and a muffled, 'It's her from the shop.'

'Hello, this is Dave. I'm very sorry, but Pansy's had some terrible news. She thought you might be able to help in some way.'

Pansy wailed in the background. 'Tell her to come here. Now.'

Dave cleared his throat. 'Do you think it would be at all possible for you to ... I mean, if it's not too inconvenient ...'

'Tell her,' Pansy shouted in the background. 'You big, useless dope.'

'Would you like me to call around now?' I said. 'I know the address.'

'Oh, thank you, Miss Merang. That's so kind.'

'What's happened?' I wanted some idea of what to expect.

'Oh, I'm sorry. Didn't I say? Elvira's been arrested.' He sounded like all his birthdays had come at once.

A Cuckoo in the House

I was still reeling from the shock of Elvira being arrested when Shakira burst into the cloakroom. 'Helen, what are you doing? You've been gone ages.'

'Sorry. Just had a distress call. I need to leave and take James with me.'

Shakira peered at the mirror and fluffed up her hair. Typically, she'd not listened. 'I've had a bust-up with Candice, and she's stormed off. Prue's had her coat on for the last ten minutes, and Malcolm's flapping about taxis. Emily's mum's waiting outside for her and Lucy, but they want to say goodbye to you. Dora's doing recitals from the show. Ruth's plastered and happy. Charles's plastered, not so happy.'

'About Charles, could you keep him entertained? I feel bad about abandoning him, but it's an emergency.'

She pouted at her reflection. 'No problem. He'll be in the hands of an expert.'

When we returned to the dining area, Snood and Swift had left. Lucy and Emily were giggling together.

Lucy tugged at my arm. 'Helen, it was so crazy hilarious. Wasn't it, Emily?'

'He didn't even notice,' Emily shrieked. That set them off again.

James shook his head in apparent despair. 'These two minxes are trying to tell you that, when the DCI stood, he had a stain at the front of his trousers in an intimate area. It was an unfortunate colour.'

I clapped both hands over my mouth. Emily and Lucy screamed.

Prue rapped on the table. 'Girls, control yourselves, please.'

I'd wondered when she was going to pipe up. She'd never have let me get away with that sort of behaviour.

I looked over at Charles, who was staring into his sticky, half-filled glass. 'Charles, I'll be with you in a minute. Just need to dispatch these two banshees.' I pushed Shakira towards him with a bottle of red. 'Emily, please apologise to your brother and tell him to send me his cleaning bill. I'm such a donkey.'

'He says you're a loose cannon, but smiles when he says it. Sorry, gotta go. Mother will be marching in at any minute. Come on, Luce. Bye, all.' Both girls kissed my cheek, and Lucy thanked me for the evening.

Malcolm tapped my shoulder. 'I will escort Mrs Mayflower and Ruth home. Transport has been organised by yours truly. It's been a right good night out, Helen, love. You've done us proud.'

I couldn't respond, as Ruth had gripped me in a drunken bear hug, and I'd spotted James trying to sneak away.

'Don't you dare,' I shouted across at him, louder than intended. Several men looked up with guilty expressions.

I had a quick exchange with Charles. He didn't protest against my dramatic exit, but by then, he was so pie-eyed he probably didn't even remember my name.

Dora interrupted her recital and seized my hand. 'Can you call into the agency first thing tomorrow?' Suddenly sober and serious, she gestured towards Mr Klondike and put a finger to her lips. 'It's really important, but I can't tell you here.'

I promised to call in, but preoccupied with thoughts of Pansy, I hardly registered her words. When I'd settled the bill, I turned for a final wave. Shakira was attempting the splits. She got stuck and shouted for help. Mr Klondike rushed towards her but must have forgotten he was on a platform, as he tripped and fell. Charles tried to pull him up, but he was laughing so much, he could hardly stand. By then, Shakira had planted her hands on the floor, with her rear in the air. Not a good position for someone in a ra-ra skirt.

'I did ask Shakira to keep Charles entertained,' I told James.

He laughed. 'You can't fault her commitment to the job. Look at Dora. She's got a face like thunder. Let's get out of here quick.' He grabbed my arm, and we ran to his car. 'What a relief to escape that madhouse. Why did you dump Charles? Had enough of him pawing you?'

'Shut up. Drive to Lexicon Avenue, and don't spare the horses. Elvira's been arrested and Pansy's in meltdown.'

Dave greeted us at the door like we were his favourite dinner party guests. Prematurely bald, with light blue eyes and teeth like tombstones, he ushered us in and took our coats. 'So pleased you could make it. Come through. Can I offer you a drink?'

So far, he'd not stopped smiling, but with those teeth, he probably had no choice. He led us through to the overheated living room where Pansy lay prostrate on a floral sofa with a box of tissues at her side.

She raised a ravaged, tear-stained face. 'You took your time.'

I was about to utter some meaningless platitude, but James cut in. 'Has Elvira been arrested, or is she just being interviewed?'

'How do I know? That's what I want *you* to find out.'

'Has she phoned you?' I asked.

Pansy sat upright. 'The pigs won't let her.'

James moved into the centre of the room. 'She has a right to let her family know where she is and is also entitled to free legal advice.'

'You a lawyer or something?' Pansy asked. Her tone was challenging, but she looked at him with interest.

'Let's just say, I know my way around the system.'

I never did get to the bottom of James's alleged criminal past.

'How did you find out she'd been arrested?' I asked. 'On Monday, you'd no idea where she was.'

Pansy left it to Dave to explain. 'We still didn't know, but yesterday, Pansy received some strange texts. Show them your phone, love.'

'Here.' Pansy threw her phone onto a cluttered pine coffee table. I scrolled down the three messages.

Sorry, I'm not there for you, my poppet. Got to hide away until I decide what's best to do

I can't tell you where I am. They might come after me

I need to hide. I'm scared. Don't forget the pram sale finishes at Mother Bear on Friday

Dave continued his tale. 'I take it you know that Eileen Newby, Elvira's sister, was murdered?' We nodded. 'Well, one of her neighbours phoned to say they'd seen the police dragging Elvira out of Eileen's house.' He finished with his broadest smile yet.

'Poor Mum,' said Pansy. 'She sounds terrified, and then the rotten police have locked her up and thrown away the key.'

Perry Mason cut in again, 'They can only detain her for twenty-four hours. Possibly get an extension if they're accusing her of a serious crime, but at some point, they'll either have to charge or release her. I'll phone them. See if I can find anything out and ensure she has legal representation.' He went into the hallway.

'That's very good of him,' said Dave. 'It's reassuring to have someone here who knows about these things, isn't it, love?'

Pansy blew her nose. 'It's nice to have a man about the house for once.'

Dave said nothing. One side of his mouth twitched, and he stared at the tea towel in his hands. When the twitching stopped, he raised a flushed face. It held the same friendly expression. 'Helen, are you sure I can't get you a drink? Tea, coffee?'

'Dave, stop fussing.'

'Actually, Dave,' I said. 'That would be very nice. If it's not too much trouble?' He obviously needed to escape. 'Tea, milk, no sugar, thanks.'

He left the room and took all the goodwill with him. Pansy and I were locked in a hostile vacuum. Neither of us spoke.

Dave shouted from the kitchen. 'Pansy, love. Would *you* like a drink? Can you hear me? Pansy?' She didn't answer and studied her nails.

I focused on a large, ornate clock that dominated the mantelpiece. An object you'd only ever display if the person who'd thrust it upon you was likely to call. A loud tick-tock punctuated the silence.

I was just wondering what Elvira had been doing at Mrs Newby's when a movement on the mantelpiece made me jump. A cuckoo shot out of the clock, gave a half-hearted coo and made a rapid retreat.

'I see you're admiring our lovely clock,' Dave said as he handed me a mug. 'A treasured memento from our honeymoon. Isn't it, love?'

Enough to put the mockers on any marriage, I would have thought.

'Where's my drink? I can't believe you've made her one and not me.' Pansy started to cry.

'Don't upset yourself, my love, I *have* made you one. Silly me, I left it in the kitchen.' Dave seemed well practised in skirting around a monster.

James returned to the room. 'Elvira's being questioned but has not been arrested. They wouldn't disclose anything else. She refused their offer of a solicitor.'

'That's because she's not done anything,' said Pansy.

'She still needs one to guide her through the system. I've rung mine and asked her to attend.'

'That's so helpful and kind of you, isn't it, Pansy?' said Dave. He expressed his gratitude all the way to the front door. 'Don't mind Pansy. She's got all those lady hormones flying about. She doesn't know what she's saying half the time.'

Yeah, right. Tell that to the cuckoo, Dave.

James's phone rang, and with a wave to Dave, he stepped into the garden.

The mention of hormones opened Dave's floodgates, and he invited me into his miserable world. Pansy had married him on the rebound from the charismatic, good-looking Paul. Dave had worshipped Pansy for years and couldn't believe his luck when she turned to him. But he knew she regretted their marriage. He was hoping the baby might bring them together. Really? I wanted to say – a massive job on a to-do list before you've even been born.'

Dave leant against the door. 'Pansy thinks she's unworthy because Paul rejected her, and I'm a poor specimen of a man because I love her. That's why she despises me.'

What could anyone say to that? I took his hand. 'I'm sure that's not true.'

'Elvira says I'm not good enough and is forever dripping poison into Pansy's ear.'

'She wants locking up.'

Dave managed a laugh. 'Did you mean to say that? Thanks for listening and sorry to burden you with—'

James shouted from the car, 'Helen, what the hell are you doing? I've been waiting for ages.'

'Sorry, Dave. Keep in touch. Call into Merangs sometime. Bye.'

James dropped me off at home, and I waved a weary goodbye. Dog-tired, I crawled into bed, but couldn't sleep. The gaiety of the show was a lifetime away. I picked over Dave's words, and sadness overwhelmed me. Pansy could at least be kind instead of bouncing her contempt off the walls.

Then I turned over what Dora had said at the restaurant. She'd had urgency in her voice and had gripped my hand with force. She must have uncovered something at Klondike's.

A Viper in His Nest

Thursday 21st May

That fairy tale princess must have got more sleep on her pea than I ever did that night. At dawn, I gave up, jumped out of bed, found my kit and went for a run. I ran through the streets of a strange new world. People stood huddled at bus stops or scurried to work with their heads down. All that going on so early, and I never knew.

The sleepless night had given me time to think and forced me into a decision about Charles. Carrying it out would not be easy, so I pushed it aside to the rigours of the run.

I returned home with a tiger in my tank and ready to roll. Dora was an early riser, so I was sitting opposite her at Klondike's by 7.30 a.m. Dark circles framed weary eyes, and speckles of last night's glitter clung to her eyelashes. I dished out more gush on the show before we got down to business.

'I'll come straight to the point,' she said, then hesitated and toyed with a plastic banana. I realised it was a novelty pencil when I spotted the squirrel sharpener. 'Elvira's been cooking the books. She's fiddled the agency out of a fortune.' Dora threw down the pencil and picked up a giant eraser that said, 'Big Mistake'.

Fraud. I'd not expected that, but could easily believe it. 'Is that why she's been arrested?'

'What? I didn't know she had. You're the first person I've told. Even my Gerald doesn't know yet. The poor ickle pet lamb.'

I doubted even Mr Klondike's late mother could have picked him out from that description. 'How did you find out?'

'Easy, once I'd got my head around the system. Elvira became complacent and careless. Hardly bothered to hide her tracks. Look, I'll show you.'

Within minutes, Dora had walked me through the intricacies of Elvira's crimes. Mr Ickle Pet Lamb must have been gambolling around with his eyes closed, not to have noticed his office manager's game.

'Are you going to report this to the police?' I asked. 'If Elvira's charged with murder, this will be the least of her worries.'

Dora's eyes opened wide. 'Gosh, I've been so focused on the fraud, it barely registered when you said she'd been arrested. Did *she* do the murders, then?'

'We don't actually know. James has put his solicitor on the case, so maybe we'll hear something soon.'

'What about Pansy?' she asked. 'How well do you know her?'

'Hardly at all, and that's more than I'd like. Oh, I see, do you think she was involved in the fraud?'

'Gerald concentrated on sales. Elvira did everything else. He hasn't a clue what Pansy did.' Dora folded her arms. 'If she worked closely with Elvira, she'd be plain stupid not to have noticed.' Dora sighed, perhaps in relief at having unburdened herself, but said she was dreading having to tell Mr Klondike.

I couldn't help her with that. I'd other fish to fry and was itching to get to Merangs. My phone had been pinging away all the time we'd been talking, and I suspected it was Charles. Each ping brought a fresh stab of guilt.

When I arrived at the shop, Prue had beaten me to it and had already tackled the party mess. She handed me a coffee as soon as I walked through the door.

'Thanks, Prue. You're spoiling me.'

'Someone has to take care of you.'

She paired the soft tone with a pitying look. For one wild moment, I thought she'd intercepted my medical results. I prepared myself for the worst sort of news and resolved to be brave. Then I remembered I'd not seen a doctor in years.

I told Prue about Elvira and the police, but she dismissed it with a flick of her wrist. 'I'm more concerned about you and this Charles.' Her face puckered in concern. 'You've not fallen for him, have you?'

'No. I quite like him, but that's about it.'

I'd decided not to see Charles again. His ardour overwhelmed me, and I couldn't reciprocate. The passion wasn't there, and my overriding feeling was one of guilt. 'It's not you, it's me'. That old chestnut.

'I hope that's all because Shakira thinks he's a cad. I can't say any more; you'll have to ask her.'

Cancel the guilt.

Prue turned her back and pretended to check the cutlery. I sneaked a look at my phone. Messages and voicemails from Charles dominated the screen. Prue swung back around. 'Shakira thinks he's married.'

Despite my resolve not to see Charles again, that knocked me off my perch. 'Well, I'm married too.'

'That's different. You've been abandoned with no chance of reconciliation.'

I managed a laugh. 'Don't spare me, Prue, please.'

'Shakira said Charles has got two phones.'

Even though I'd rejected him, a slight stab of betrayal pierced my confidence. 'Don't worry about me, Prue. My heart won't get broken.' I had to stop myself from saying, 'again.'

James arrived. We became busy, and I concentrated on the tea room until Ruth turned up, wreathed in smiles, full of joy and bearing gifts. Flowers for me and an exquisitely wrapped package for Shakira.

'I wanted her to have something nice,' Ruth said. She was no longer the glamorous goddess of last night, but an oversized schoolgirl in a navy blazer. She wanted to linger, but could see we were busy. 'We've not had time for a proper chat. What about that dinner date? You could come to my hotel after work tomorrow?'

How could I refuse? 'That sounds perfect. I'll look forward to it.'

She went away humming a song from the show.

Pansy's husband, Dave, fetched up next with an enormous bunch of tulips. 'I just wanted to thank you for last night,' he said, zapping me with his high-voltage smile.

I looked around in a panic, hoping no one had overheard and got the wrong idea. 'James did all the useful stuff.'

'But you were very kind. It's all such a worry, and Pansy is delicate.'

Yeah, like a barbed-wire fence.

We sat at a table, and Prue brought coffee and strawberry cream tarts. Dave relaxed, and I seized the opportunity to toss in some guileless grenades. 'You've got such a lot of stuff for the baby. Pansy said Elvira bought it all?' Dave mumbled something non-committal. 'Very unselfish of her. She can't be rolling in money, still working full-time at her age?'

He avoided my eye and fiddled with his cup. I surmised he knew or had an idea about Elvira's alternative income. I changed tack. 'I know Elvira's been unkind to you. Was she as mean to her sister?'

'Don't know much about her, but that Vincent, he was a total slimeball. Good riddance, I say.' Dave's voice turned shrill. 'Vincent took both sisters to the cleaners. That was *their* business, but when it was going to affect us. I mean, Pansy.' He banged his fist on the table and made me jump. 'I had to ...' He pursed his lips, shook his head and attempted a brittle laugh. 'Sorry, just listen to me prattle on. Excuse me, a moment; I must just go to the little boys' room.'

Disturbed by the vehemence of his reaction, I didn't know if I'd pressed the right or the wrong buttons.

James slid into his seat. 'Our friend seems overexcited. What have you said? Look out, he's back. I'm gone.'

'Please excuse my outburst, Helen. Pay no attention to my nonsense. It's just the stress coming out.' Dave looked so woebegone; my heart went out to him.

'Of course, Dave. I completely understand. Anytime you want to offload, I'm always available.' Cheesy, but what else could I say?

'Thanks. Very sweet of you. I'll have to go now. Pansy will be wondering where I am.'

There's more chance the cuckoo gives a fig, Dave.

Prue and I worked flat out for the next hour or so. I'd turned my phone to vibrate, and it pogoed in my pocket like a crazed little creature. As we viewed the wreckage of the tea room after the rush, the phone bounced with a new urgency, and I sensed it was Pansy.

Her shrill voice spat into my ear. 'You're to blame. You put that stuck-up bitch there. Who does she think she is? I've got a right to what I'm owed. I need that money to buy a pram.'

'Sorry, Pansy. I don't know what you're talking about.'

'I've rung Klondike for my wage. That actress friend of yours said to ask my mother where all the money's gone. What did she mean?'

I tried to stay calm. 'Pansy, do you really not know? Dora's seen the accounts.'

'If she makes any accusations about my mum, I'll make some about Klondike.'

My hand shook as I searched through the functions on my phone. Did I have a voice recorder thingy? 'Pansy, what exactly are you saying?'

'I'll say he's a dirty old man. That he said rude things to me and put his hands where he shouldn't. I'll say much worse if I have to.' Her voice rang so loud, I had to remove the phone from my ear.

'Did Mr Klondike do any of those things?' I thought of how Dora would take the revelations.

'No. But I'll say he did. They'd believe poor little pregnant me against that big, sloppy fool. Mud sticks. No smoke without fire.'

I shuddered at Pansy's casual mendacity. The damage she could wreak. No wonder Dave was stressed. Never mind a cuckoo in the clock; he had a viper in his nest.

'Pansy, that would be lying, and you're also threatening blackmail.'

'Yeah, so what? I don't care. Just keep your traps shut and no one gets hurt.'

Despite the gravity of the situation, I laughed. 'Pansy, we're not in a gangster movie. And get this, I've recorded our conversation.' *Fingers crossed, I have.* 'The penalties for slander and blackmail are severe.'

She hung up. The phone rang straight away. I answered without looking. 'What now, you malicious cow?'

'Is this a bad time to call?' asked Charles.

Oh, bugger. If I'd noticed it was him, I wouldn't have answered. I needed to speak to Shakira first. 'Sorry, just having a bad day. And, sorry for rushing off last night.'

'You can make it up to me this evening, hun.'

'Go with your gut instinct' was the dating advice. Well, my guts had sunk. All I wanted was an early-to-bed, peaceful night. I told him this, and he ended the call without saying goodbye.

Prue had closed the tea room and was busy clearing up. I told her to leave it to me and insisted she go home. She didn't argue, so I knew she was tired. I had a quick exchange with James. He'd not heard from his solicitor, and I updated him on Elvira and Pansy.

'What a toxic, malevolent pair,' he said with distaste.

'I feel sorry for Dave. I think he's teetering on the edge.'

'What? On the edge of their cauldron? Step down, Mother Teresa; you can't save every mutt that offers its paw.'

After James wandered back into the shop, I texted Shakira and asked her to pop down. We could talk while I finished the cleaning. I handed her Ruth's gift as soon as she arrived.

She tore at the wrapping and squealed. 'Helen, you won't believe what Ruth's given me.' Shakira's eyes glittered with tears. 'The Bottega clutch.' She clasped it to her breast. 'I feel like a lady.' She promenaded the tea room as if it were Milan. 'I must ring Ruth.'

'Before you do, please dish the dirt on Charles. You've told Prue he's a cad.'

'A what? I said he's a player. He's got two phones, and you know what that means? I've seen 'em both.'

'So, you think he's married or in a relationship?'

She stroked the bag. 'Not sure. Something doesn't quite add up. Just be careful.' It struck me, Ruth had said the same. 'Can I go now, Miss? I need to ring my new best friend.'

Another day done. The takings were high. James had created a dazzling new window display and had just waltzed off, pleased with himself. I was about to turn the sign to closed when someone rattled the handle. I didn't like to refuse latecomers. It was money in the till, after all, but it was Charles.

'Would you believe I was just passing?' he said with a sheepish grin.

'Not on your nelly.' I forced a smile.

'I was desperate to see you again. Helen, hun, please come out for a quick drink with me. Please.' His wheedling tone did nothing to entice.

I sighed and closed my eyes. 'I told you earlier, I'm exhausted and just want to go home.'

'I could come back with you and give you a relaxing massage?'

'No, I'm sorry.' I could hardly conceal the distaste in my voice.

'Helen, I can't take no for an answer.' He changed to mock stern. 'I need to tell you something. It's important.'

He wasn't going to give up. 'Okay. One quick drink,' I said, half intrigued. One last drink with him. What harm could it do?

Get Me Out of Here

Charles and I went to Bangles again. *Déjà vu,* except this time I wasn't quivering with anticipation, and we didn't have the spectre of Malcolm looming over us. Charles queued at the bar while I pondered the dating game and my fickle nature. How I wished our stars could have aligned. I had so wanted to adore him.

I glanced over at Charles surrounded by an attentive group of women. When he saw me looking, he swirled his index finger, swivelled his hips and pointed at me. He swaggered over with a satisfied smile. 'Sorry, couldn't get away. The women folk are, er, very friendly.' He loosened his tie. 'Scarily so.'

I wanted to say, 'Around these parts, Malcolm's considered a catch,' but said instead, 'We're not used to such handsome men in Buttersley.' He smirked, and I regretted the flattery.

He plonked four outrageously large cocktails onto our table. He'd already started on one of them.

'Just the one drink, I said.'

'Yeah, sorry. Two for one. I got confused.' He grinned like he'd done nothing of the sort. 'Cheers.' He finished his drink.

'Let's hope you're not so confused when buying properties or you'll end up bankrupt.' Charles looked blank. 'Your burgeoning portfolio?'

'Yeah, gotcha. I was just thinking how gorgeous you're looking tonight.'

That must have been a line from a seduction bag of tricks. Either that or his standards were low. I'd not even untangled my hair.

I sipped at my drink. 'What did you want to tell me that's so important?'

'Let's just chill and have a drink first.'

So he wants to string this out. I sat back to relax and at least enjoy the cocktail. 'Sorry again for rushing off last night. Did Shakira look after you?'

'And some.' He winked. 'She's a whole lotta fun that one. Top girl.'

'Did she tell you I was married?'

'No.' The colour left his face except for a red mark on his cheek.

'Technically, still married, but I'm separated. Zack lives abroad.'

Charles exhaled and gulped down cocktail number two.

'Are *you* married?' So what if I was being unsubtle?

'Nope. Not married, engaged or in a relationship. I'm single and wanting to mingle with you.'

I flinched and couldn't decide if he was telling the truth or not. Either way, I didn't care. He reached across the table to take my hand.

I snatched it away, pointed at the far wall and said, 'Oh look, there's ... er, something over there.'

'No need to be nervous. I don't bite. Well, maybe I do, but only in a nice way.' He recaptured my hand and stroked it. I thought of the unwashed breakfast dishes I'd left in the sink. He suddenly dropped my hand and pulled down the corners of his mouth with his fingers. 'I've got bad news for you, hun.'

'Is this what you wanted to tell me?'

'No. But here's the thing. We've only a short time together before I leave for Brazil.'

'Brazil? Fantastic.'

His brow creased. He'd possibly expected tears. I had to stop myself from punching the air in relief.

'No biggie. I'm over there all the time. That reminds me. 'Excuse me a nano.' He pulled a phone out of his jacket. 'Yes, efficient as always. Gloria, my PA, has booked the flight.'

'Do you use a separate phone for business?'

'Sure do, hun. Imagine if I sent old Gloria a sizzling text meant for you. She's over 50 and the size of a bus.'

'That's not a gentlemanly thing to say.'

'Whoa, feisty. Love it.' He downed his third cocktail. 'Thing is, even if she were hot, I'd only have eyes for you.'

'If you're going to Brazil, does that mean you've tied up Vincent's affairs? Have you heard from the police?'

Charles brought my hand to his lips. 'Let's talk about us. We need to see as much of each other as we can before I leave.'

I removed my hand. 'Sorry to press you, but what else did you need to tell me? I've finished my drink and need to go now.' That sounded ungracious, but I felt hounded and trapped.

'Stay there, hun. I'll get you another.'

That's not what I meant, and he knew it. His fan club was pleased to see him back at the bar.

I stood to ease my aching back and spotted Emily and the DCI in a corner booth. Without thinking, I cannonballed into their conversation. 'Hello, you two. We must stop meeting like this.' In my haste, I'd lost control of the volume. My booming voice could have filled Buttersley's theatre.

They both jumped. The DCI recovered first. 'Ms Merang, a pleasure as always.' His smile was warm but brief. He turned back to his sister. 'Emily, say hello.'

'Hi, Helen.' She put a hand to her forehead and bowed her head. 'I don't want to talk right now. Sorry, I'm a bit ...'

'No. *I'm* sorry. I'll leave you to it.' Only last night, Emily had been helpless with laughter. Now she had a face full of tears.

I grimaced and scuttled back to my seat. Our table was still empty. Charles had his arms around two women at the bar. At least he was deriving some enjoyment from the evening.

The DCI's voice broke into my thoughts. 'We're leaving now. Emily's just gone to freshen up. Sorry for the rude reception, but she's having problems at college.'

'I shouldn't have barged in like that. It's a trait of mine.'

He smiled. 'Can't say I've noticed.'

'Why aren't you at the station putting the thumbscrews on Elvira?'

'I've got people to do that for me.' He grinned, and I grinned back.

Charles came between us with his elbows held wide. 'Can anyone join the party?' He slammed four more cocktails onto the table.

'Just leaving, Mr Newby,' said the DCI. He held a jacket out to Emily as she approached.

'Yes, please move along. Nothing to see here,' Charles called out as they walked away.

The DCI paused, drew back his shoulders, but continued to the door.

Cringing, I wanted to run after him and say, 'Whatever it looks like, he's not with me.'

Charles stared until they had left. 'Who does that jumped-up copper think he is? My taxes pay his wages.'

Apart from flirting on the back of his good looks, Charles had no social skills. How the hell did he do any business deals? I vowed after tonight, I would forsake all men and embrace celibacy. Take the veil, maybe or road test a wimple at least?

He pushed one of the cocktails towards me.

'Charles, I'm really tired and couldn't drink another.'

'You managed well enough the other night. You're a lot more fun with a few drinks inside you.' His voice now had an edge.

'What were you so desperate to tell me?' I was only interested in case it was something to do with Vincent.

'It'll keep until I take you out tomorrow.'

To hell with the wimple, where do I sign for the nunnery?
'I'm meeting Ruth tomorrow evening.'

His face hardened. 'What? You'd rather see that mad bitch than me?' Charles banged the table with his fist, causing the drinks to spill. He'd regret that part at least.

Heads swivelled around. It would be up on the Buttersley network already.

'Congratulations.' I gave a slow handclap.

He narrowed his eyes. 'What for?'

'Against stiff competition, you've won The Misogynist of the Month Award.'

'Very funny. I'm serious. She's scary.' He took a long drink and wiped the back of his hand across his mouth.

'You came to Vincent's funeral together. You seemed to be on good terms then.'

'Yeah, but she offered to come, no strings attached, and I thought she'd got the message by then, so I took her up on it. I was glad of the support.'

'What message?'

Charles nibbled his lip. 'Look, this doesn't sound good, but I'll level with you. I might have led Ruth on a bit. It amused me she could even think I found her attractive. I mean, look at her. She's man-sized. Why would I go there? So I put her straight. I could have maybe handled it better. She didn't take it well.'

A sour taste swirled in my mouth. 'Thanks for the drink, Charles. I'm leaving now, and *my* message to you is, we won't be meeting again.'

He grabbed my wrists. I broke free and would have liked to say I flounced off in triumph, but I didn't. Catching my foot in some careless woman's handbag, I dragged it halfway across the bar like a crocodile clamped to my ankle.

Charles caught me as I was about to kick the bag in crazed frustration. 'Helen, please don't go. What's wrong? I thought you liked me.'

'Get this thing off.' He bent down to untangle my foot, and I noticed the beginnings of a bald spot at his crown. 'Thank you. I just want to leave now.'

He let me go, but his last words echoed all the way home. 'Don't think this is the last you'll hear from me.'

I've never been so relieved to close my door to the world. Snowy's face peered around the living room door. She trilled like a bird and ran towards me. I picked her up, and she nestled into my shoulder.

Our peace was broken by my phone. Charles, again. I ignored it. Once in bed, I listened to his slurred messages. The last one removed any vestige of guilt I might have felt. 'I could have any woman in this bar. No woman walks out on me. You're not that great anyway, and your hair's a mess.'

I had to agree with him about the hair. I noticed James had rung, so I phoned him back.

'So you left old Lover Boy drowning his sorrows?'

I sighed. 'Your mother told you.'

'She's got a mole at Bangles. Much as I'm uninterested in your tawdry affairs, have you sent Charles packing?' I held the phone away and stuck out my tongue. 'I can see you,' said James. He laughed, and I felt back on home turf.

'I won't be seeing Charles again. Is that why you called?'

'No. I've spoken to my solicitor. Elvira's confessed to both murders. Will you tell Pansy or shall I?'

I jumped out of bed and shrieked. Snowy fled from the room.

A Fever of Speculation

Even though I'd pointed the finger at Elvira, I could hardly believe she'd committed both murders. Snowy eventually climbed back into bed, and as she gently snored, James and I talked for over an hour. We started with Elvira's motive and immediately fell out.

'Passion. It's a story of thwarted love and revenge,' I said.

'Barbara Cartland cobblers.'

'So what's your theory then, Clouseau?'

'The murders are about money, but I'm struggling to see how Elvira fits in with that.'

Relegated to the edge of the bed by Snowy, I shifted my position. 'Maybe Eileen found out about Elvira's scam at the agency and threatened to report her? Also, Vincent was a financial drain on Elvira.'

'You can't deny that both murders point to your lover boy. I've done some research on Ruth's father. He died enormously wealthy. Ruth hinted that Claudia left Vincent all her money. That will now go to Charles.'

I sighed. 'I'm aware of that, but I just can't believe Charles is a murderer. The police believe his alibi. And he's a vegan.'

James laughed. 'Putting his food preferences to one side, how do you rate the investigative powers of the police so far?' I didn't have an answer to that, and he raised his voice. 'Doesn't it say something to you that Eileen was killed before Vincent?'

'Dates are immaterial in a crime of passion,' I insisted. 'Also, you seem to be forgetting, Elvira has confessed.'

'If Eileen had survived Vincent, all his inheritance would have gone to her and not Lover Boy.'

I wanted to scream. I didn't know which irritated me the most: James calling Charles Lover Boy, his overly patient tone, or his dismissal of Elvira's confession. I'd also done my homework. 'It depends on the figures, James. I can go into detail if you're not *au fait* with the current rules on intestacy.' *Jog along with that, mate.*

'It would still have been a significant amount. We all have a price.'

'And you, James, don't always have the last word.' I plonked down the phone before he could reply.

I mulled it all over into the early hours. I still saw it as a crime of passion, despite what James said. I pictured Elvira as a ruthless, vengeful monster. But then, she'd displayed genuine grief at Vincent's funeral. That could have been remorse. She had access to both properties, but what about the workman seen leaving Vincent's, and would she have been able to move his body to the cupboard? She was only a slight woman. And why would she shove the body of her lover into a cupboard, anyway?

At dawn, I threw back the sheets and went for another early run. On the home stretch, I realised it was the confession itself that was bugging me. I would have expected Elvira to brazen it out.

Entering the high street, I noticed knots of scruffy strangers hanging about. Two men were peering into Klondike's window. *They must be reporters.* Despite once being a victim of their dubious practices, I had the shop open by seven, with a sign advertising takeaway coffee and cake. I was tempted to add, 'Served from under the murder scene' until I remembered it was now Shakira's flat. By eight-thirty, I'd sold out of cake and was hoping Shakira would deliver on time.

She didn't let me down, but was in a rush. 'Gonna show the press around the flat of death as soon as I've put my face on. Ka-ching ka-ching.'

'Good luck with that. Mention Merangs, but say nothing personal about me.'

Shakira winked. 'Don't worry. I'm all the personality they'll need. Gotta go, but need to tell you this first. Guess who I've just seen at The Greasy Spoon, scoffing a full English?'

'Hmmm, let me think. James – my body is a temple – Jones?'

'Close, but wrong. Charles.'

I gasped. 'No?'

'Bacon, sausage, eggs, black pudding, the whole caboodle. I wouldn't touch that disgusting dried blood stuff if you paid me.' Shakira made a choking noise. 'Plus a round of toast. Thought you said he was a gluten-free vegan?'

'Are you sure it was him?'

'Defo. Didn't look like his pretty-boy self, though. More like a rabid jackal that'd not eaten for weeks.'

Had I driven Charles to meat and wheat? I pictured him trawling the high street for a lamb to slaughter and slap between two slices of bread. Charles and I needed to have a civilised, sober conversation so we could part as friends. Or did we? That old mantra from Prue rang in my ear. 'Why do you want everyone to like you?' I'd think about it later.

Buttersley had awoken in a fever of speculation. The tea room buzzed with Salem-style accusations. Customers I'd previously thought sane denounced Elvira as a devil worshipper, a malfunctioning cyborg, or a contract killer who couldn't say no.

James said he'd rung Pansy, and she'd accused him of foisting an incompetent solicitor onto Elvira, one who was also corrupt and in collusion with the police.

At two-thirty, a ripple ran around the tea room, and everyone rushed outside. Dora was issuing a statement from the agency steps. I sent Lucy to spy. James and I watched from the shop window. Dora had dressed for the occasion in a 1980s power suit with a Margaret Thatcher handbag.

'What could you possibly say,' I asked James, 'when your office manager has run amok and killed two tenants? Arguing it's against company policy can only take you so far.'

'Whatever she's saying, it's going down well.'

A minor cheer rang through the crowd. I spotted The Silent Sisters bobbing their heads at the back. The police arrived and encouraged people to disperse.

Lucy flew back with eyes like fairy lights.

James opened the door. 'Spill the beans, Tinkerbell.'

'Omigod, Dora rocked it. Class.'

Malcolm followed Lucy. 'Have all the women in this town gone mad? Dora thinks she's still on stage, and I said all along it was that Elvira.'

I patted him on the back. 'Yes, Malcolm, you did. How perceptive of you.'

James raised his eyebrows at me, but I needed to butter Malcolm up, as I'd a favour to ask.

Customers trickled back, and the rumour mill soon cranked up to churn out more demented bilge. By late afternoon, I was flagging. Two sleepless nights had taken their toll. I had never known the tea room so busy. The noise had reached a crescendo, and we'd run out of teapots. I told myself to be positive and consider the takings. I'd not rung Charles and was thinking of cancelling Ruth.

At the end of service, Lucy and I sat slumped at a table with our feet resting on cushions. Malcolm had made a pot of tea. As he placed it on the table, James ushered someone through from the shop.

'Who's this berk?' asked Malcolm under his breath, but not quietly enough.

'It's me, Dave, Pansy's husband. I've had to come in disguise. I couldn't risk being seen.' Dave wore an Afghan coat with bits dropping off, aviator sunglasses and a battered fedora.

I drew back a chair and introduced him to Lucy and Malcolm. 'Sit down and join us, Dave.'

He removed the sunglasses and sat next to me. His coat reeked of wet sheep. 'Pansy's sent me out to buy hairspray.'

I poured him a cup of tea. 'I'm surprised she's focusing on hair products under the circumstances.'

'What circumstances? Oh, you mean Elvira's confession?' Dave asked like he had multiple crises spinning at once. 'Pansy needs it for the newspaper interviews she'll be doing.'

'She's traumatised then?' I asked.

He killed his smile. 'Yes, very much so.'

'She needs to be careful what she says to the papers,' said Malcolm. 'How much are they paying her?'

Dave coughed. 'It's not about the money. Pansy's doing it to help others in a similar situation.'

'So, what do you think of your mother-in-law being a double murderer?' asked Malcolm.

Dave flashed a nervous smile. Lucy put her hand to her mouth, and I wanted to kick Malcolm. Had he over-sugared his tea?

Dave was saved by his phone ringing. 'Hello, love. Yes, I'm on my way. Just popped into Merangs. No, I won't.' He looked towards me with a guilty expression. 'Yes, coming now, dearest. Don't get upset. Be there in a jiffy. Love you. Love you.'

'I should be going home, myself,' said Malcolm. He rose and stretched.

I told Lucy to clock off. James had already left. I was looking forward to some time alone at Merangs.

It took an hour to clean the tea room, but I enjoyed the peace and quiet. I was glad I hadn't cancelled Ruth, after all. A relaxing evening would do me good. I'd still not phoned Charles. He'd left numerous voicemails and texts.

Scrolling down my phone, I saw a text from an unknown number.

STAY AWAY FROM HIM

My eyes darted around the empty tea room as if someone might jump out of the shadows. No longer wanting to be alone, I collected my coat and bag, did a final check, and flicked off the lights. As I walked up the high street to Ruth's hotel, I considered the text. Was it a warning or a threat, and who the hell had sent it?

Hotel Acrobatics

The shops had closed, and the high street was deserted. All was quiet, except for running footsteps behind me. The steps became louder, and someone shouted my name. I froze.

Charles was breathless by the time he caught up and gasping for air. 'What do I have to do to get your attention?' His voice sounded gruff from the exertion.

'Sorry, I didn't hear you,' I lied.

'I've been trying to get hold of you all day.'

'I know, but we've been extremely busy at the shop.' Why did I feel guilty? '*And,* we didn't part on the best of terms.'

'You're right. My bad. I said all the wrong things. Can't we just start again?'

I'd not yet reached the chapter in my dating book on how to end a relationship. That in itself was too ambitious a term. It had only amounted to a couple of haphazard dates. I needed to extricate myself without shattering his ego.

I took a step back. 'Charles, you're all a girl could want — the dream package.' So far, so good, and he wasn't denying it.

His puppy dog eyes locked onto mine. 'I sense a but?'

I took a deep breath and slowly released it. 'I don't think we're right for each other.' There, it was out.

Charles seized my arm. 'But, you're perfect for me. Just the right fit. Listen, I've got a few days before I leave, and we could have some fun together.' He gave one of his winks. 'You'd like that.'

This wasn't going to be easy. 'I'm sorry I can't fall in with your plans. It's a shame but ...'

'Another but?'

'The best-laid plans of mice and men and all that.'

'Helen, stuff the mice, and I'm the only man you'll ever need.' He had regained both his breath and his swagger.

I needed to throw him off. 'Do you know where the line originates?'

'I can live without knowing.'

'It's from a poem. The poor little mouse lost her house.'

Charles pinched the bridge of his nose.

According to James, I had a particular talent for obfuscation, and perhaps it had done the trick here. 'I've got to go now. I'm meeting Ruth at her hotel.'

'I'll walk there with you.'

My God, does he never give up? I set off at a vigorous pace. 'I'm already late,' I threw over my shoulder. I trotted all the way and was sweating profusely by the time we arrived.

For the second time, Charles was breathless. I felt a tiny bit sorry for him. We stood on the steps of the hotel. I glimpsed the soft lights of the bar through a window on the left. I needed to ditch Charles there and then. The doorman lurked within earshot, and I didn't want a scene.

My visits to The Butterdish were rare, and I'd so looked forward to revelling in the whole experience. I'd already neglected the couchant lions at the bottom of the steps.

I usually rested a hand on each, but under pursuit, I'd forgotten to do so. I then liked to admire the original gas lamps at the main entrance, but with Charles in tow, the magic had gone.

Any sympathy for him vanished when he said, 'Will The Hulk be lurking in the bar?'

'I won't invite you to join us. We don't want Ruth getting the wrong message again, do we?'

Charles put his head down. 'Yeah, sorry for going on about her. If I leave quietly, will you promise to see me tomorrow?' The wheedling tone had returned.

Seizing my last chance, I said, 'Charles, you're an acesome, stand-out guy.' Speak his language, I thought, and I might get through. 'You've got it all going on, but it's just not happening for me.' I paused and then added for good measure, 'My bad.' Could it be any plainer?

'Cool. No worries,' he said with a smile.

Did I dare hope we'd reached an understanding? 'Bye, then.' I held out a tentative hand to shake a final farewell.

'Ciao. Laters, hun.' He lightly smacked my rear and then danced down the steps like a deluded Fred Astaire.

I shook my head and ran up the remaining steps. The doorman doffed his hat and ushered me through the heavy door into a bygone world of quiet opulence. Ruth was seated at a window table in the bar. She had a gin and tonic waiting for me, which I could have downed in one.

'Cheers. Good health,' she said. We clinked our glasses, and I relaxed into the plush armchair. 'You look like you needed that. Are you ready for another?' She beckoned a waiter over. 'And, before you say anything, it's all on me.'

'Ruth, I'm too tired to argue, so thanks very much.' I sank further into the chair, waiting for the gin to blur my edges.

We immersed ourselves in nostalgia and swapped our childhood memories of the hotel. It was always a birthday treat for me, and Ruth said her father used to bring her once a month for afternoon tea.

'I was a proper daddy's girl,' she said. 'He was such a wonderful man. Did you know he was famous in his field?'

'I heard he was an inventor?'

'Yes. So clever. His inventions helped people and made him pots of money.' She continued at some length, and I'm ashamed to say I glazed over. 'I've so much to thank him for. I just wish ...' Her eyes misted, and I patted her hand in a totally inadequate way.

On our third drink, she described her shock at Claudia running off with Vincent. 'I was eleven and mortified that my mother was having "relations", as I called it. We'd only just done sex lessons at school.'

'Omigod, those appalling sex lessons. Do you remember the graphic pop-up textbooks that could take your eye out? How did the teachers keep a straight face?'

Ruth smiled but continued her narrative. 'One night, not long after Mother left, I found Dad crying. Then she came back to collect me, and I hardly saw him again. We wrote to each other, and I've kept all his letters. He died when I was thirteen.'

The soft lights reflected Ruth's tears, and I had to dab at my own eyes. I reached across to hug her. 'You must have hated Vincent? And how did you feel about your mum?'

'I despised them both. I know that sounds harsh, but things are so black and white at that age, aren't they?' I nodded in agreement. 'I didn't make it easy for them.' She attempted a laugh. 'They were two lovebirds with a big brooding crow in the middle of their nest. Then Vincent flew, Mother collapsed, and I had to pick up the pieces. I ended up feeling sorry for her.'

'Vincent came back, though, didn't he?'

'Fleeting visits. He kept her dangling. Mother saw it as an epic romance and believed they would eventually marry. That's why she gave him money whenever he asked.'

Ruth broke off as a waiter arrived to take our food order. We'd not even opened the menus. I left Ruth to order for us both while I went to the ladies. I tried to walk in a straight line.

A visit to the ladies was another of my Butterdish rituals. First, I liked to linger in the ante-room, which was the size of a ballroom. Tonight it was all mine to enjoy, and I flitted from table to bureau, switching on the tulip-shaped lamps and plumping the cushions. I gravitated towards the row of tall windows and threw myself onto one of the deep couches nestling underneath. As a child, I used to recline on the chaise longue and pretend to give orders to my servants.

Mindful of Ruth, I jumped up and headed to the far corner where a door marked 'lavatories' was hidden by a floral screen. After the stateliness of the ante-room, the utilitarian aspect of this area was always a shock. Four large open-topped cubicles faced two bath-size sinks.

I didn't notice the lock on my cubicle door was stiff until I tried to exit. It wouldn't budge, but after three double gins, I wasn't one to panic. Sober, I would have called hotel reception, but a gin-based confidence induced me to stand on the toilet seat and launch myself over the door.

In the two-second planning stage, I'd clocked the features of my door. Although high, it had the bonus of a large, ornate handle. On the downside, the protruding coat hook might prove tricky, but since when had life been a full bowl of cherries?

The door held up well, and as I clung to the inside, with my arms hooked over the top, I felt pretty pleased with my progress. Placing my foot on the handle, I hauled myself over, leant forward, and began the descent.

Stuck upside down, with my skirt around my ears, I realised I'd not thought this through. The top of the door dug into my soft bits, and as I clung to the handle, nausea rose in my gullet. Not since I'd languished under the weight of Vincent's dead body had I felt so helpless. What else could I do but laugh? It must have been the rush of blood to my head.

Then two things happened at once. My phone started ringing from inside the cubicle, and two voices sounded in the ante-room.

An Oversized Bat

As I stared at the toilet floor, two pairs of shoes came into view. The first was a sensible pair of brown brogues which supported matchstick-sized legs. The second pair could have belonged to a doll, and held chubby short legs in sparkly pink tights. I raised my head in a friendly greeting, and the young girl's scream rattled the windows. She hid behind the old lady, who was the size of a pencil.

'Sorry to alarm you. I'm having a spot of trouble. My name's Helen, by the way.'

'I hope this isn't my birthday surprise,' said the old lady.

The child risked a peep and squealed. 'It's not, Granny. It's really not.'

'Now that's sorted, let's go find someone to help, shall we? Stay there, Helen.'

I'm not going anywhere.

'We'll be back with the cavalry. Won't be a tick.' She put her arm around the child and ushered her out.

Hanging there, I reflected on how arbitrary measures of time could be so cruel and deceptive. I appreciated that an old lady might not be quick on her feet, but as the minutes dragged by, and the blood drained down, I wondered if she was enlisting her cavalry one by one and sending them on basic manoeuvres first.

Finally, just as my arms had gone numb, a loud, authoritative voice boomed out in the ante-room. 'Man in the room. Man in the room.'

The outer door opened. 'Here she is,' said the old lady, as if I needed pointing out.

The doorman helped me down gently and without any fuss. It might have been any one of his Friday night duties.

Once upright, I wanted to smother him in kisses. My effusive thanks were interrupted by my phone ringing from inside the cubicle.

The hero looked at the door and sighed. 'I should have brought my tools.' He gently touched the door, and it swung open. 'You must have, er, dislodged it, Miss, with your acrobatics. I'll be on my way now.'

'I feel such a fool,' I said to the old lady as I picked up my bag.

'Nonsense. It's the most fun I've had in years, and I'm ninety today. I'll just spend a penny, and then you can walk me back to my table and help blow out the candles on my cake. There are so many of the damn things.'

I glanced at my phone while waiting. Two missed calls from Charles. I sent Ruth a quick text and noticed I'd received one from an unknown number.

'I'm Matilda,' shouted the old lady. She'd left her cubicle door ajar.

We made our way to Matilda's table, arm in arm. She introduced me to her family, and we all sang 'Happy Birthday'. I blew out my fair share of candles, scattered vouchers for Merangs and then bounded back to the bar.

I'd been gone a total of thirty minutes. 'Ruth, I'm so sorry.'

'I thought it was something I'd said until I got your text.' She smiled. 'I just assumed you'd bumped into some friends. Don't mean to be rude, but your face is bright red, and your hair looks like it's been plugged into the mains.'

'I've been hanging about like an oversized bat.' I recounted the tale, and Ruth laughed until she started choking, and I had to thwack her on the back.

'I'll just pop to the ladies, myself,' she said when she'd recovered. 'Then we can go through to the restaurant.'

As she walked away, I pulled a mirror out of my bag and then hastily shoved it back in again. Why spoil the evening by looking at that? Beyond patting down my hair, there wasn't much else I could do. I remembered the text on my phone. I knew it wasn't going to be nice, but even so, I flinched.

BACK OFF YOU BITCH

It had come through when I was outside the hotel with Charles. As I contemplated this, another popped up.

YOU THINK EVERYONE LIKES YOU. YOU'RE WRONG

Definitely not a friend, but on the upside, my anonymous texter had a good grasp of grammar. Ensconced in the convivial and comfortable Butterdish, I did as Scarlett O'Hara would do and told myself to think about that tomorrow.

In the restaurant, Ruth and I continued our conversation where we'd left off. Ruth confirmed Claudia had bequeathed Vincent all her money, and that it was a considerable fortune.

'You must have been bitter about that,' I said. 'Most people would.'

'A mixture of emotions, really. I was incensed she'd been exploited by Vincent. Part of me felt sorry for her, but I was also angry. I resented how she'd squandered her money on such a low-life.'

I had to ask the obvious. 'Did you not feel cheated out of your inheritance?'

'No.' Ruth shook her long, dark hair. 'Honestly, no. I didn't.'

I must have looked sceptical, as she gave a slightly false laugh. 'Dad made provision when they divorced. He settled most of his share in a trust fund for me. I always considered Mum's money her own and had no expectations.'

'But you must have felt angry on behalf of your dad?'

'Yes, absolutely.' She stabbed at her steak. 'What an insult to all he'd achieved.'

'Sounds like you could have cheerfully murdered Vincent yourself.' I can't believe that came out of my mouth.

'I'll drink to that, even though it's in terribly bad taste to do so.' She held up her glass and grinned. 'The only thing is, I would have had to murder Charles, too. Why would I stop at Vincent when I thought the money would then go to Charles? You must know by now, I'm not his number one fan.'

I pictured Ruth striding through town, a hunting rifle slung over one shoulder and a brace of Newby men over the other. I put down my cutlery. 'I've told Charles I don't want to see him again.'

She gasped. 'When did you tell him? And why don't you want to see him again?' Her eyes remained fixed on my face. 'Sorry, that's none of my business.'

'I don't mind. Plain and simple, he's not for me.' I explained how I'd tried to ditch him gently, but he wasn't taking no for an answer.

'He won't like that.' Ruth's eyes gleamed. 'He's the one normally throwing the women overboard.'

'Is that why you told me to be careful?'

Ruth hesitated before she answered. 'Partly. I made a fool of myself over Charles. I thought he liked me, wanted a relationship, even, but I'd misread the situation. I was the one who couldn't take no for an answer.'

I wanted to ask what the other part of her reason had been. Even though she was baring her soul, I sensed she was holding something back. 'He must have encouraged you?'

She stared at her plate. 'He led me to think we might have a future together. Hardly credible, I know.'

'He's certainly a smooth operator.'

Ruth nodded. 'I found him exciting and dangerous.'

Steady on, Ruth. He's hardly Lord Byron.

'In fact, the attraction I felt towards him explained how Mother had been ensnared by Vincent. Unlike her, though, I did come to my senses.'

Both mother and daughter would have been easy pickings for the Newby men. It made me all the more determined to shake Charles off. Time to change the subject. 'Have you heard about the murder confession?'

'How could I not? It's all around town. Who's this woman who's confessed?' Ruth topped up both our glasses.

I took a quick sip of my wine. 'She works for Mr Klondike.'

'Is she the dragon or the sulky, incompetent one?'

I laughed at her accurate descriptions. 'Dragon.'

Ruth screwed up her face. 'But what was her motive for murder?'

I outlined my thoughts on it being a crime of passion, and Ruth appeared to be weighing it up, but then again, she may have been considering her dessert options.

'I see what you mean, but I'm not sure it all fits. What does James think?'

I swept that away with an impatient hand. 'Him? Oh, he's got no imagination. He just thinks it's all to do with money.'

'He may have a point. It does sound more likely.'

'You're as bad as him.' I grinned across at her, and we clinked our glasses.

We moved on to more general topics, with no awkward pauses. That might have been due to all the alcohol we'd consumed, but I found her such easy company. I was tempted to tell her about my anonymous texts, but something held me back.

Towards the end of the evening, Ruth gave a tentative smile and said, 'I'm thinking of moving back to Buttersley. I've found my cousins here, and there's also you and Merangs.' Her voice slightly trembled, and she disguised it with a cough.

'That would be fantastic.' I probably overdid my enthusiasm, but she deserved encouragement. 'I'll drink to that.' We clinked our glasses together for the umpteenth time.

The Dating Jungle

Saturday 20th May

Alcohol was a depressant. I'd tick that box to agree. I awoke in the early hours with palpitations and acute paranoia. Charles had already texted that his Brazil trip had been postponed. *Acesome.*

Pushing that particular horror to one side, I fixated on the anonymous texts. I'd received another during the night.

YOU ATTENTION-SEEKING WHORE. KEEP YOUR GRUBBY PAWS TO YOURSELF

In my fragile state, it landed like a punch in the guts. What had I done to provoke such vitriol? My paws might have been grubby, but I couldn't recall the last time I'd pinned someone down in a half-nelson. Attention seeking? Fair point. I might hold my paws up to that. But whore? I'd never had the chance.

Too weary for another early run, I reached for my book, *The Dating Jungle.* It neither held my attention nor sent me back to sleep. I could have searched online for news on the murders, but my appetite for gossip had gone. I threw back the sheets at five.

In the mirror, I couldn't believe how fresh-faced I looked, considering my alcohol intake and lack of sleep. My curls bounced, my eyes sparkled, and even more incredible, I'd no hangover.

Sipping a glass of juice at the kitchen table, while Snowy wolfed down her food, I had a flash of inspiration. The reason for my bright eyes and bushy tail could only be due to hanging upside down for nearly thirty minutes. Maybe I should squeeze in a bat routine on every night out?

I called at Mr Choudray's to buy a copy of each daily paper. From the horde of reporters yesterday, I anticipated a big Buttersley splash. Not one to miss a trick, Mr Choudray had shipped in extra copies and stacked them in towers next to the counter.

'Miss Merang, you must be wanting a packet of mints to go with your purchase. No? Then I'm thinking you would like to buy our most popular Cup-a-Soup? Mulligatawny. Limited edition. Reduced. Very exclusive for our more discerning customers.'

'I'll have a bag of pear drops, please.'

Mr Choudray beamed as if I'd bought his entire shop. 'An excellent choice, Miss Merang.'

I always left Mr Choudray's with a smile on my face and an unplanned purchase in my pocket.

At Merangs, I scanned the headlines. 'Small-town Buttersley Battens Down its Hatches as a MURDERER Runs Amok'. It was too much to process without a strong cup of tea. I stood listening to the reassuring hum of the fridges. Perhaps I should have opened early, as plenty of reporters still buzzed around. But for once, I couldn't face being on my own in the shop. Needing to see a friendly face, I slipped on my coat and ran to Prue's house.

Prue's face might have been friendly, but it was difficult to tell. It was smothered in thick white cream and shielded by a canopy attached to her hairnet. That and the heavy cambric gown suggested an outfit for beekeeping rather than bed.

In the morning chill, I shivered on her doorstep. 'Sorry, it's so early. Can I come in?' Never mind the old camel and needle routine; it would have been easier to access a secretive communist state than cross Prue's portals unannounced.

She folded her arms. 'I hope you've got a good reason for calling so abominably early and getting me out of bed.'

That was exactly the welcome I'd expected, and I took comfort from her predictable reaction. Maybe I should have taken one of Mr Choudray's Cup-a-Soups to smooth the way?

'Sorry, but I couldn't sleep and wanted your advice on something.' That was true, but also my passport in. An appeal to her mothering instincts worked every time.

'Well then, don't just stand there, letting the cold in.' Prue shifted a couple of inches so I could squeeze past. 'Leave your shoes in the hallway. Go through to the sitting room and switch on two bars of the fire. I'll be with you shortly.'

Prue's sitting room could have staged a period drama. The sort where characters displayed impeccable manners and rigid deportment. The dark, oppressive furniture lowered my mood, and I wasn't tempted to sit on one of the Queen Anne-style chairs. They stood like sentries at the four corners of the room and looked as uncomfortable as hell.

I noted, not for the first time, how Prue must have compromised her lifestyle to accommodate me as a messy teenager. How many times must she have regretted that promise to her dying best friend? When I lived there, my scatty approach had driven her mad, and she was not beyond flinging my possessions in the bin. As soon as I left for university, she set up her show home.

I closed my eyes as a pendulous clock ticked my life away. I could not imagine the room ever being warm. The two bars of the electric fire might well have been bananas for all the heat they generated.

Ten minutes later, Prue entered, regal in her floral housecoat. She'd wiped off the face cream and ditched the headgear. 'So, Missy, what's got you out of bed so early?'

I hesitated, not wanting to plunge straight in with the anonymous texts. 'I seem to have upset someone.'

'That young man, Charles?'

'Well, yes. Possibly. I mean, probably, but that's not what I meant.'

Prue pinched the end of her nose. 'I can't offer advice if you don't spell out your problem. Let's go through to the kitchen. It's warmer in there, and I need to soak my prunes. Make sure you turn the fire off.'

The kitchen was a whole lot cosier. Most of the equipment was familiar. Even the kettle was over twenty years old. I read out the nasty texts as Prue bustled about. When I'd finished, she stood with her hands on her hips.

'Poison pen letters, that's what they were in my day. When people could still hold a pen.' She tutted. 'Some things never change, though.'

'Such as?'

'Plain jealousy. That's what it is.'

'But who would be jealous of me?'

Prue's face froze like a contestant on a quiz show who'd been asked an impossible question. She turned her back and filled the kettle a second time.

We sat at her little table, eating white-bread toast. The Light Programme – as Prue still called it – played in the background, and we dissected the texts. Finally, Prue removed her reading glasses and put them away. 'As you use your phone for the shop, all and sundry will know the number.'

'Nice to think it's not necessarily my closest friends who want to stab me in the back.'

Prue poured another cup of tea. 'The texts coincide with your dating Charles. Are you sure he's not married or in a relationship?'

I was about to confirm his single status, but paused. What did I know about him, other than he wouldn't take no for an answer? According to Ruth, there were plenty of discarded women in his wake and a long queue for his attention.

I fiddled with my phone. 'If the texter was his wife or partner, would they resort to anonymity?

'You've encroached on someone else's territory. They are warning you off and hoping to make you feel bad about yourself. These texts come from someone troubled and deeply insecure.' Prue spoke with authority. 'As soon as you sever ties with Charles, the texts will no doubt stop. And that's that.'

I lifted my shoulders. Prue's no-nonsense approach had empowered me. I would tell Charles where to get off with no equivocation. I wasn't going to put up with his harassment any longer. My switch had flicked back to positive.

I smiled and reached my hand across the table. 'I had a lovely time at The Cavendish last night, Prue. It brought back fond memories of my birthday treats there.' I covered her small hand with mine. 'Thanks for everything you've done for me. I owe you such a lot.'

Prue did not quite succeed in hiding her pleasure. Her face flushed a delicate rose, and she removed her hand to dab at her eyes. 'Get along now, you big softie. You've got a shop to open, and I've got my prunes to rinse.'

I rushed back to Merangs. Lucy had already arrived and was leaning against the door frame, intent on her phone. When she looked up, her eyes flashed like diamonds, and she flung out her arms. 'Helen, there you are. I've got so much to tell you. It's totes crazy. You look nice, by the way.' She paused for effect. 'You won't believe it, but Sadsville has literally gone insane.'

As I unlocked the door, I thought she was talking about Buttersley in general, until I realised she was referring to some drama at college.

She prattled on as we set up the tea room. 'Like everyone, literally, everyone's walking around with slapped-bum faces.'

Although soothed by her chatter, I missed most of the detail. I tuned in again when her voice rose.

'What do you think? There's been a savage vibe for weeks. She's like ultra upset.'

'That's terrible,' I'd no idea what she was talking about.

'She might call in today. She'll need an extra big hug.' Lucy's brow puckered, and she prodded my shoulder as if I wouldn't be up to the job.

'Absolutely. Hugsville all the way. In fact, give her these as a gift from me.' I handed over the pear drops.

We had another busy day in the tea room. The newspaper coverage had attracted sightseers, with darting eyes and swivelling heads. James channelled them all to me, but I didn't feel up to the scrutiny of their hungry stares. I phoned Malcolm, who said it would be right up his street. He arrived within minutes, wearing his best blazer.

He held the visitors in the palm of his calloused hand. 'Look up,' his patter began. 'Directly above your heads, the first body was found hidden away in a cupboard.' He repeated it so often, you'd have thought there was a locker room up there, stuffed with dead bodies. 'I was first on the scene of the second murder and had to direct the police.' He lowered his gaze to the floor. 'There's talk of me being in line for a commendation.'

As with Prue, earlier, a surge of love overwhelmed me. Malcolm was always willing to help and forever on my side. I told him what a fantastic job he was doing, and how the shop couldn't operate without him. His face lit up, and he straightened his back. A button flew off his shirt.

I scrabbled around for it under a table. 'If the media run with the story, Malcolm, you'll be famous.'

'Don't worry, Helen, love; I'll still do your decorating next week.'

The customers kept on coming. I'd no time to think of Charles or the toxic texts. I'd wanted to visit Dora and Mr Klondike to check how they were coping, but I didn't get the chance.

By mid-afternoon, I could have done with a spell upside down. Just when my fizz was nearing empty, who should stroll in but Charles? I should have told James to bar his entry.

He handed me an enormous bunch of roses. 'How's my girl?'

'Oohs' and 'Ahhs' emanated from the tables. Charles's smile swept the room, and he gave a silly bow.

I handed the flowers to Lucy and took him to one side. 'Listen, I am *not* your girl and *never* will be. Why can't you accept there's nothing between us? Leave me alone. I never want to see you again. And while you're at it, call your dogs off.' I prodded his chest as I spoke, pushing him towards the door. I'd never in my life been so direct and deliberately hurtful.

Charles laughed. He planted his hands on my shoulders. I flinched. 'Hey, Hels, you *are* my girl. You just don't know it yet. Laters, hun.' He sauntered to the door and blew a kiss before he went out. His insouciance rattled me. His behaviour was bizarre, and I was out of my depth.

Late afternoon, a rumour rippled around the tea room, confirmed by a few short lines in the local evening paper. A woman had been charged with the murders. That could only be Elvira, but more of a surprise, two others had been taken in for questioning.

Preoccupied with my messy personal problems, I paid scant attention. Only a few days before, I would have been agog with speculation.

As the last customer left the tea room, Emily arrived. She stood in the doorway, twisting her hands together. Lank, dull hair hung around her pale face.

Lucy rushed up and swamped her in an enthusiastic hug. 'So glad you came.'

'I had to get out of the house. Mother won't leave me alone. She's at me all the time.' Emily's face crumpled, and tears ran down her face. Lucy led her to a table while I made them both hot chocolate. 'She can't make me go back,' said Emily, vigorously stirring her drink. 'She literally has no idea how vile they are.'

I gathered she'd left college after falling out with a group of girls, and her mother was insisting she go back. 'What does your brother say?'

'Him? It's nothing to do with him.' She clattered the teaspoon onto the saucer, and it fell to the floor.

I recalled their disagreement in Bangles when she'd flounced off. DCI Swift probably agreed with her mother.

Lucy retrieved the teaspoon. 'Emily's agreed to come to mine for a sleepover. We're going to get wine and chocolate.'

Relieved to be useful, I grabbed two bottles of wine from my stash, made up a box of truffles from the counter, and persuaded James to take the girls home. 'Can you drop off these roses to Prue while you're at it?'

Ten minutes later, they all left, with Emily more cheerful and James grumbling all the way out. Relieved to be on my own, I did an express clean, telling myself it wouldn't matter for once. Just as I was leaving, the shop phone rang, but I ignored it.

Walking home, I relished the fresh air and escape from work. James was going to call around later with one of his magic hampers. I didn't rush, enjoying the soft, friendly breeze. The streets were quiet, so it was easy to detect that I was being followed.

Sticks and Stones

As I quickened my pace along the high street, the paranoia from the early hours resurfaced. Fearing it could be the anonymous texter wanting to escalate their threats, I almost fainted in relief when I realised it was Charles. He made little effort to conceal himself. Either he wanted me to know he was there, or he'd taken his gumshoe lessons from Malcolm. He shadowed me all the way home.

Once home, I slammed the door shut and dragged the stiff bolt across. It snagged my fingers, and I howled in pain and frustration. Snowy, wandering into the hallway, froze at the commotion. I rushed into the living room and closed the curtains. If Charles was lurking out there, I didn't want to know.

I hoped James wouldn't be too long with his food hamper. I'd not eaten all day and tried to fool myself it was the food I craved when really, I needed my friend. His car pulled up in the drive, and I ran to the door. As James crossed the threshold, I clenched my hands to avoid flinging them around his neck. Then, like a lapdog, I followed him into the kitchen and stood as close as I dared.

James took a step back. 'What's wrong? You're not usually so pleased to see me.'

'Nothing.' I forced a smile. 'I'm just thrilled at the size of your hamper.'

James grinned. 'That's what all the girls say.'

My fears fluttered away. 'I've got the cutlery out. Do you want me to do anything else?'

He lifted his head from the hamper. 'Switch on the oven, would you? It's the pristine silver thing over there.'

I flicked back my curls. 'I'm a busy businesswoman running my business. I don't have time to cook.'

'Pour me a large glass of red then, if your schedule allows.'

'Of course, but you'll be drinking alone tonight. I'm on the wagon.'

An hour later, I pushed my chair back from the table. 'James, those spinach, feta and pine nut tarts were divine, and the salted caramel cheesecake, your best ever.'

He permitted a smug little smile. 'I'd give you the recipes, but I might as well hand them to the cat.'

As I cleared the table, I told him about Charles. I didn't mention he'd followed me, just that he wouldn't take no for an answer.

'That fella's a loose cannon. An egomaniac.'

I considered firing back, 'It takes one to know one,' but the new clingy me swallowed the retort. 'Ruth *did* warn me about him. She's got history there. I think she's holding something back.'

'We need to know what that is.' James tapped the spoon on his dish as if to emphasise his point. 'If the harassment escalates, you need to contact the police.'

I'd not expected that reaction. And he didn't even know the half of it. I tried to laugh it off. 'The police already think I'm a joke. There's only PC Daz who would listen, and he can't even look after himself.' I pointed to a photograph in the newspaper. It featured Dora, holding her arms up in triumph with the Thatcher handbag dangling from one arm and Daz from the other.

'You need to take this business seriously.' James stroked Snowy under her chin, and the floozy jumped onto his lap. 'I know I'm banging on about this, but I'm convinced Charles is involved in the murders.'

I steadied myself at the sink. My hands shook as I reached for the tap. I was so used to James's flippant approach that this serious side rattled me. I diverted his attention to the newspaper coverage. Buttersley had made all the front pages. Merangs had received several mentions.

James stretched out his legs, but Snowy held on. 'Don't worry. The publicity won't harm the shop.'

'No. We're smelling of roses so far. Malcolm's considering charging for his autograph. But I'm worried about the effect on Mr Klondike's agency. You know they're still calling it 'Death Lets', despite Dora's best efforts?'

'I know. Even I feel sorry for Klondike.'

I spread the newspapers out on the table. In *The Sun*, Pansy reclined on a couch, wan and pensive, her sharp features softened by the distant lens. *The Times* featured Pansy and Dave together with the camera catching them at an awkward moment. She had contorted her face in fury, or maybe pregnancy wind, and he was staring ahead with his mouth open wide.

'He could trap wild animals with those teeth,' said James.

Pansy had granted 'exclusive scoops' to two publications. Elvira, she stated, was innocent. She'd been coerced into confessing, and there would be heads to roll. I pictured Snood's head rolling down the high street, shouting, 'You members of the public get out of my way.'

I sat down and patted my knee as an invitation to Snowy. She stayed with James. 'Have you heard Elvira's been charged with the murders? They must believe she's guilty.'

'Not necessarily. They would have had no choice but to either charge or release her. They'll be trying to find corroborative evidence.'

'What about the couple the police have taken in for questioning? That must be Pansy and Dave, don't you think?' I raised my voice as I appeared to be talking to myself. 'Maybe they're involved? Dave did say something strange in connection with the murders. I didn't think much of it at the time, but it was an odd thing to say.'

I could have said, 'Dave wanted to be my sex slave,' for all the reaction I got from James. He was too absorbed in the newspapers to hear.

I stopped talking, and he lifted his head. 'Look at this. "The scene of the crime".'

Shakira's overly made-up face leered out of *The Daily Mail*. With a plunging neckline and mussed-up hair, she'd draped herself around the flat like a footballer's wife in a trashy magazine.

Like old Queen Vic, I didn't want to be amused. 'Vincent died up there, but she's prancing around showing off her boobs.'

James laughed. 'Hey, misery guts, lighten up. Actually, Shakira's given me an idea on how we can help Klondike.'

Snowy awoke and dug her claws into his thighs.

That's more like it, girl.

He shook her off, and she flounced out of the room. James winced and clutched his leg.

I smiled. 'Toughen up, softie guts.'

We moved into the lounge. The cold hallway drove Snowy to join us. She stretched out on top of the sofa and laid a paw on James's shoulder.

'I think she likes me.'

'You've always had a way with the girls.' He'd had a lot to drink, so I dived in to ask about his criminal past, as alleged by Snood.

James sighed. 'I can't deny I ran wild for a few years, got arrested here and there, but Snood exaggerated. I may have been violent when provoked, but was never a Death Row contender.'

'I don't want you roughing up Charles on my behalf.' I half-believed he might.

He yawned. 'No chance. I don't have the energy to beat up a cushion these days. So, when were you planning to tell me about these nasty texts you've received?'

Prue must have told him. The unexpected softness in his tone brought tears to my eyes. I rubbed away at an imaginary stain on my sleeve. 'I was going to get round to it. Prue says they're linked to Charles. What do you think?'

'Let's have a look.' I handed James my phone, and he read them with a frown. He shrugged. 'Probably linked to him, but it could just be a coincidence.'

'Who else are they referring to, if not Charles? I don't have men coming out of my ears. Oh no. That doesn't sound right.' I wrinkled my nose at the image.

'Just saying. It's not always the obvious explanation.' He left the sofa to crouch at my side. 'You have a lot going on at the moment. Prue and I agree …'

'That's a first.'

He took my hand. 'We're worried about you.' My tears dropped onto our hands, and I scrambled around for a tissue. As I loudly blew my nose, James continued. 'Prue and I both think you should report Charles and the texts to the police. Don't waste time. Go to the top.'

I forced a smile. 'Who, Snood? She'd take one look at the texts and say they didn't go far enough.'

'Not her. I meant DCI Swift.'

'Swift? He's too high up to deal with this.' Surely, James was taking it far too seriously?

James narrowed his eyes. 'You'd be surprised. I've seen how Swift looks at you.'

'Like I'm the village halfwit?'

James patted my hand and returned to the sofa. 'Yeah, it's possibly pity, but I think he likes you.'

After James had left in a taxi, I stacked the dishwasher and replayed our conversation. How could DCI Swift view me with anything but contempt? I ran through the litany of mishaps I'd placed before him. Sugar cubes popping out of my bra, a poorly executed twerk, dropping a curry into his lap and then diving in with my hankie. Worst of all, my parading around with that peacock Charles and him being rude to the DCI. What shockingly poor judgement I'd displayed. My face burned in shame.

And now James and Prue were insisting I run to the DCI about Charles's strange behaviour. How humiliating would that be? And what did it amount to? Charles, not being able to take rejection? Swift was the head of the local police, not a relationship counsellor.

As I plodded upstairs with my cat and cocoa, I decided to shove it all out of my mind and stay in bed for the whole of Sunday. A day off from the world might calm it all down. As I undressed, I made the mistake of checking my phone. Another text had arrived.

HOW COULD ANYONE LIKE YOUR UGLY FACE?

I shouted, 'Sticks and stones may break my bones,' and hurled the phone out of the room. 'But words will never hurt me,' I whispered to Snowy as the tears ran down my face.

I burrowed down into my welcoming bed and must have nodded off straight away. Charles invaded my dreams. I knew it was a dream, so I wasn't scared, just damned annoyed.

He was climbing up my drainpipe in his skinny black jeans, a sack of salad on his back and a demented gleam in his eye. 'Rapunzel, Rapunzel,' he chanted, 'let your curls down.'

I chuckled in my sleep at the thought of reporting that to the DCI and realised I was awake, not dreaming. I switched on the bedside lamp and knocked over my cup of cold cocoa. Fully awake and about to swear, I paused to listen. Something had rattled against my window.

A Day of Rest

Spilt cocoa on the shagpile was the least of my worries. Someone was outside my bedroom window, making a noise. With shaking hands, I fumbled for my phone. 'Snowy, where the hell is it?'

She opened one eye, closed it and curled into a tight ball. I wanted to do the same. A shot of adrenaline surged through me, I grabbed my heavy-duty hairbrush, roared like a Zulu warrior and ripped back the curtains to find nobody there. Emboldened, I opened the window and stuck my head out into the night. A drainpipe had come loose and was clanking against the wall in the now feeble wind. No one in their right mind would have attempted to climb that decrepit old thing.

I slapped my chest in relief, blew out a deep breath and staggered back to bed. Wide awake, with no chance of sleep, I could have done with a cup of tea, but couldn't face going downstairs. I sat bolt upright and waited for the sun to rise.

I had a couple of hours to think about life's rich tapestry and all its vicissitudes. Helen Merang, moderately successful in business but hopeless at everything else.

Counting my blessings, I started with those I loved who loved me back. On the fingers of one hand, I had digits to spare. Should I designate one for Zack? If he had loved me, he wouldn't have left. Did I still love him? I didn't remember stopping, only becoming numb. It was easier to cope with rejection from afar. If Zack had remained close by, I might have ended up a full-blown stalker.

Maybe that was why I empathised with Charles and his raw desperation. His actions set me on edge, but surely he wouldn't hurt me? When the sting of rejection had passed, he'd soon realise he was being ridiculous and give up the chase. I couldn't bring myself to report him – yet.

The radio alarm blared into my thoughts. Sunlight poured in through the window. A familiar voice shouted from below, and pebbles pelted the glass.

Enraged, I jumped out of bed and planted my feet in a sticky cocoa mess. 'Deal with spills immediately,' Prue would say. Why was she always right?

Charles stood beneath the window, grinning and waving both arms. 'I wanted to see your morning face,' he shouted so all the street might hear.

On the best of mornings, after a nourishing sleep, I often resembled a ghoul who'd been tipped out of a coffin. As I stared Charles out, the grin slipped down his face, and he stumbled backwards. 'I was, er, just passing. Laters.' He ran down the street without looking back.

'See,' I said to Snowy. 'That confirms he's harmless.' Maybe if she could speak, she'd say I was deluded? I closed the curtains, cleaned up the cocoa and climbed back into bed. About to congratulate myself on seeing Charles off, I paused to wonder if that daily dose of horror had made Zack reach for his suitcase and run far away.

Confident that Charles would not return, I dozed off and dreamt of Shakira rolling down the high street in a giant shoe. The heel snapped off, and she tumbled out. Candice laughed like the devil and pelted her sister with macaroons.

A banging on the front door awoke me. *What now?* I was about to prepare the boiling oil when Ruth called my name.

'Hope I'm not disturbing you,' she said as I opened the door. 'Oh, you poor thing.' Her face furrowed in concern. 'Are you ill?'

Snowy had followed me down. She froze, yowled and ran back up the stairs.

'Sorry about that,' I said. 'We're not at our best on a morning. No, not ill, just tired. Come through to the kitchen.'

'I won't stay long, but it's such a glorious day, I fancied a walk. I've brought these.' She placed a bag of warm croissants on the table.

'I'll fire up the coffee machine. Thanks for dropping by. I can catch up on my sleep anytime.'

Ruth tilted her head to one side. 'Is something wrong? You're not your usual sparkly self.'

I paused in opening the cupboard door. Should I tell her? Why not? I turned around. 'Charles is stalking me. Prue and James say I should report him to the police.'

Ruth nodded vigorously. 'Absolutely right, you should.'

'I'm not sure. I feel a bit sorry for him.'

'What if he becomes violent? You don't know what's behind that mask of charm. He's used to getting his own way, especially with women.'

'Oh, don't say that. I'm sure Charles wouldn't be violent.' I tried to push away the memory of him gripping my arm in Bangles. I fumbled with the packet of coffee until it tore apart, and the precious brown powder spilt onto the worktop. 'Now look what I've done.'

'You sit down.' Ruth pushed me gently onto a chair. 'I'll make the coffee.'

Taking deep breaths, I gradually relaxed as the aroma of freshly brewed coffee worked its magic. I reached for my cup. 'James is convinced Charles is involved in the murders.' I wanted Ruth to dismiss that as nonsense.

About to take a drink, she placed her cup back onto the saucer. 'All the more reason to report Charles, then?'

'But if he *were* involved, surely the police would know?'

'Maybe they haven't got all the facts, or haven't investigated properly? What about all those miscarriages of justice we hear about?'

I didn't have an answer to that.

Ruth tactfully changed the subject and left soon after, saying she wanted to enjoy the sunshine. I went back to bed. Snowy trotted down for breakfast, returned, washed her face, then, exhausted, fell back asleep. I recalled what Ruth had said about Charles and how she echoed James's view. Yes, she knew Charles better than I did, but I just couldn't see him being the violent, dangerous type.

I found the nasty texts more threatening, as if someone was watching me and waiting to pounce. I shivered and drew Prue's old knitted cardie around my shoulders. I'd not told Ruth about the texts. I wasn't sure why exactly, only that I didn't want her thinking I was a total disaster zone.

I dozed on and off all day, and my phone remained silent. It was reassuring that even texting trolls took a day off from their fire and brimstone.

I awoke on Monday, revived and ready to tackle the world. I marched to work in the early morning sun. Yesterday had given me time to think. Although Charles and the toxic texts had elbowed the murders from the forefront of my mind, I was certain of two facts. Neither Charles nor Elvira was involved.

The elusive thought remained – a detail someone had mentioned that wasn't right – a memory I just couldn't grasp, and I shook my head in frustration.

My thoughts turned to Merangs. Malcolm would be decorating this week. It was our annual Forth Bridge affair. He painted a section at a time, and although he tried to keep out of our way, it always ended up in a turf war with James.

Malcolm was reading a newspaper outside the shop when I arrived. 'Have you seen the latest about Elvira?' He thrust the paper towards me.

The headline ran, 'Grandmother Brutalised and Starved in Rat-Infested Cell'.

What? Elvira may not have featured on my list of loved ones, but nobody deserved that. They'd been banging on about prison reform on the news, only last week, but I didn't realise it had come to this.

Wait A Minute. 'Malcolm, this is a woman held in Bangkok, not Buttersley, England. Put your glasses on.' I read out the story. "British pensioner, Enid, confesses to the murder of her husband on their holiday of a lifetime. Her daughter, Hazel, aged 43, pictured at the door of her four-bedroom bungalow, refused to comment. A neighbour and family friend said, Enid is a lovely woman who wouldn't hurt a fly"'.

I could see how the article had confused Malcolm, as it compared the two cases and played on the granny angle. It featured Pansy holding her baby scan photo and patting a non-existent bump. 'My baby may never know its grandmother', ran the predictable copy.

I continued to read the paper after I'd unlocked the door. Another article demonised Vincent and dredged up his former flings. None had a good word to say about him. 'A charmer with menaces', said one. Mrs Newby hardly got a mention. Did she have no one to mourn her? Had the poor woman even had a funeral? I couldn't see Pansy putting herself out for her aunt, and Elvira was indisposed.

'There's another picture of Shakira on page three and an interview,' said Malcolm.

'Let me see.'

She'd toned down the make-up and wore a white blouse under a yellow gingham apron. Smiling like a Stepford Wife, she held out a tray of 'delicious' cakes. 'Mr Klondike of Klondike Estates on Buttersley High Street, opposite Merangs, is my knight in shining armour', it read. 'I was homeless with two small children, and he came to my rescue'. She threw in the terms 'local hero, benefactor of Buttersley' and 'munificent sponsor'. Apparently, Mr Klondike had fixed it for her to live in one of his prestigious properties at a subsidised rate. 'I'm an entrepreneur, and he recognised my contribution to the local economy'. I saw the hand of her scriptwriter. 'It should be called The Klondike Kindness Agency'. She'd probably gone off-piste there. 'He also helps people at the very bottom of the pile. Those like my poor sister, Candice'.

'I see you're impressed,' said James from the doorway. I'd been so engrossed, I'd not noticed him arrive. 'Not bad,' he added. 'Even though I say so myself.'

'I thought you'd be behind it, but anything that helps Mr Klondike, I suppose.'

'Here, grab two of these.' He held Shakira's trays in his arms. 'Merang's celeb phoned me. She's busy with the media all day, and could I collect our order?'

'Whatever next?' said Prue, who'd rolled up behind him. 'It's not like you to be so obliging.'

'Good Morning, Prue,' James replied. 'Been gargling with vinegar over the weekend, have we?'

'Those trays are in my way,' said Malcolm, just to get in on the knockabout.

'Why don't I make us all a drink?' I said.

Prue followed me into the tea room, muttering, 'Get me away from all men.'

Monday meant Maureen and an everlasting mint tea. 'I could murder my hairdresser,' she announced. 'She's let me down at the last minute. Double-booked. Why didn't she cancel the other client?'

'I don't know, Maureen.' *Do I look like I care?*

The Silent Sisters had followed her in, and she turned to them. 'Don't say Sandra's cancelled you two as well? What do you think about all this murder business? I'll tell you what I think.'

Ten minutes later, Maureen interrupted her monologue and peered over the sisters' shoulders. 'Look what the wind's blown in. Buttersley's answer to Elizabeth Taylor.' She looked Dora up and down. 'In her later years.'

Dora looked like she barely had the energy to pick up her handbag. It was a different woman who had commanded the stage less than a week ago.

Prue took Dora by the arm and beckoned me over. 'You sit down with Helen, dear, and I'll bring you a coffee.' Prue guided her to the table furthest away from Maureen.

Once seated, Dora covered her face with her hands. 'Helen, it's been unbearable. You won't believe what people are saying. As for Gerald, my poor little lamb has lost his vim. He can't even wag his ickle tail.'

I tried to erase the vision she'd planted in my head and took hold of her hands. 'Why don't you tell me all about it, Dora?'

Red Herring Ballcocks

It disturbed me to see Dora so down. It was like some cataclysmic event had turned off the sun. She bent her blonde tresses to reveal an ugly stripe of dark grey roots. After her initial outburst, she didn't speak further but stared at the table.

'So, is the rental business really that bad?' I asked.

'Yes. No. I mean, it was. Some landlords withdrew their properties, and a few tenants upped and left, but it's all settled down now.'

'That's good then? You had to expect some collateral damage.'

'I know.' Dora gave a fleeting smile. 'Most have been loyal. But then, the agency *has* been on the high street forever.'

'Well then, what's upsetting you so much?' The mean thought occurred that Dora might be milking the situation and enjoying the drama. But I dismissed it immediately. She would never method act to the extent of exposing her roots.

Prue placed two coffees on the table, and I pushed one towards Dora. 'You know what Buttersley's like. They'll move on to something else next week.'

'I know, I know.' She heaped four sugars into her coffee. 'It's Gerald. It's knocked the stuffing right out of him.' I pictured a deflated double mattress haemorrhaging feathers onto the floor. Dora sighed. 'He's taken it very badly – like it's a personal attack. It's not just the dead bodies in his properties, but what with Elvira cooking the books under his nose, he's lost his confidence.'

No stuffing. No confidence. No ickle wagging tail. What's left of the man? 'Have you reported the fraud to the police?'

She shook her head vigorously, causing the plastic earrings to slap against her cheeks. 'No, he won't hear of it. And does it even matter now? Murder trumps fraud, after all.'

'Dora, it's not like a game of Rock, Paper, Scissors.'

'You're right, I know. But my poor lamb thinks it will damage his reputation even more. And it won't recover his money. Things couldn't get any worse.'

James's voice boomed from the doorway, 'Hey, Dora. What do you think of Pansy trying to blackmail Mr Klondike?'

My hands clenched. I could hardly believe James had been so indiscreet, especially with Maureen about. I whipped my head around. 'James, has the ointment helped with your intimate problem? Or is it still inflamed?'

James slammed the door shut. Message received and understood.

Dora sat open-mouthed. I recounted the phone spat with Pansy, but was vague about the false accusations she'd made about Mr Klondike.

'That's all we need.' Dora pressed a finger and thumb against her eyelids and groaned.

'Pansy knows I recorded her threats, so I don't think she'll pursue it. Besides, she's too preoccupied with all the media attention.'

James crept up to our table. 'Sorry about that. Unforgivable, I know, but boredom created temporary insanity. Malcolm's been giving me a dart-by-dart account of all the tournaments he's never won.'

'Don't apologise. I needed to know about Pansy and her little games.' Dora's eyes blazed. 'That little madam, I *can* deal with.'

James had brought in the papers and showed Dora the interviews with Shakira.

She smiled and drew back her shoulders to expose her magnificent cleavage. 'That should help. Gerald will be chuffed. How sweet of Shakira.'

'You need to run with this,' James said. 'I know the editor of *The Bugle.* I could get him to do a feature on the agency, underlining how long it's been on the high street. Tell Mr Klondike to dig out the vintage photos.'

'James, you're such a darling. Gerald will be thrilled.' Dora rose quickly, and her chair fell back. She pressed James to her bosom and kissed the top of his head. 'Must dash and tell Gerald the good news. Love to you both.' She blew kisses and gave Maureen and the sisters a cheery wave on her way out.

'What's she got to be happy about?' asked Maureen.

James went back to his counter, and Prue and I worked steadily until after lunch. It had been over twenty-four hours since the last nasty text or contact from Charles. Not that I wanted to tempt fate, but a wisp of hope made me think they'd both run out of steam.

Maureen was on her second mint tea when Dave arrived. He'd decked himself out in Oxford bags, false sideburns, and a Dr Who scarf.

'You might think it's over the top,' he said, 'but I can't risk being recognised. The reporters follow me. It's like I'm being watched all the time.'

Perhaps he could feel Maureen's eyes boring into the back of his head.

'How are things?' I asked. 'I've heard the police questioned you?'

'Yes. Just helping with their inquiries, you know. The thing is, the police don't know what to make of Elvira. She's clammed up after her confession. They've brought in a psychiatrist from London.'

'What did the police ask you and Pansy?'

He stared at the floor. 'They interviewed us separately.'

I wasn't letting him get away with that. 'Dave, the first time you came to Merangs, you said something that puzzled me – you had to step in when Vincent's actions affected you and Pansy?'

'Oh, that was nothing. Water under the bridge. A family tiff. You know how it is.' He spooned the full contents of the sugar bowl into his cup. 'What a silly billy. Look what I've done.' He bared his teeth like a nervous horse.

I decided he wanted to spill the beans, but needed encouragement. 'Dave, is there something you should tell me?'

He nodded. 'It's about Pansy.'

'Yes?' *I didn't think it would be the cuckoo, Dave.*

Dave cleared his throat. 'The police asked Pansy about Elvira's movements on the day of Vincent's murder. Pansy didn't tell them the whole truth.'

I sat forward in my seat. 'Really?'

'Pansy said Elvira never left the office all day.' He flicked his tongue over badly chapped lips. 'But I called in during the afternoon, and Elvira wasn't there.'

'Won't Mr Klondike have told them Elvira went out?'

'He'd have no idea. She came and went as she pleased. What's more, when he got the call to enter Vincent's flat, Elvira had returned to the office, but she followed him out. It's been worrying Pansy.'

'But she hasn't told the police?'

Dave shook his head. One of the sideburns dropped to the floor. I saw his dilemma. He wouldn't want to shop Pansy, but would quite like to cement the case against his mother-in-law.

'So Elvira could have gone to the flat anytime in the afternoon?'

He shrugged. 'She told Pansy, "It's best you don't know".' He tugged at the scarf, which had coiled around his neck like a boa constrictor.

'I can see how difficult it all is for you, Dave.'

He flashed his teeth. 'I knew you'd understand. You're such a caring person.'

Knowing his womenfolk, I couldn't take that as a compliment. 'Did you just want to tell someone, or are you seeking advice?'

Dave smiled, which left me no wiser, so I plunged in. 'You should tell Pansy to come clean. She could maybe tell the police that the pregnancy is playing havoc with her memory?' I was like a dog with a bone. 'You could sell it to Pansy by saying Elvira wouldn't want her to get into trouble for lying.'

He nodded in a way that indicated he'd do nothing of the sort. Picking up his phone, he frowned at a text that had just arrived. 'Sorry.' He rose in haste. 'I have to go now. My Pansy-petal needs me.'

Run out of hairspray again?

Dave hurried away, tripping over his scarf at the door. I followed him into the shop to update James on the Pansy-liar revelations.

James shook his head. 'Red herring bollcocks. Dave's desperate for Elvira to be guilty. He can see the promised land slipping away. When will you admit Charles is at the crux of all this? Have you reported him to Swift, yet?'

I shook my head.

'Well, now's your chance.'

I looked over my shoulder to see the DCI and Emily. As I took a step towards them, the door opened again.

'Helen, hun. I'm here.' Charles rushed towards me with his arms held wide.

Beauty and the Bakes

As Charles repeated my name, the last person I expected came to my rescue. Maureen was just leaving when I grabbed her sinewy arm and fired her like a missile towards Charles. 'Maureen, here's someone who's dying to meet you.' I doubted she'd heard that statement before.

Charles switched on the autopilot charm. He stretched out his hand and disarmed the she-wolf with a single smile. She wriggled into her kitten costume and offered a playful paw.

From a distance, I saw how Charles operated. His workings lay before me like the exposed mechanism of a clock. Never mind all that – I turned towards the Swifts. I hadn't noticed their familial likeness before. Both tall and lean, they moved with an easy, natural grace. Emily wore a simple, elegant dress, and her brother looked the business in a crisp white shirt. I wanted to snatch a private word with the DCI, but how could I discuss my problem when it stood only yards away?

'I'm under orders to sample one of your famous milkshakes,' the DCI said, as Emily tugged at his sleeve. 'What flavour's the most pop—?'

'C'mon, bruv. We've not got much time together.' Emily dragged him into the tea room, and he gave an apologetic grin over his shoulder.

I yanked open the tea room door behind them and yelled, 'Banana!' My old problem with volume had resurfaced. They both jumped, and Emily shrieked. I mumbled a quick apology, registered Prue's horrified face and slammed the door shut. 'I'm under a lot of stress,' I said, staring hard at Charles.

He'd already processed Maureen. She'd skipped away giggling like a child. He stepped towards me and cupped my face in his hands. 'My girl needs to chill.'

My blood boiled. 'Charles. Please, I'm working and how many times? I'm not your girl.'

'Your customers love me, darling.' He winked. 'Why not take the rest of the day off and come out with me?' He pulled me closer. His breath smelt stale and he needed a shave. His skinny jeans bagged at the knees, and he'd done his shirt buttons up all wrong. 'I'm going to kidnap you and keep you all to myself.'

I twisted my head around to summon help. James was serving a customer, and although I would have welcomed his intervention, it would have broken the first rule of Merangs. 'Till transactions are sacrosanct, except in the case of a refund.' Where the hell was Malcolm?

I pulled myself away and stamped on Charles's foot. 'I've told you. I'm working. Leave me alone, or I'll call the police.'

He winced. 'I'll leave you to play shop now, hun, but we need to get it together ASAP.' He backed away, blowing the usual kisses. 'I'll be back.' His attempt to impersonate Arnie made me cringe.

As soon as the shop floor was empty of customers, I released my frustration by running around in circles, flailing my arms and screeching like a chimpanzee. I gave it my all until I banged up against a solid torso. Raising my lolling head, I met the eyes of the DCI. He held a takeaway cup, and I instantly noticed two things: he'd gone large on the milkshake, and I'd knocked the contents down his shirt.

He looked down his front. 'You can see from the yellow froth, I followed your banana recommendation.'

Mortified, I muttered a quick apology and fled to the toilet.

In my wake, I heard James say, 'She's under a lot of strain.'

I remained in the cubicle for ages. They would just have to cope without me. I couldn't face the DCI again, never mind report Charles. The enclosed space made me feel safe. Maybe that and hanging upside down were all I had left.

I'd once thought it trendy to decorate the cubicle with a map of the world, and I traced my finger across and wondered where my wandering husband might be. I swore in annoyance. If Zack had not waltzed off to God-knows-where, I wouldn't have become embroiled with Charles and ended up showering a senior policeman in a banana milkshake.

I'd been wrong about Charles giving up the chase. Fingers crossed, I was right about the nasty texts.

A rap on the door broke my hermetic seal. 'You can come out now,' James shouted. 'Swift's gone.'

'Just doing my weekly detailed check,' I said, as I reluctantly emerged. 'Yes, everything appears to be in order in there.'

'Helen, it's me you're talking to, not some dollop who doesn't know you.'

'Was the DCI very annoyed?'

James folded his arms and leant against the door frame. 'I told him it was his own fault. He knows you've got form and should have had the foresight to bring a spare set of clothes.'

'You're lying, I hope?'

'Yes, but I did suggest, the next time you meet, he should throw food and drink down himself and save you the bother. He seemed to like that.'

I couldn't help but laugh. 'What about Emily?'

'She was already sulking, according to Prue. Swift took a call just after they sat down. Something urgent had cropped up. That's why he had to leave. He'll be away for the rest of the week.'

I returned to the tea room. Prue didn't refer to the incident but threw me a scornful glare. The afternoon plodded on, brightened only by the arrival of Shakira.

'Greetings, earthlings. What's new with you? But first, guess what I've been doing.'

'Buying cheap shoes,' said Prue. That was tart even for her, but Shakira didn't seem to mind.

'I've been showing the reporter boys around town. The Elvira story is thinning out, so they've widened their interest. Photo opps for me.'

'I'm looking forward to your next spread,' said James, who'd followed her into the tea room.

'Cheeky.' She punched his arm. 'Guess who I just saw, knocking the gins back in Bangles?'

'Charles?' I answered.

She nodded. 'Making a bit of a show of himself with the young waitress. Then I saw Dave in the Dog and Duck, looking miserable and throwing pints down his neck.'

Prue sniffed. 'I hope with all this gadding about, you will continue to honour your commitments to Merangs.'

'Obvs, you're my bread and butter. But I've not told you my best news yet.' Shakira looked around to see if we were paying attention. 'I've got a gig on local radio.'

'As a presenter?' I asked, hoping not to sound incredulous.

'No. It's an interactive bake-along show. Listeners will make a cake at the same time as me.'

James laughed. 'What? Then you'll all get together and eat a radio?'

'Don't be ridiculous, James,' said Prue. 'They've been cooking on *Woman's Hour* for years.'

'Anyway, we needed a name for the show, and I came up with Beauty and the Bakes, but ...' Shakira paused, and with precision timing added, 'my *agent* suggested Buttersley Bakes.'

'*You've* got an agent? *You?*' James put a hand to his head and pretended to faint.

Shakira nodded and smirked.

'Good for you, Shakira,' I said. 'You deserve a break.'

'Thanks, Hels, and I *will* make Merangs my priority.'

'For now at least,' muttered Prue.

Shakira's bubble could not be burst by Prue's negativity. She prattled on about her good fortune before remembering she had to be somewhere else. A woman of some importance, she bustled away and left us all in the shade.

Prue and James remained together, united in their scorn of Shakira's escapades. I moved away to sneak a look at my phone. It had been pinging away in my pocket. I scrolled down the inevitable texts from Charles.

They started harmless enough. I was his girl, and he wasn't going to let me go. But they gradually became more aggressive and illegible – probably in line with his drinking.

Typical of my poor timing, I'd missed the opportunity to report it to the DCI. I should have told him, and he was now away on urgent business – not to mention stain removal. I couldn't face Snood but wondered if it would be worth telling PC Daz?

The afternoon dragged. I wanted it to end, but at the same time, dreaded closing time, and the possible arrival of a drunken Charles.

After Prue left, I sidled up to James, who was cashing up his till. I nibbled my thumb as he counted.

He looked up from his figures. 'What's wrong? You've not even asked how much I've taken.'

'I was just about to.'

'You need a wingman,' he said. 'Someone to see you safely home.'

'I'm fine,' I lied, hoping he might offer to come round with one of his hampers.

'Unfortunately, I'm tied up most of this week on my furniture restoration course. It's knobs and knockers tonight, and I can't miss that.'

'No, I can see how that would be unmissable. Good to know I come second only to door furniture.' I tried to keep my voice light, but it betrayed me with a wobble.

James mock-punched my arm. 'I've arranged for Malcolm to walk you home, and he'll stay with you as long as you want.'

Malcolm gave a cheery wave with his paintbrush.

'I'm not a game of pass the parcel,' I shouted in petulance. James compressed his lips and stared at the ceiling. I wrung my hands. 'I'm sorry. I'm sorry. I know you're trying to help, and it's my own fault for getting into this mess.'

James shrugged, collected his coat and left with a curt goodbye. I wanted to run after him to apologise again, but that would only delay him from his knobs and knockers, and I didn't want to alienate him further.

'Helen, love,' called Malcolm. 'What time do you want to leave?'

I pulled myself together and said I'd be ready in twenty minutes.

It was a warm, mellow evening when Malcolm and I left the shop. We agreed to take the long route home and enjoy the final rays of the dying sun. We strolled down the high street eating ice creams. Malcolm discoursed on the importance of surface preparation in the average decorating project, and I admired the trees in the distance.

Charles followed at a distance, like a lame and needy dog. And, despite his belligerent texts, that was how he appeared to me. I didn't believe, or maybe just didn't want to admit, he could be dangerous. Yes, he disturbed me, but in all our confrontations, he'd scarpered off, and I was sure he meant me no harm. He just wanted the attention and devotion I couldn't give. Prue would say I was gullible, and James would add, 'Just plain stupid.'

At my front door, Malcolm planted his feet on the step and said he would stand guard. 'For as long as it takes for the bugger to realise he's not welcome here.'

Tears of gratitude gathered at the backs of my eyes. 'I'd rather you come inside, and I'll make us both something to eat.' Malcolm loved his food, and I wanted to do something nice for him.

A conflict played out on Malcolm's face. He licked his lips but then shook his head and jutted out his jaw. 'I've got a job to do.'

I won him over by saying he needed food to keep his strength up. We agreed I'd put the kettle on while he did a final sweep of the street.

'The bugger seems to have hopped it,' he said when he eventually came in. 'He'll keep well away if he knows what's good for him.'

I handed Malcolm a mug of tea. 'Thanks. What would I do without you? Now, sit down and relax. You've earned it.'

After finding some oddments in the freezer, I put the microwave through its paces. Malcolm complimented me on the random elements of our meal as we sat side by side on the sofa with trays on our knees. We watched reruns of *Are You Being Served?* and for several hours, I forgot about my problems.

At ten, I stretched and yawned. 'Time for my cocoa and bed, Malcolm. Thanks for looking after me, but I'll be fine now.'

'I might just hang about outside to check the coast is clear.'

'You could always sleep in my spare room?'

Malcolm scratched his chin. 'Yes, I need to stay, but I'm best at ground level and ready for action, so to speak. I'll sleep on the sofa.'

While he did his final security check, I fetched pillows and a duvet and made up a makeshift bed. Then, in the kitchen, I filled a pan with milk for our cocoa but made the mistake of checking my phone. My anonymous texter had struck again.

HOW MANY MEN DO YOU WANT? WHY CAN'T YOU STICK TO ONE AT ONCE?

My eyes flew to the window as if someone was spying on me, and the milk bottle dropped from my hand. So much for hoping they'd given up. How naive. I threw my phone on the table.

Reassured by the presence of my guard, I must have fallen asleep as soon as my head hit the pillow. In the middle of the night, my phone rang. The caller display said Pansy, but after I'd fumbled about, she'd rung off. What could she want? Although curious, I couldn't face speaking to her. It would do in the morning.

A gentle tapping coming from downstairs woke me in the early hours. I thought I'd imagined it until I heard a distinct but soft knock on the front door. I shot up, and my heart raced. Then I remembered Malcolm, but I couldn't detect him stirring. I got out of bed and stood at the top of the stairs. The floor beneath my feet vibrated at the snoring coming from Malcolm's lair.

As my guard dog slumbered, I stood for several minutes but heard nothing more. Eventually, my tingling cold feet drove me back to bed. Perhaps I'd imagined the noise? The ridiculous notion struck that it might have been James testing out his new knockers. I laughed out loud, but all the same, I was glad to have Malcolm there, sleeping or not.

I was snuggling back down when Pansy called again. I managed to answer this time, and her voice filled the dark room.

'Is he with you?

'Who?'

'Dave. Who else?'

Her querulous tone annoyed me. 'Pansy, why would Dave be with me?'

She stifled a sob 'Well, he's not come home. Where is he? I thought you'd know.'

A Collision Too Far

Pansy had grabbed my attention with her early-hours phone call, but why did she think I knew or cared where Dave might be? Her conviction made me wonder if it had been him knocking on my door.

I turned on the bedside lamp. 'Pansy, it's three in the morning. Have you only just noticed he's gone?' I'd no compunction at being sharp as she'd offered no apology for disturbing me.

'Of course not, but you know how it is?'

'No, not really.'

Pansy gave her 'dealing with an idiot' sigh. 'I've got a lot going on. There's Mum to worry about, and all the interviews I have to do. I need to keep the flame alive. That Bangkok bitch is getting more publicity than me, and she's on the other side of the bloody world.'

A fragment of a song came to mind. A record that Prue used to play on her antique player. The New Seekers had wanted to teach the world to sing in perfect harmony. They'd have had no chance with Pansy. How did the song go? I must have started singing snatches, as Pansy reined me in.

'What the hell are you going on about teaching people to sing for? This is serious.'

The song died on my lips. 'I take it Dave's not answering his phone. Have you contacted the police?'

'No, I thought he'd be with you.'

Back to that again. I couldn't keep the impatience out of my voice. 'Why the hell would Dave be with me?'

'He's always at that fancy shop of yours, or droning on about you.'

'He's only been a couple of times. I hardly know him.'

'Yeah, whatever.' A muffled sob travelled down the line.

A smidgen of pity for Pansy crept in, and I recognised her vulnerability. Her mother was on a murder charge. She was pregnant, and her husband had suddenly gone missing. Life couldn't be easy. She possibly had no one else to call.

'The last I heard of Dave, he was in the Dog and Duck, knocking back the pints. He's probably gone to a mate's house to sleep it off. Have you had a row?'

'None of your business. He lost contact with all his mates when we got married.'

Bet you made sure of it. 'Pansy, other than ring the police, there's not much you can do at this hour. Try and get some sleep. I'll call you back later.'

Silence at the other end, and then I caught another faint sob. 'Make sure you do.' She rang off.

Lost in thought about the complexities of relationships, I spent the next five minutes staring at the blank screen of my phone.

Eventually, I switched off my lamp, but my mind raced with speculation about Dave and his Dr Who scarf. I couldn't get back to sleep.

I rose at six. So did Malcolm. He trundled off home for 'a wash and a shave' and I set off for a long run. All the time, my phone pinged in my pocket, and when I stopped near the river, I'd received three texts from Charles. I'd gone from the slag of yesterday to a graceful gazelle. I eyed a privet hedge with suspicion. He might have been behind it, watching me, or had he watched me set off from home? Why weren't the demands of his business calling him back to wherever he lived?

Home had always been my refuge, yet I shied from going back. Fuelled by anger, I ran too fast, and after ten minutes, my lungs were ready to collapse. Pansy lived in the vicinity. Tough if I woke her. I rang to say I was on my way.

She answered the door with a white, tear-stained face, vampire eyes, and a dirty dressing gown. 'Yes?' she said, standing firm at the door.

A promising start. 'Have you heard from Dave?'

'No.'

I stared her out. If she wanted help, she'd have to drop the hostility.

'You'd better come in.'

The house was a midden. As she led me through to the lounge, I caught sight of plates stacked high in the kitchen, with leftover food hanging over the sides and tipping onto the floor.

Entering the living room, I wrinkled my nose at the cloying floral scent with its undertones of fried meat and garlic. The mantelpiece had turned into a shrine of feminine clutter. As I gingerly negotiated the piles of pizza boxes and magazines littering the floor, my feet stuck to the carpet.

Even the cuckoo clock had a sad air of neglect. The shutters were down and there was no tick-tock.

Pansy followed my gaze. 'Dave's not here to wind it up.'

Or clear up after you. Although by the state of the place, he must have been off duster duties for quite a while.

I was thirsty after the run, but Pansy didn't offer me a drink. Not that I would have accepted one anyway. 'Has Dave ever gone off before?'

'No.' She chewed her lip and pushed a greasy strand of hair from her face.

'You both must be under a lot of pressure,' I said in the hope she'd open up.

'*I am.* Not him. It's *my* mother in prison. Dave doesn't even like her. Happy to take her money, though.'

'Could he have gone to his own mother's?'

'She's dead.'

'Any other family member?'

Pansy stared as if I'd asked if Dave was the exiled prince of some exotic dynasty.

'He's nowhere to go.'

My God, and I thought my life was bad.

'Have you rung the hospitals?' Pansy picked at her nail polish. 'In case he's had an accident?'

She didn't bother to reply, and I was running out of patience and ideas. I suggested again that she should contact the police. That did ignite a spark.

'What? Ask them jailers for help. They'd as soon arrest him as find out where he is.'

'Why? Has he broken the law?'

She evaded my eyes. I gave up and left, telling her I'd discuss it with James and be in touch.

I was glad to escape. Apart from Pansy irritating me, I'd become cold and uncomfortable in her miserable house. I turned over our conversation as I sprinted home. At least it distracted me from Charles and where he might be lurking.

Back home, Snowy welcomed me with enthusiasm. Bending to stroke her chin, I reflected it was only a week since my vegan date with Charles. I'd skipped off in anticipatory delight, full of hope and expectation. Now I couldn't wait to see the back of him.

After a quick shower and a vague wave of the hairdryer, I walked briskly to Merangs. I glimpsed Charles, only the once. That was on the high street, and I told myself he possibly had a legitimate reason to be there. He looked like he'd slept in his clothes. If he stepped out of line again, I resolved to contact the police.

When Lucy arrived at the shop, she announced, 'Charles is hanging about outside. What's happened to him? He looks all crumpled and beat up.' Luckily, she moved on to a convoluted tale about an argument with Emily and didn't require a response.

It was a typical Tuesday morning in the tea room; the reporters and rubberneckers had all but disappeared. It was a relief to be back to the normality of The Silent Sisters and other regulars.

After the late morning rush, I went through to the shop to update James on the Dave situation. I drummed my fingers on the counter. 'So, what do you make of it?'

'Not much, other than he's fed up with his despotic shrew of a wife.' James was more interested in gift-wrapping boxes of Buttersley Biscuits than listening to me.

'I think there's more to it than that.' I raised my voice to gain his attention. 'I told you before, Dave has a guilty secret.' *You weren't paying attention then, either.* 'Something to do with Vincent.'

'Forget it, you're barking up the wrong tree.'

Exasperated, I turned to Malcolm, who was assiduously painting the shelves. 'Malcolm, you're doing a magnificent job as always.' Although lacking the creative flair of James, he was just as skilled, but without the attitude. 'Can I get you a cup of tea?'

'I'll just finish this tricky bit here first. Look, can you see?'

As he pointed to a section, we both startled at the unfamiliar sound of James shouting in anger. 'Get out. Leave. You're not welcome here.'

Who else but Charles? He ignored James and bounded towards me. Malcolm – what was he thinking – seized his large paint bucket as a shield and jumped in front of me. I covered my eyes and missed the collision, but the exclamations did not bode well.

As I peeked through my fingers, a pool of White Linen Whisper lapped at my feet. Both Charles and Malcolm were covered in the stuff, and James was laughing like he'd never stop.

Charles scarpered, dripping paint to the door. Prue had only just entered, looking smart in her navy coat – the one she wore for her women's group lunches. Charles missed her by a whisker; so one disaster at least was averted.

'What's going on?' she demanded.

'Don't step …' I couldn't get my words out quickly enough.

Prue made no sound as she skidded across the floor. Crouched low like a surfer, she almost reached dry land but lost her balance at the coat stand. Malcolm grabbed a flailing arm. That would have saved the day, had he resisted the urge to draw his loved one towards him. Prue came to rest against his wet plumage of White Linen Whisper.

For a few seconds, silence prevailed. Malcolm, not realising what he'd done, beamed with pleasure. The poor sap probably expected Prue to be grateful.

As she peeled herself away, James said, 'White suits you, Prue. You should wear it more often.'

Falling down a rabbit hole might have been less of a shock to Prue. Fortunately, she seemed too stunned to notice the coils of false hair that had fallen from her beehive. They now floated in the paint like strange little fish.

Lucy emerged from the tea room. After a brief survey of the disaster scene, she led Prue away with the promise of a nice cup of sweet tea.

Her efficiency galvanised me into action. I flipped the door sign to closed, told Malcolm to use dust sheets to soak up the mess, rang Candice, begging for assistance, and snapped at James for being no help whatsoever.

By late morning, Merangs was open, and we were all back in position. Prue had departed, muttering, 'It's a madhouse,' as she swept past in *my* coat. She'd refused to speak to any of us, which took the tune out of poor Malcolm's whistle.

I chose a quiet corner to ring Snood. I'd no choice but to report Charles.

'Yes, what do you want? Have you information about the case?' she asked, without preamble.

'No, it's ...' I hesitated, not sure what to say.

'Is it about Snowy? What's wrong?'

'No, she's fine and sends her best.'

'Well then?'

I launched into a long exposition about Charles. She cut me short. 'I'm aware of the situation. It's being dealt with. Goodbye.'

I'd not expected that. After some reflection, I concluded James had beaten me to it. I didn't expect Charles to disappear overnight, but I was reassured.

After closing, James hung around as I cleaned.

'Are you not gracing the world of furniture restoration tonight?' I asked.

'No, the second part's tomorrow. When you're ready, I'll show you where Dave's hiding.' James cocked his head to one side and gave his smug, 'I'm so clever' smile. 'Hurry up. I haven't got all night.'

Ding Dong

How did James know where Dave might be? Surely, he was bluffing? All the same, I rushed my cleaning routine and regretted I'd told Lucy to leave early.

Ready to leave, I found Malcolm bent over the sink, rinsing his brushes. 'It's important to look after your tools,' he said as if they were all he had in the world. 'Will Mrs Mayflower ever forgive me for ruining her coat?'

I placed a hand on his shoulder. 'It's about time she updated her wardrobe and got a new one. Don't worry about that; James and I are tracking down a missing person tonight, and we need your input.' The repetitive action of wiping the tables had freed my mind to think, and I'd had an idea of where Dave might be.

'Just like last time, when we found a dead body?' Malcolm asked, his eager eyes glinting.

I nodded. 'I'm hoping this one's still alive.'

He flicked the water from his brushes with a firm hand. 'I'm in.'

James set his lips in a rigid line when he saw Malcolm had joined the gang.

I directed Malcolm into the back of the car and sat next to James. 'Seeing as we're going fishing in the same pond as before, Malcolm should be with us.'

The slightest upturn of James's mouth confirmed I'd reached the correct conclusion about Dave. We drove in silence to the street near the church.

Eileen Newby's house had the same air of neglect. The overflowing bin had not been emptied. We sent Malcolm round the back, and James rapped on the front door. Nothing stirred. James knocked again, and I glimpsed a movement behind the grimy net curtains at the window nearest the door.

'Let him know it's you,' said James. Unsure what to do, I didn't move. 'Shout through the letter box, for God's sake.'

'What shall I shout?' I recalled James's own encounter with the letterbox and didn't relish the prospect.

'Anything. Ding Dong, Avon's calling, for all I care. As long as he realises we're friends, not foe.'

A whiff of decay hit the back of my throat as I opened the box and shouted, 'It's only me.'

Footsteps pattered in the hallway, and then a dishevelled Dave flung open the door. The rough-around-the-edges style suited him, though the scarf had seen better days.

'Lovely to see you.' He beamed as if we'd arrived for a civilised evening of mah-jong.

He had something green, possibly seaweed, stuck in his teeth, and I couldn't peel my eyes away. 'Pansy's worried about you, Dave. Did you stay here last night?'

Dave cut his smile. The green bit now dangled out the side of his mouth. 'I'm surprised she even noticed I'd gone. Pansy's only interested in herself.'

I had to stop my head from nodding in enthusiastic agreement.

Malcolm joined us, and James turned away. 'I'll wait in the car.'

I ignored James. 'But Dave, you're her rock. She needs you.' *Probably can't afford a cleaner, for one thing.* 'Maybe it's the baby hormones making her selfish.'

'No, it's all that media attention. She's obsessed with being in the limelight.'

He'd hit another nail on the head, so I told him Pansy was upset. If strapped to a lie detector, I'd have changed that to extremely annoyed.

'Woman trouble,' said Malcolm with a shake of his head. 'I know how it is, mate.'

Dave turned to Malcolm. 'I've treated her like a princess.'

'You can't win whatever you do.' The relationship guru warmed to his theme.

Dave shook Malcolm's hand. 'You're so right, my friend.'

'You need to show 'em who's boss,' said the man who'd commit hara-kiri for Prue.

I needed to turn this conversation back on track. 'So, Dave, what are your plans? You can't stay here another night, surely?'

'I'm not ready to go back. Pansy needs to show she appreciates me, and besides, there's the ...' He put a hand to his mouth and hung his head.

'Let me tell Pansy you're safe, at least?' I said.

'Yes, you can tell her that, as long as you add, I'll come back when I'm good and ready.'

Great. That'll go down well, coming from me.

'Look, mate, Helen's right,' said Malcolm. 'This here's no place to stay. Come back to mine, have a shower, a few beers and then see how you feel.'

Dave didn't give it a second thought. He pumped Malcolm's hand like a thirsty man at a well. 'Just let me grab my stuff, and I'm all yours.'

Who'd have thought Malcolm would have been the one to rescue a delicate situation?

Minutes later, Dave emerged with a plastic carrier, locked the door, tried the handle twice, and then stowed the key in his wallet as if it were the Koh-i-Noor.

A wise man – who knows what needy relative might turn up next. I wondered how he'd got hold of the key in the first place.

James made no comment when I told him to drive to Malcolm's. The new best buddies sat together in the back and cemented their bond with a debate over beer.

'Prickly Hobgoblin's the best of your pale ales, I think you'll find,' Dave was saying as James pulled up at the gate. 'Thanks for the lift, James. And to you, Helen, for being such a friend.'

'Pale ale, you don't know what you're ...' Malcolm's voice trailed off as they ambled up his path.

'Right, that's *The Odd Couple* dispatched,' said James. 'Let's see *you* safely home.'

'You make me sound like a problem.'

'You are.'

I'd half a mind to start an argument, but a yawn engulfed my words, so I sat on my hands and stared out of the window. James patted my head as if I were a little dog.

I was nearly asleep when we arrived at my house. I fumbled with the car handle. 'Thanks for the lift.'

James unclipped his seat belt. 'I'm coming in with you.'

'No, I'll be fine. It's still daylight, and I'm practically at my front door.' I didn't want to be reduced to a helpless victim who needed round-the-clock supervision.

'I'll just come as far as the door, then. It could do with a lick of paint, by the way.'

Tiredness made me rude and ungrateful. 'Drop the nanny routine, and keep your nose out of my decorating decisions.'

I regretted my sharp words as soon as James drove off. He was only trying to look after me. And he *was* right about the door.

As I fished in my bag for the key, I realised I'd received no anonymous texts all day. My gut instinct told me they'd ceased, and feeling lighter, I hummed the New Seekers song as I inserted the key in the door.

I cut the song dead when a hand clamped over mine. Screaming like a banshee, I kicked like a mule. The hand released mine.

'Helen, hun, I only want to talk to you.'

I turned to see Charles in paint-stiffened clothes, hopping around the lawn, clutching one knee. He launched himself back towards me. 'I've things to say.'

'Why can't you leave me alone?' I yelled. Spittle and snot flew out of me. I started up the banshee wailing again, convinced the neighbours would rush to my rescue. Not a curtain twitched. *Must be a good night on the telly.*

Charles spoke in a reasonable tone. 'I didn't mean to scare you. I just want to know why you don't want me.'

James had told me not to engage with Charles, as it would only feed his obsession. But I had liked him once. Surely the odd cliché or two couldn't do any harm?

'I don't know, Charles. That's just how it sometimes goes. Some things are not meant to be.' *There, that should do it.*

It did it all right. Charles grabbed hold of my wrists and shouted in my face. I couldn't break my hands free. He had the strength of ten. 'You led me on, you whore bitch.'

More enraged than scared, I took a step back and swung a foot in the direction of his groin. Charles collapsed on the ground and groaned. For one scary moment, I couldn't find my key until I remembered it was in the lock. I turned it with a clumsy hand, got through the door and then slammed and bolted it behind me. With my whole body shaking, I gasped for breath.

Charles had looked capable of anything. Maybe even murder. He pounded on the door and shouted threats of what he would do to me. Why had I not taken him seriously before? In my conceit, I'd thought he'd never harm me. I sat at the foot of the stairs with my arms wrapped around my knees. With my energy all spent, I couldn't move.

After about ten minutes, Charles must have exhausted himself. The shouts became weaker and then ceased altogether. I rose from my spot with relief. My arms ached, and my legs had stiffened.

But Charles started up again. This time, in a wheedling tone, coaxing and begging me to let him in. When this failed, he banged his head against the door and wailed like a baby. Whatever the neighbours were watching on the telly, it could not have equalled that.

The situation was too much to deal with on my own. As I scrambled around for my phone, I recalled Snowy had shot out the door when I fell in. The poor thing was out there with Charles.

Ruth to the Rescue

My confrontation in the garden with Charles must have frightened Snowy. I'd not let her out before. Maybe she was hot-pawing it back to Eileen's right now. Why not? Everyone else did. I added Snowy to my list of worries.

I rang Snood and steeled myself not to blurt out Snowy had bolted. Never mind the lunatic on my doorstep; I didn't want Snood thinking I was a careless cat owner. She didn't answer, and I couldn't think of what to say in a message. Should I ring the emergency number? Would it be classed as an emergency, or would I be wasting police time?

It had gone quiet out there. Perhaps Charles had exhausted himself and left? I risked a peep out of the living room window. Charles's face and hands were pressed against the window, his mouth contorted into a Munch-like scream. I shrieked and fell backwards onto the floor.

I called James, but it went to voicemail. Maybe he was still mad with me? 'I need you right now,' I cried into my phone.

There was no point in ringing Malcolm. He would be well stuck into his Hobgoblin brew with his new best mate. I couldn't subject Prue to that carry-on, so I rang Ruth.

She grasped the situation immediately, told me to hold tight, and she'd be there before I knew it. 'And, Helen, don't disconnect the call. Keep talking, so I know you're okay.'

It was a comfort to be no longer completely alone. I watched Charles from behind the curtain and relayed a commentary back to Ruth. 'He's walking around the garden. He seems to be searching for something. He keeps looking over his shoulder to see if I'm still watching.'

'Stand well away,' she advised. 'He may be looking for a rock to hurl through the window. Don't hesitate to ring the police if he does.'

I jumped smartly back. *Please hurry up, Ruth. The windows aren't double-glazed.*

Ruth arrived within ten minutes. By that time, Charles lay prostrate on the lawn. As the gate clicked open, he casually lifted his head, but then his whole body jerked upright when Ruth swooped down the path.

She didn't mince her words and shouted, 'Why are you terrorising Helen?'

Charles matched her volume. 'Get that big ugly nose out of my affairs.'

'Helen wants nothing to do with you.'

'You're just a big, jealous bitch. I dumped you, and now you won't let anyone else have me.'

I hid like a coward behind the curtain. Should I go out and show solidarity with Ruth, or would that only inflame the situation?

Ruth took a step towards him. 'If you know what's good for you, stay away from Helen.' She'd somehow injected steel into her normally wispy voice.

They squared up to each other like boxing hares.

'What are you going to do? Have me followed like ...' Charles fell silent, or more accurately, fell unconscious after Ruth punched him. He lay sprawled out on the path in a lifeless heap. I rushed outside.

Ruth was cradling her right hand in her left. 'What have I done, what have I done? I didn't mean to hit him so hard.' Her voice wobbled. 'What if I've killed him?'

That knocked Snowy off the top spot of my worries. *Should I call an ambulance? Think, Helen, think.* 'Ruth, call for an ambulance, and I'll check his pulse.'

I knelt by Charles, grabbed his arm and searched for a beat. Nothing. I tried to take my own pulse. No, I didn't have one either, even though my heart banged away like a military drum.

Ruth dropped to my side. 'Sorry, I can't ring. I've lost my phone. It was in my hand just before I hit him.'

'Use the landline in the house. No. Wait a moment. I think he's coming round.'

Charles opened his eyes and smiled into mine. 'That's my girl.' His eyelids fluttered, and a trace of the smile stayed on his lips.

Ruth and I stared at each other in palpable relief.

'Charles,' I said. 'Can you stand?'

'Course I can. Where are we going?'

'*You're* going back to your hotel.'

'Why? Have I had too much to drink?' Charles opened his eyes wide and tried to move his head.

We heaved him to his feet, and after a few Bambi-on-ice moments, he managed to stand. Then, leaning against the fence, he prodded his jaw. 'What happened?'

The street was quiet and still. It underlined how loud the performance must have been. We stood in silence, an awkward social group.

I wondered if Charles realised he'd been knocked out. I was about to suggest he should go to the hospital and be checked for concussion when a siren sounded in the distance. Maybe one of the neighbours had rung the police, after all?

Charles cocked his head like a nervous dog. The siren grew louder. He threw me a look of reproach, stumbled through the gate and took off in a slow, lop-sided run. The siren peaked and passed.

I turned to Ruth, who was still nursing her hand. She looked like she might burst into tears. I knew how she felt. There wasn't much to laugh about. At least she'd found her phone. Charles had fallen on top of it.

I took hold of her arm. 'Rocky Ruth to the rescue,' I said, trying to raise a smile. 'Come inside. You need hot, sweet tea.'

'I'm hoping you've something stronger.'

Ruth sat at the kitchen table and iced her hand with a bag of frozen peas. I made the tea and searched for the brandy. We each threw back a large measure and then recounted the scene with Charles, embellishing it more each time we spoke. Eventually, we created a *Tom and Jerry* version that satisfied us both.

But despite the laughter, I couldn't erase the image of Charles dragging himself off like a wounded animal. All the more tragic for one who'd been such a peacock.

Thoughts of fur and feathers drove me to the door. 'Snowy, Snowy,' I yelled over and over again until I sounded like a wintry weather forecast stuck on repeat. I'd let my pet down and failed to protect her.

Ruth rang for a takeaway, and I called James on his landline. 'Ruth's here with me. We've had an ugly scene with Charles. She's going to stay with me tonight.'

'That's good.'

'Did you not receive my message?'

James sighed. 'I've not looked at my phone.'

'Please, can you update Pansy about Dave, as I can't cope with Miss Uppity right now?

'If I must.'

I was going to tell him about Snowy, but he rang off. Tears of self-pity pricked my eyes.

Maybe I'd caught him at a bad moment, but James had shown little interest.

Ruth enveloped me in her capable arms. 'Don't worry. Charles *will* get his comeuppance, and Snowy *will* come back. Cats always do.'

I appreciated her concern and forced a smile. 'You're right. Let's have some wine with our pizzas.'

We downed several glasses but could not recapture the adrenaline-fuelled hilarity of before. I rang the hotel to check Charles had returned. I knew the receptionist, and she confirmed he was in his room. We both raised a glass in relief.

While Ruth opened another bottle, I returned to do my Snowy routine at the door. Nothing stirred. I trailed back to the kitchen full of despondent thoughts. After one more glass of wine, I'd had enough and was thinking of cocoa and bed.

Ruth looked like she could continue all night. 'It's so nice to just sit and chat with a friend.' She stretched out her long legs. 'It's not something I'm used to.' I banished all thoughts of bed. Ruth deserved a friend and not just for her actions tonight. 'Are you worried about something other than Snowy?' she added. 'You keep looking at your phone as if it might bite.'

I hadn't realised it was so obvious. The last anonymous text had arrived this time last night. If another didn't come soon – fingers crossed – that might be it. My optimism had no grounds, but I wouldn't let that get in my way. There was no point in confiding in Ruth if they'd stopped.

I forced a smile. 'Sorry, this Charles thing has made me nervous. I reported him to the police, by the way.'

'And what are they doing about it?'

'A good question, Ruth. I've no idea.'

Ruth leant forward. 'Are you going to tell them about this latest incident?' Perhaps she was worried Charles might report her for assault?

'I don't want to ring them after I've had a drink.' The memory of my drunken phone call to Snood still filled me with shame. 'Let's discuss it in the morning?'

Ruth had been about to take a sip from her glass. She put it back on the table, frowned, and then picked it up again. She didn't look at me but fiddled with the stem.

'Ruth, a moment ago, you asked what was worrying me. Now it's my turn. Is there something on *your* mind?'

She sat up straight and nodded as if she'd reached a decision. 'I'm sorry about not speaking out earlier, but there's something I've not told you about Charles.'

What's in a Ringtone?

I'd suspected all along that Ruth was hiding something about Charles. I wanted to slap my hand on the kitchen table and shout, 'I knew it. I bloody knew it.' Instead, I said, 'What haven't you told me, Ruth? It's obviously bothering you.' My sympathetic tone belied my raging curiosity.

'It could be nothing. I might even be wrong.' She peered into her empty wine glass.

I filled it up. 'We won't know unless you tell me.'

She bit her lip. 'I may get into trouble with the police for withholding information.'

Talk about backtracking. I wanted to shake her. 'For God's sake, Ruth, just spit it out.'

Ruth's eyes widened at my harsh tone. 'Oh, okay. It's to do with Vincent's murder.'

'Yes?' I tried to regain my encouraging voice.

'Charles said he was abroad at the time.'

'Yes, that's his alibi.'

'That's the time when I ...' her face flushed, and she avoided my eyes. 'I was sort of stalking him after he rejected me. I couldn't help myself.'

I put down the bottle and placed my hand on her arm. 'I understand, Ruth.' And I did. She was a vulnerable and inexperienced woman. Charles had thrown her a few crumbs, and she'd been captivated. He'd then callously dumped her, and she would have needed answers.

Ruth cleared her throat. 'I rang Charles the day Vincent died, just like I had the days before and after.' I nodded in encouragement. 'He didn't answer. I rang again and again.'

In my bitter experience, that's what stalkers did. 'Did you eventually speak to him?' I couldn't see where this was going.

'No. The thing is, it wasn't a foreign ringtone. It should have been, shouldn't it, if he was abroad?'

My first thought was, yes, but then I wasn't sure. Maybe we could call someone abroad, but the only person I could think to call was my wandering husband. I could hardly ring Zack and say, 'Just testing'.

'It may depend on whether a phone is switched on, or if it goes straight to voicemail. Can you remember?'

Ruth closed her eyes. 'It did go to voicemail eventually, but only after it had rung several times. And it was the usual ring tone.'

I suddenly remembered. 'Charles has two phones. I've seen both of them. He possibly took his work one with him, and you were ringing the one left at home.'

Ruth massaged her temple. 'Yes, that's probably it. But – and this is embarrassing.' She shielded her eyes with her hand. 'As I said, I rang over and over, day after day. If he was abroad for several days, surely the battery on the phone left at home would have gone flat at some point and then straight to voicemail?'

My head ached. My cat had gone AWOL, and all I wanted to do was collapse into bed, yet there we were, dissecting the details of telecommunications. 'Do you know how long he was away?'

'No, but he travels to far-flung places – or so he says. With the length of the flights, it would probably have been a few days at least.'

'Surely the police would have been all over his alibi? From what you say, I assume you've not told them?'

Ruth shook her head and started to cry. 'I'm sorry. I've been such a fool, but I didn't know what to do. I thought there was no point once Elvira confessed.' She raised her eyes to mine. 'And you were dating Charles. I didn't want to spoil it for you.'

I squeezed her hand. 'Let's sleep on it. You are staying, aren't you? I'll discuss it with James tomorrow.'

Although exhausted, I couldn't sleep. Visions of a disturbed Charles invaded my head. Then there was Ruth and her conundrum. Was she expecting me to question Charles's alibi with the police? That led on to Dave and Pansy. Something dodgy had gone on there. Was that linked to the murders?

My thoughts skedaddled, returned and gained a crazy momentum. Although desperate for sleep, I fought against it in the fear I would miss Snowy scratching at the door.

The birds started their chorus ridiculously early and sang like they were on some productivity bonus. Minutes later, my alarm woke me, which should have been impossible as I wasn't even asleep.

Remembering Snowy, I galloped downstairs, flung open the door and interrupted the postman, bending mid-post at the bottom of my door. Confronted by my bare, unshaven legs, he covered his embarrassment on the upward journey with a tuneless whistle. I tried to cover mine by clawing at my skimpy vest.

'Morning,' I mumbled.

He coughed, fled down the path and threw me a tortured glance from the gate.

There was no sign of Snowy. I shuffled through to the kitchen and made two cups of tea. I knocked tentatively on Ruth's door. She was sitting up in bed. Her face had sagged during the night, and the dark circles indicated she hadn't slept well either.

She put a hand to her head. 'Sorry, I had far too much to drink last night. I went on and on about Charles. Forget all I said.'

'Easier said than done, Ruth. If you're right about him not being abroad, this could be serious.'

'I know, but I could be wrong. I don't want to waste police time or stir up trouble for Charles.' She raked her fingers through her hair. 'I don't suppose, er, you could ...'

'Do your dirty work for you?' I laughed to show I was joking, but I wasn't. I could already hear Snood's incredulous snorts.

'Only if you want to.' She smiled brightly; now she'd pushed it on to me. 'I'm so sorry. I've made such a mess.' The smile faded. 'I'm hopeless,' she added when I didn't respond.

'Sorry, but I was just thinking I've nothing to offer you for breakfast. I've only got cat food or defrosted peas.'

'No problem. I've arranged to have breakfast with my cousin.' Ruth stretched her long, powerful arms over her head. 'Shall I give you a lift to the shop?'

'No, but thanks for the offer. I fancy a walk to clear my head.'

'What if Charles jumps out at you, and I'm not there to punch his lights out?' She giggled in her high-pitched way, and an unexpected tide of irritation rose within me.

'You've seen him off. I don't think he'll be hanging around this morning. Although ...' A thought occurred. 'Would you be available for escort duties this evening? James is leaving early for his furniture course.'

'No problem. I'll sleep here again if you like?'

We parted the best of friends, though I was slightly irked she'd not mentioned Snowy. We each made our promise. I would contact Snood, and Ruth would pick me up at closing time.

I was looking forward to the walk to work, as I'd a brand new pair of shoes to put through their paces. I sashayed down the street in my red high heels. The sun shone and reached through to my bones. It recharged my optimism and made me think all would be well. Every so often, I smiled down at my shoes.

Near Merangs, I did a silly skip of a run to avoid a car and went over on one heel. The heel snapped, and I hobbled towards the shop. What was it with heels nowadays?

Malcolm had arrived before me. He was leaning against the door, reading his newspaper. I'd given him a key, but he was reluctant to use it. I presented him with my shoe and asked him to do his best.

When I handed him his first cup of tea, he'd already fixed the heel. 'I've bodged it the best I can. It'll last you through the day, but you'll need to take it to the cobblers for a proper mend.'

'Thanks, Malcolm. You're a superstar.'

As I pulled up the shop blinds, I reflected that it was a normal Wednesday like this, six weeks ago, when we found Vincent's body. My life must have been so dull back then.

James arrived early. He drew me into a bear hug and murmured a 'sorry' into my curls. He smelled of lemons and musk, and his muscles felt hard beneath his soft cotton shirt. I could have stayed there all day.

We exchanged our news. Pansy had expressed relief that Dave was safe and had even thanked him for the call. He laughed when I said Ruth had knocked Charles out, but he abruptly stopped when I told him the rest.

'Ruth will be correct,' he said. 'That creep won't have been abroad. I can't understand what the police are playing at. You must ring them at once.'

'Stop bossing me around. I intend to ring, but surely they'd have been all over his alibi from the start?'

'I've said all along, Charles is involved. It's obvious.' James thumped the counter. 'He had the most to gain.'

We were interrupted by Shakira clattering in with her trays. 'Morning, my lovelies. I'll just put these down here. She looked at our faces. 'I'm picking up a bad vibe here. I'm sensitive like that. Hope you two's not had a barney.'

'No, everything's fine. James is being an arse as usual. I'll bring you both a coffee.'

'Thanks, doll. Hey James, I've had a great idea. Listen to this: I'm gonna turn flapjack on its head and insert ...'

Shakira's voice faded as I closed the tea room door. When I returned to the shop with their drinks, she'd moved on to Buttersley *goings-on*.

'What's all this about Prue and Malc doing a spot of love wrestling in a paint pool? I'd have paid money to see that.'

Malcolm popped his head out from behind the truffle cabinet, paintbrush in hand. 'It wasn't like that.'

'Oops, sorry, Malc,' said Shakira. 'Don't mean to offend. I know you've got a hard spot – I mean soft spot for Prue.'

'Get away with you,' said Malcolm, flicking his hands in angry pretence, but loving the attention all the same.

'Speak of the devil,' said Shakira, 'here she is.'

We all turned to the door. Prue marched in and barked out, 'Good morning.' Her glare indicated she'd heard the devil reference. 'Shakira, how many times have I told you to take your trays straight through to the tea room?'

'Just going. On my way, now.'

'If I've told you once, I've told you a thousand times.'

This set Prue's crosspatch tone for the rest of the day. She was probably still smarting over her ruined coat. She'd not bothered to return mine.

I phoned Snood several times, but it always went to voicemail. In the end, I left a carefully composed message, querying Charles's alibi and that he was continuing to stalk me.

So far, so good on the malicious texts. I didn't want to dwell on why they might have stopped, as I feared I might jinx them into starting again.

With Prue in a prickly mood, the day seemed to last forever. We weren't busy, and I longed to slouch at one of the tables and rest my head in my arms.

Prue, still in a huff, left early, and so did James, saying he needed to prepare for Knobs and Knockers part two.

After I'd cleaned the tea room, I chatted with Malcolm as he washed his brushes and tidied his equipment. He folded his dust sheets into neat piles and inspected each paintbrush with reverence. It soothed me to watch his methodical routine.

'Hey, Malcolm, the shoe has lasted me the day.'

'Glad to hear it, but you still need to get it properly fixed. Now, Helen, love, do you want me to wait for you, and we can leave together?'

'No, you're fine, thanks. You go. Ruth will be here any minute, and she's going to give me a lift home.' My phone vibrated in my apron pocket. 'That's probably her texting to say she's outside.'

I closed the shop door behind Malcolm and read the text. Ruth was on her way but held up in traffic. That suited me. It gave me the time to tweak a few things in the shop.

Ten minutes later, I was standing at the counter, head down, checking the day's figures when the shop door opened.

'Nearly done, be with you in a moment, Ruth.'

'Take all the time you want, hun.'

Why did I not lock the door? I looked up into the smiling face of Charles. He wore a prominent head bandage, which he'd carefully accessorised with a sharp new suit and a shiny black gun.

Bang Bang

Charles smiled as he pointed the gun at my head. 'Ah, I see I've finally got your attention.' He thrust the gun forward to emphasise his point, and his hand slightly shook. 'Move into the tea room where no one can see us. Go on. Move!'

I wasn't about to argue. My thoughts scattered like wildebeest when faced by a lion. Yesterday, Charles had taken a knock on the head. It could have pushed him over the edge. Concussion could do strange things. I once tripped on the high street and knocked myself out. When I came round, I couldn't stop yodelling. *Why are you thinking about that? You'll be hysterical next.*

With a pounding heart and trembling knees, I shuffled into the tea room and gazed around, conscious that I might never see it again. The posies of snowdrops on each table brought a lump to my throat.

With a steadying hand on each thigh, I leant against a table and tried to speak as if Charles had just popped in for a cup of Earl Grey. 'What can I do for you?'

'You can give me some answers for a start. Why did you run away from me? Why wouldn't you speak to me? Why did you reject me in the first place?'

'Your intensity put me off.' The truth, but I could have worded it better. *Get a grip, girl.*

Charles grunted. His nostrils flared, but not nearly as wide as the muzzle of his gun. 'No bitch rejects me. I'm the one who does the hiring and firing. Geddit?'

His bravado was starting to crumble. Sweat trickled down the side of his face, and his eyes furiously blinked.

A spark of anger flashed within me, and I clenched my fists. This was my shop. I was a successful businesswoman, and I wouldn't bow down to his warped view. 'Oh, for God's sake, Charles, grow up.'

Possibly, I'd gone too far. My nerves jangled, and my knees knocked, but at the same time, I couldn't believe he'd shoot me.

Charles glared. 'We could have been dynamite together. But you didn't give us a chance.' He jabbed the gun further towards me. 'Straight on to the next man you were. Making eyes at that copper in charge.'

How unfair. I'd never even looked at the DCI in that way. Thinking about it, though – and this was so patently the wrong time to do so – Swift had an attractive, boyish grin, and he'd taken my various food assaults in good humour.

'Look at me. Look at me,' Charles shouted. He waved the gun in my face. 'Say you're sorry and you want to make it up to me.'

I could only blurt out what was on my mind. 'Ruth will be here any time soon.'

'More target practice, then.' He shrugged as if proud of this line and added, 'I couldn't miss *her.*'

If Charles had planned this better, he would have locked the shop door. Too late for that; Ruth called my name from the shop. I hesitated, not wanting to invite her into the danger zone. She didn't wait for an answer and yanked open the tea room door as if it were cardboard.

'Helen, you in ...' Ruth appraised the situation in seconds and unexpectedly laughed. She filled the space with her girlish giggles. They had a slightly jarring edge.

Charles bristled and jutted out his chin.

'Oh, Charles, is that the best you can do?' She wiped tears of laughter from her eyes. 'Prance in here with your toy gun and wave it around?'

Talk about poking a big stick. I wanted to tell her to shut up, but couldn't speak.

He gripped the gun with both hands. 'This isn't a toy. Don't come any closer.'

Ruth walked towards him, her arms outstretched. 'You don't have the balls to carry a real gun.'

It looked real enough to me. 'Careful, Ruth.' Too scared to watch any more, I closed my eyes.

'Look at you,' she sneered. 'You're like a cornered rat. What are you going to do now?'

Charles fired the gun.

A Loose End

As the gun went off, the three of us screamed. My heel snapped and the chandelier shattered. Charles stood open-mouthed, with the gun at his feet. Ruth kicked it out of his way and pounced.

'What do you think you're doing? Get off me,' he shouted. In the soft glow of the lamps, Ruth was wrestling him to the floor. His limbs flailed like an octopus as he tried to resist.

Ruth had the element of surprise and the strength of ten. He protested even louder when she whipped off her scarf and bound his hands behind him. As a final humiliation, she tied him to a chair. 'Get me something else to tie him with,' she said.

I ran to our 'odds and ends' drawer and threw its contents onto the floor. Grabbing some cord, I ran back to Ruth. She snatched it out of my hand.

'I'll call the police,' I said, feeling the need to show initiative.

Ruth gasped for air. 'Let's get some answers first. The police will take him away, and we'll be none the wiser.'

She had a point, but Charles was dangerously unpredictable, and I wanted the experts to remove him as soon as possible. Although we had control of the situation, that could easily change.

'I just wanted Helen to talk to me,' said Charles. 'I wasn't going to harm her.'

Ruth picked up the gun and examined it. 'You were aiming a loaded gun at her face. Why can't you accept she's not interested in a loser like you?'

'You didn't think that when *you* were chasing me.' Charles snarled like a dog under attack. 'Gagging for it, you were.'

'You deceived me with your fake charm. You were only after my money.'

'Too right I was. What else have you got? I had to down a bottle of wine before I could even stomach a date with you.' Charles pretended to be sick on the floor.

Ruth bent to the level of Charles so she could spit her fury into his face. 'A parasitic drunk, just like your father. He leached off my mother for years. All that money my daddy made, and Vincent squandered it on drink.'

Superfluous to their hate-filled tango, I wanted to say, 'Hello, I'm still here.'

'Like mother, like daughter.' Charles sneered. 'Vincent would have earned it all right, having to put up with that whining wreck. She can't have had any complaints. She left him all her money.'

Ruth's eyes blazed. 'Yes, and when you learnt Vincent had inherited it, you dropped me like a brick.'

'If you'd not looked like a bull in a dress, I might have stayed for double the money, but there's only so much pig-ugliness a man can take.'

Ruth made a strange noise, part sob and part roar of rage. Her next move shocked me. She pulled Charles's head back and struck him with the butt of the gun.

Charles made no sound. His head dropped to one side, and blood seeped out of his ear.

'Ruth, Ruth,' I shouted. 'What are you doing? It's Buttersley, not the O.K. Corral.'

She ignored me but bent down to Charles and hissed into his bleeding ear. 'However much money you have, you'll always be cheap. Always a wannabe in your fake designer gear.'

Fake designer gear made me think of Shakira. Was she upstairs in her flat? Had she heard the gunshot? Unrealistic to hope she'd called the police, but it would be a comfort to hear her clomping down the stairs.

That old, elusive thought nagged away. Something I'd heard but not registered at the time was pushing its way to the surface. Fake designer gear had led me to Shakira. Why did that lead to something important?

'Ruth, I'm going to call the police *now*.'

She prodded Charles with the gun. 'And you couldn't wait to get your hands on the money. You killed your father and, before that, you murdered his wife, so you would inherit.'

'You're mad,' said Charles. His voice was slightly slurred. 'I didn't even know he had a wife. I may be a liar and a cheat, but I'm no murderer.'

'You lied to the police. You weren't abroad.' Ruth was acting like she wanted to break him and force a confession.

'So, I lied, but the police accepted my alibi.' Despite his bound hands and bleeding ear, Charles spoke with conviction. 'What about you, Ruth? Where were you when Vincent died?'

Ruth turned the gun over in her hands. She glanced at me and then quickly away.

'Miles away from here,' she said, 'if you must know, but I'm not the one under suspicion.'

I gasped, 'But, Ruth?' I'd finally made the connection and couldn't stop myself from blurting out, 'You *were* in Buttersley.'

She swung round towards me, her eyes questioning and wide. 'Helen, why do you say that?'

'Because ...' *There's no turning back now.* 'On the morning Vincent died, Shakira tripped over a dog and snapped her heel. When we mentioned this weeks later, you said it was a Louboutin shoe. How did you know?'

'Oh, that.' Ruth's face brightened, and she flashed a ready smile. 'Shakira had already told me about it.'

I smiled back as if I believed her, but we'd crossed a line. 'That explains it then. You had me wondering.' I tried to appear casual. 'Look, let's just call the police and get this over and done with, and then we can go have a drink together.'

Ruth moved closer to stand by my side. 'Too late, my friend,' she said. 'You know, don't you?'

My mind went blank, and my body turned rigid and cold. What did I know? Only that Ruth had been in Buttersley on the day of Vincent's murder.

'What, what?' shouted Charles from the other side of the room.

Ruth took a run and pistol-whipped him again. His head snapped back, and he cried out in pain. She stood over him. 'Shut up, you moron. I need to think.'

I needed to do likewise, but my brain had turned into mush. Ruth came back to me. Charles groaned from the other side of the room. He possibly needed medical attention.

I wanted to step back as she leant too far into my personal space. 'Helen, you see why I had to kill Vincent, don't you?'

I nodded. Not trusting myself to speak, I dug my nails into my palms. Charles had scared me earlier, but that was nothing like the icy fear that Ruth instilled.

'Daddy was a fine, brilliant man. We were such a close family until Vincent ripped us apart.' She held the gun in one hand and took my hand with the other. 'It broke poor Daddy. All that he'd worked for, gone. You *do* see, don't you?' She tightened her grip.

'Of course, I do. And it must have been so hard for you. You were only a child.' *Keep her talking. Buy some time.*

My brain had started to work. Shakira must have heard the shot. She should be up there in the flat at this time, feeding her kids.

Ruth smiled and released my limp hand. 'I couldn't blame Mother. She was just weak. When Daddy died, even though a child, I vowed to get my revenge.'

'So you'd been planning it a long time then, Ruth?' *Damn, Shakira takes the kids to her mother's on a Wednesday.*

'After *he* humiliated me,' Ruth pointed at Charles, 'I devised a plan to get rid of them both.'

'I'm sure they deserved it.' The main shop lights were still on. The door wasn't locked. The key was in my handbag. *Anyone might walk in.*

'Holding Vincent's head underwater as he thrashed around was so satisfying. I did it for Daddy.' Ruth sounded like a child reciting a gruesome fairy tale.

'And what about Eileen Newby?' I asked, but did I really want to know?

'Oh no.' Ruth looked shocked. 'No, I didn't enjoy killing her. I'm not a monster, Helen. Let's chat about that as we go through to the shop. You need to lock up.'

All hope left me then. Ruth was a calculated, efficient killer, and no doubt, she'd made her plans for me,

I glanced back at Charles as she nudged me into the shop. His head lolled, and he made no sound. As I turned the key in the main door, I wondered if I'd ever open it again. There wasn't a soul on the high street.

'I'll take the key, Helen. You won't need it any more, but I'll put it back in your bag afterwards. Now, where was I? Oh yes. I needed a motive for Charles, so the murders would be pinned on him. I had to sacrifice Eileen to my purpose.'

I nodded and smiled, recognising Ruth's need for approval. It wouldn't do to antagonise her. She turned off the shop lights, and with the gun nestling in my back, we returned to the tea room. I grabbed a chair for support, but my ice-cold, shaking hands couldn't get a grip,

'I just can't understand why they didn't arrest Charles,' she continued. 'He had no alibi. I'd had him followed for weeks. All he did was laze in bed all day.'

Ruth stared at me as if I could supply the answers. What did she expect me to say, 'Oh what a shame it didn't work out. Better luck next time?'

As if reading my thoughts, Ruth said, 'This time they'll be in no doubt. It's not what I intended, but it'll have to do.'

'What do you mean?' My voice shook, but not as much as my legs.

'It's such a shame, as we've become great friends, but I'm going to have to kill you.'

'Ruth, no. You can't mean it? Why?' My voice soared to the ceiling.

'I've no choice, Helen. Blame Charles. He's ruined all my plans. Him and that stupid Elvira woman.' Her wispy voice rose with petulance as if they'd spoilt her tenth birthday party, but her wide eyes shone with a manic, self-righteous zeal. I could hardly believe this was the pleasant woman I'd served a cup of tea in bed that very morning.

'Why don't you just escape while you can, Ruth? Charles hasn't heard any of this, and I won't give you away. You're my friend. I'm on your side.' I tried to sound calm.

'Sweet of you.' Ruth patted my arm. 'But, no. I have to see it through and tie up all the loose ends.'

So that's what I've amounted to, a loose end. A memory of Zack on our wedding day popped into my head. He'd said he was the luckiest man in the world. James would have to tell him he was a widower. Hopefully, he'd be grief-stricken and mourn me forever.

'And, sorry about this,' continued Ruth, 'but I'm also going to have to rough you up before I shoot you.'

I struggled against my rising panic. She had a gun, she was stronger than me, but I wouldn't go down without a fight. From my behaviour so far, she'd expect me to be compliant. *Keep her talking. Keep her talking.* 'Why, Ruth? You must have a good reason.'

'I need it to look like you put up a struggle against Charles – before he shot you, I mean. It'll be our little secret he didn't.' Ruth laughed and dug me in the ribs with the gun as if expecting me to join in. 'Thoughtful of him to bring his own gun.'

Three cheers for Charles.

I edged nearer the connecting door to the shop. If she was going to shoot me anyway, I should make a run for it. We'd be visible in the shop, and I might be able to fling myself through one of the windows. Ruth moved with me.

'And after you've killed me, what will you do?'

'Kill Charles, what else?' She shrugged. 'It's not what I planned. I wanted him to suffer and waste away in prison, but this will have to do. I'll make it look like he turned the gun on himself.'

Having silent hysterics, I pictured James standing in the tea room doorway saying, 'Hey, Prue, you don't expect to find two dead bodies on a Wednesday, do you?'

Thoughts of James galvanised me into action. 'Look at Charles, Ruth. He's broken free.'

As she turned, I ran for the connecting door and pulled at the handle. The door opened slightly before Ruth dragged me back by my hair and hit me so hard my whole body shook.

That was when the lights went out, and the gun went off for the second time.

My Hero

After the gun went off in the dark, there was a moment of silence. Then Ruth cried out, 'I've shot myself in the foot.'

Oh dear.

I stood like a statue as a brief and noisy skirmish took place around me. When Ruth spoke next, I couldn't make out what she said. Her muffled voice came from somewhere down by my feet.

A tiny beacon of light shone into my face, and a familiar voice said, 'Helen, it's me. I've tripped the fuse. Go into the shop and flick it back on. I've got the situation here under control.'

I did as was told. My whole body hurt like hell, and I'd banged my head when Ruth had hit me, but adrenaline powered me through. I returned breathless to find Malcolm sitting on a mound of dust sheets, holding his mobile phone.

He flicked off the torch function with a flourish. 'The gun's on the floor over there. Pick it up with a serviette, and put it out of the way. Then come and sit on here with me. I need your weight – she's a big 'un. Chop, chop. Be as quick as you can.'

Hello, Malcolm the Masterful.

As we both sat on top of Ruth, Malcolm phoned the emergency services. How could I ever have laughed at this man? If Prue didn't want to marry him, I would do so like a shot.

'My foot hurts,' cried Ruth. 'It's bleeding.' She didn't attempt to move.

'You'll get medical attention soon enough,' said Malcolm.

I sat in a daze and couldn't speak. I tasted the metallic tang of blood and realised my nose was bleeding. I listened intently to Malcolm but could hardly follow his monologue.

'As you know, Helen, I'm particular about my brushes.' Even in my fuddled state, I wondered where that was going. Malcolm handed me his hankie. 'I'd just got my key in the door at home when the thought occurred I hadn't cleaned my best brush, or at least couldn't remember doing so. I must have got distracted. Maybe I had cleaned it, but I just wasn't sure.'

'Mm-hmm,' was all I could manage.

'Well, I couldn't settle. I was in a right pickle, but then I thought, Helen won't mind if I let myself in with that key she gave me. I had to come back and check.'

Malcolm shifted his position, and Ruth groaned. 'Can you imagine the state it would have been in tomorrow morning? The brush, I mean. Stiff as a board.' He chuckled.

I finally found my voice. 'Malcolm, if you'd not returned when you did, I would have been in that condition myself.'

Ruth made no attempt to move, but her sobs and protests filtered through the dust sheets. Charles softly moaned from the other side of the room. I'd forgotten about him.

'I was surprised to hear voices in the tea room,' Malcolm continued. I was going to come straight in, but something made me stop at the door. "Hello", I said to myself. "Someone's up to no good". I had to act fast, so I tripped the fuse and just charged in with my decorating sheets.'

'The SAS couldn't have reacted any better than you, Malcolm.'

He put his arms around me. He smelt of turpentine and bacon. His tweed jacket prickled my face, but I wanted to stay there forever.

The emergency services arrived in minutes. Suddenly, the tea room was full of bustling uniformed figures. While paramedics attended to Ruth and Charles, the police led me and my hero through to the shop. A female officer draped a blanket over my shoulders, but it did little to quell my shivers and shakes.

The police had cordoned off the shop. Flashing blue lights festooned the high street, and the place was thick with personnel. Snood strode up and down outside, shouting into both her phone and radio.

They dispatched Charles and Ruth in separate ambulances and huddled Malcolm and me into two police cars. A crowd had gathered, and I waved to Dora and Mr Klondike, who were holding hands and staring, open-mouthed.

I could hardly recall the journey to the police station and my arrival. A cup of scalding tea restored my senses, and I became conscious of a hard plastic chair pressing against my legs as I waited in a dingy room.

Fortunately, it wasn't Snood who questioned me but a genial older detective. I prattled on about my ordeal as he sat with his arms over his belly. Every so often, his watery eyes caught mine, and he would gently shake his head as if the ways of the world were a complete mystery to him.

Worn out, I slumped onto the desk. The detective left the room, and I must have fallen asleep, as I awoke with a start when he re-entered.

'You're free to go, Ms Merang. Don't leave the country.' He smiled, so I took that as a joke. 'We'll need to speak to you again.'

He led me through to a grubby reception area. James was leaning, white-faced, against a wall. I ran into his arms and sobbed.

He stroked the back of my head. 'Come on. Let's go.'

'What about Malcolm? We can't leave him here.'

'They released him earlier. I've already taken him home. He's told me part of what happened.'

As James drove, I related the events in a disjointed, haphazard way. I'd held it together when telling the detective, but with James, the enormity of it all, and what might have been, hit me with such a force, I couldn't find the words.

'I'll stay with you tonight,' he said. 'Don't argue.'

I turned to face him. 'I won't. Please don't leave me.'

We arrived at my house to find Snowy on the doorstep. I cried again. As I bent to stroke her, she climbed onto my shoulder and buried her head in my hair.

The next morning, I woke from a long but fitful sleep. Even though my body ached, I'd never felt so glad to be alive. How many folks could say they owed their lives to a forgotten paintbrush?

James drove us to work. I stared out of the window at a bright, shiny world and gulped at the thought of it spinning along without me.

The police had removed the cordon from the shop, and Prue met us at the door. 'After the *goings-on,* we're going to be extra busy, so I've come in early, and Lucy will be here soon. No slacking, you two.'

'Oh, Prue, I'm so pleased to see you.' I burst into tears yet again. I clamped Prue against me and noticed her own eyes were moist.

'I can't bear to think of it all,' she murmured into my curls.

When Malcolm arrived, we all cheered. Prue kissed his cheek. 'I will always be grateful to you.'

Malcolm blushed and smoothed down his oddments of hair. Dave had trailed in behind him.

'Can we have a quiet word, Helen?' said Malcolm with his newfound authority. 'Dave has something to tell you.' I led them to a table away from the customers. Malcolm prodded Dave's arm. 'Go on, son. Spit it out.'

Dave looked at the floor. 'I'm so sorry, Helen, but Pansy and I did a terrible thing. It's been eating away at me.' Dave shredded two serviettes as he spoke. I moved the rest out of reach and told him to sit down.

He confessed they'd gone to Vincent's flat the night before the murder. Pansy had wanted to confront Vincent about involving Elvira in a daft, money-sucking Ponzi scheme.

Beads of sweat spotted Dave's forehead. 'It ended in a terrible row. Vincent was drunk, barely knew what he was saying. We got into a tussle, and I knocked him out.'

'So?' I said, shrugging at Malcolm. 'He probably deserved it.'

'Yes, but the thing is, Pansy searched through all his things and found a stash of money under the bed. And we took it home, with Vincent still out cold.' Dave fidgeted in his chair. 'I'm talking about a lot of money.'

Malcolm tutted.

After my experience the night before, it would take a lot to shock me. 'How much?'

'Thousands of pounds.' Dave twisted his hands together. 'After Vincent's murder, we didn't know what to do, as it could have been seen as a motive. I hid the money. Then Elvira confessed and complicated it even more. We argued about it all the time. I wanted to hand it in, but Pansy ...'

'Didn't want to part with it,' I said. 'Dave, on the subject of money, were you aware Elvira was stealing from Mr Klondike? Much of the money seems to have been splurged on equipment for *your* baby – thousands of pounds maybe?'

He looked away and cleared his throat. 'I did wonder if she was up to something.'

I tapped his shoulder to make him focus. 'The money you found technically belongs to Charles. You can either hand it to the police, or there is an alternative. I won't spell it out, but it would do as compensation. Either way – you can't keep it.'

'You're right. I'm going straight home right now to tell Pansy exactly what to do. Elvira's caused enough trouble, and Pansy's allowed it.'

'Good for you, son,' said Malcolm.

'Thanks for giving me houseroom, Malcolm, but it's about time I left. Don't want to outstay my welcome and all that.'

'You do what's best for you, son, but I've enjoyed your company.'

'I'll leave you to your touching farewells,' I said, rising from the table. 'Prue's signalling that I've been sitting down too long.'

In the next few days, life got back to normal. We remained ridiculously busy, and Malcolm became a local hero. The infamous paintbrush peeped out of his top pocket as a permanent feature.

My initial euphoria dwindled into lethargy and then into a sense of anti-climax. I also reflected on how stupid I'd been over Charles. By being too nice and wanting to spare his feelings, I'd sent him mixed messages. I needed to toughen up.

Both Prue and James complained that since the events of 'that night', the police had kept us in the dark.

'We have a right to know the full story,' said Prue.

Exactly a week from 'that night', DCI Swift phoned to say he would be calling at Merangs after we closed. His manner was terse and abrupt.

We all wanted to hear the denouement, as James called it, so I got everyone together, including Dora and Mr Klondike. We gathered in the tea room, and it was almost a party atmosphere. James had brought champagne and was just topping up our glasses for the second time when the DCI entered. We all stopped talking and turned with an air of expectancy. He stalled and blinked as if he'd walked into a searchlight.

His eyes scanned the room and landed on me. 'Ms Merang, could I have a private word with you? It's important.' He abruptly turned and walked back into the shop.

He had never looked so serious before. As I trailed after him, I wondered what I'd done wrong. What if, in my blundering way, I'd done something to compromise the case against Ruth?

That's that, Then

I followed the DCI back into the shop, thinking how attractive he looked when serious and preoccupied.

He stood in the middle of the floor. 'The shop's looking ... er, nice.'

Nerves made my tone sharp. 'You didn't need a private word to say that. What's wrong? Have I done something to jeopardise the case against Ruth?'

'What?' He looked like he'd never heard of Ruth. 'Sorry, no. You've done nothing wrong.'

I let out a deep sigh. 'That's a relief. I've been known to blunder in without thinking.' Swift's mouth twitched like he wanted to smile, but it wasn't allowed. I tapped my foot. 'So, what is it then?' Were we to stand there all night while he admired the shop?

He cleared his throat and produced a formal, official voice. 'You were the victim of some anonymous texts.'

'I was.'

'I'm assuming they've now stopped?'

'They have.'

He scratched his chin. 'Good. Yes. That's good.'

Wait a minute. How does he know? I took a step forward. 'Did Prue or James report them?'

'No. No need.' He coughed and addressed his words over my shoulder. 'I found out by other means. I know who sent them.'

'How? I mean, who?'

He finally looked at me. His eyes had misted. He pressed a finger against his forehead. 'My sister, Emily.' I opened my mouth, but no words came out. The DCI had gone from handsome to haggard. 'She confessed. It's not the first time she's done such a thing. I've seen all the texts she sent you.' His face flushed, and I suspected that mine did too. 'I fully understand if you want to make an official complaint.'

Had a pile of rubble been dumped on my head? 'But why? Why did she send them?'

'She's a deeply troubled girl. Always has been. She needs professional help. We've arranged it before, but she refused to take it.'

Swift looked so lost; I wanted to reach out to him. 'On reflection, she did seem up and down, but ...'

'It's like she's two people.' He was eager to talk now. 'Most of the time, she's a lovable, vivacious young woman, but then she gets something into her head and turns into a vicious monster.'

I still didn't get it. 'Why send them to me?' I repeated. 'It may sound pathetic, but I thought she liked me.'

'She did. I mean, she does, but ...' Swift stared at the floor. 'She picked up on something.'

'Sorry, what do you mean? Picked up on what?'

'She noticed *I* like you. She wants all my attention, and she was jealous.'

Jealous? He likes me? Swift risked a direct questioning glance, and heat blasted up from my toes. I smiled. He moved towards me, and I reached out my hand towards his.

The tea room door flung open, and Shakira stuck her head out. 'Yo, what's going on? We're all waiting, and I need to get off soon. Got a new date tonight, and I already know he's gonna be Mr Right.'

Swift grinned at me, and I couldn't take my eyes off his face. I'd forgotten all about the denouement. 'We thought you were here to spill the beans about Ruth and the murders.'

'I thought my officers had already given you the relevant information? No?' He frowned. 'I can see why you all need to know.' He pulled back his shoulders, straightened his tie and said, 'Lead the way.'

Back in the tea room, Swift stood in front of us, fully in command of both himself and the situation. Prue and Malcolm nodded their approval before he even opened his mouth.

'Don't ya just love a man with authority?' whispered Shakira. 'Wish he were mine.'

A frisson of excitement and anticipation ran through me. I would have to get used to calling him by his first name. I dug deep into my memory bank and came up with Tom. I repeated the name over and over in my mind and had to force myself to concentrate on his words.

As an introduction, Tom stated that Ruth had made a full confession, and there was no doubt she had committed both murders. Her motive was revenge, and the catalyst was her mother's death.

Tom cleared his throat. 'When Ruth wound up Claudia's affairs, she was staggered at the money Claudia had given Vincent. Even more so when she learnt the terms of the will.' He looked around at us all. 'She freely admitted to her bitterness against Vincent, who had not only destroyed her father but ended up with his money.'

I hardly listened but stared at Tom's face and noted for the first time how his cheeks dimpled when he smiled. Now and again, his slate-coloured eyes fixed on mine, and I had to look away in fear I would gasp in delight.

In the warm glow of my happiness, I could afford to be generous. 'I feel a bit sorry for Ruth.'

Prue shook her head. 'You soft, silly goose.'

Tom smiled at Prue as if she'd said the most delightful thing. 'Charles accompanied Vincent to Claudia's funeral, where he first met Ruth. He already knew her to be wealthy and assumed she would inherit. He spotted a money-making opportunity.'

'But Charles was so flash. I thought he were loaded,' said Shakira.

Tom nodded. 'The impression he liked to create.'

James nudged me and whispered, 'Told you.'

I fidgeted in embarrassment and looked away as Tom continued. 'Ruth was initially besotted with Charles. They had a few dates. He told her Vincent's treatment of Claudia was despicable, but his intentions were honourable. He hinted they might even get married.'

'The cad,' said Prue. Malcolm vigorously nodded.

'When Charles discovered Vincent had inherited, he dropped Ruth. In his statement, he said it would be less of a chore to extract the money from his father than to continue a relationship with Ruth.'

Everyone tutted, and Shakira swore.

Tom raised an eyebrow at her and gave a faint smile. 'Ruth hired a private investigator and found that far from being a high-flyer, Charles couldn't hold down a job. The investigator also uncovered that Vincent had a wife. This led Ruth to hatch her murder plan.'

'Which was what, exactly?' asked Prue.

'She planned to destroy them both,' said Tom. 'Kill Vincent and frame Charles for the murder.'

'But first, she killed Eileen,' I said.

Lucy gasped. 'Why kill that poor lady?'

'To substantiate the motive for Charles,' said James, who couldn't stay quiet for long. 'With no wife and Vincent dead, Charles would inherit the lot.'

Tom nodded. 'Ruth saw Eileen as necessary collateral damage. She knew Eileen led a lonely life, so her body would not be immediately found. She calculated this would blur the lines of the investigation regarding alibis.'

I jumped in. 'But, with Eileen's death going undiscovered, she had to wait a while before she killed Vincent.'

'Exactly.' Tom locked his eyes on mine, and my face went hot. 'It had to be obvious that Eileen had pre-deceased Vincent.'

'Why did she assume Charles wouldn't have an alibi?' asked James.

'This is where she came unstuck. From her investigator, she knew Charles had a fixed routine. He slept every day until noon, and then watched TV for the rest of the day, alone.'

I was puzzled. 'He must have been doing something else that day, something unexpected that Ruth didn't know about?'

Tom flashed me a warm smile, which gave me what Mum used to call a *Ready Brek* glow. 'Well spotted. Unlucky for her, Charles started a job the morning Vincent died. It was in a call centre where his every move was monitored. He couldn't possibly have committed the murder. True to form, he quit the job a few days later.'

'But surely,' said James, 'Ruth can't have expected Charles to be convicted purely on motive, and opportunity?'

It would have been petty to remind James that he'd thought it was Charles all along.

'No,' said Tom. 'Ruth visited Charles after Vincent's death to offer her condolences. They had a drink together, and Ruth slipped a sedative into his wine. When he fell asleep, she brought out the murder weapon she'd used on Eileen, wrapped Charles's hand around it, and then hid it in his wardrobe. She expected the police to be suspicious of him from the start.'

'I can't believe it of Ruth,' said Lucy. 'She seemed such a nice, generous person.'

That woke Shakira up. 'Do I have to give up my Bottega clutch?'

'And what about the actual murder of Vincent?' asked James.

'Yes, the fateful day that involved Merangs.' Swift looked around the room. 'Ruth disguised herself as a workman. She even had a fake ID from a utility company. Once inside, she clobbered the unsuspecting Vincent from behind with the drill from her tool bag. This rendered him semi-conscious, and she dragged him to the bathroom. Stripping his clothes off, she pushed him into the bath and turned on the taps. Claudia had once said Vincent had a fear of drowning. Ruth wanted to maximise his suffering.'

'Terrible, terrible,' Prue muttered to herself.

'As the water rose, Vincent regained full consciousness and put up a fight. Unfortunately, he was at a disadvantage from his position in the bath, and Ruth is an incredibly strong woman. Ruth says she enjoyed the fight so much, she gave no thought to the water spillage and possible consequences.'

If I'd not been on the other end of Ruth's gun, I would have found that impossible to believe.

'Poor Vincent,' said Lucy and began to cry. I put my arms around her, and Malcolm offered his hankie.

'Ruth then had her second piece of bad luck, as she describes it.' Tom had everyone's attention again. 'Vincent had only just stopped struggling when she heard Mr Klondike on the stairs.'

Mr Klondike sat up straight, and his chins wobbled. 'Just think.'

'Ruth hid in the wardrobe until Mr Klondike fled. She was about to emerge when she heard someone else. She saw the reflection of a fleeing woman and suspected the woman may have glimpsed her before running back out.'

'Elvira?' I asked.

'Indeed,' said Tom. 'I'll come back to her. Ruth needed to act fast.'

'Why didn't she just get the hell out of there?' asked Shakira. 'She'd done what she wanted, killed Vincent, I mean.'

'Not quite,' said Tom. 'She wanted it to look like murder, remember? As it was, it could have been classed as suicide or even an accident. After the drowning ...' Tom ran a hand through his hair. 'She'd intended to disfigure Vincent, so there would be no doubt it was murder, but she no longer had time.'

Prue slowly shook her head. 'Shocking. Quite shocking.'

'Ruth knew Mr Klondike would call the police,' said Tom. 'She dragged Vincent out of the bath, wrapped him in sheets and stuck him in the cupboard. She then shoved the sheets to the bottom of the linen basket. As she was leaving, she spotted Vincent's mobile phone and grabbed it. She was going to keep it as some sort of trophy, but threw it into a bin on the high street. She left before the police arrived.'

James nudged me and whispered, 'Cue Arse and Alien.'

'So what about Elvira?' asked Malcolm.

'Yes, Elvira. She confirmed she entered the flat after seeing Mr Klondike run out. She didn't go into the bathroom, but from the angle of the mirrors in the bedroom, she saw a figure about to step out of the wardrobe.'

'But why confess to the murders?' I asked.

'From what the psychiatrist says, Elvira had been living on the edge of her nerves for some time. After the funeral, she convinced herself the murderer had recognised her. She feared she would be next. Guilt about her sister, Eileen, and also something else she refused to disclose was preying on her mind.'

I almost felt sorry for her, too. 'So, the confession was a means of escape and also a cry for help?'

'Yes,' he agreed. 'She's still under medical supervision.'

'Ruth must have been puzzled as to why Elvira confessed,' said Dora.

'She put two and two together and realised Elvira was the woman who'd followed Mr Klondike into the flat,' said Tom. 'She was more concerned about why Charles hadn't been arrested.'

'What about Charles?' asked James. 'Weren't you supposed to be keeping an eye on him after I'd reported his stalking?'

My face burned, and I inspected my nails. Tom, for the first time, blustered. He said his team, in his absence, had been short on manpower and had not communicated as effectively as they should.

Prue came to his rescue. 'What about we all have a nice cup of tea?'

'Surely, we can do better than that,' said James. 'We've drunk all the champagne, but there's always Helen's gin?'

We stood in a noisy group as James poured out doubles, and Prue fussed around for the tonic.

Tom attached himself to my side, so close, the heat of his body made me sizzle, and I almost swooned with joy.

I proposed a toast. 'To Malcolm, my hero.'

'I'll second that,' said Tom as he grabbed my spare hand.

Malcolm blushed but puffed out his chest. Even more so when Prue patted him on the back and said, 'Hear! Hear!'

'Mud in your eye, Malcolm,' said Shakira and knocked back her drink. 'Gotta go now, folks, and meet Mr Right.'

She returned seconds later with a man in tow. 'Hey, I found this handsome, tanned beast on our doorstep.' I assumed that was her date until she added, 'He's here to see you, Helen.'

I'd hardly glanced at him. As I peeled my attention away from Tom, James rushed forward.

'Zack, mate. You're back. Great to see you.' He held his arms out wide. 'Welcome home.'

The Next Book

Fancy Death At Merangs

When Merangs branches out into party planning, Helen's delighted to land her first job. But that's before ...

The biggest diva in town wants the dance floor turned into a beach, the food painted gold, and a world-famous DJ flown in for the night. The guests must dress as movie stars, and, to top it all, she'll knock 'em dead with a show-stopping stunt.

Helen's determined to make it a night to remember. Few will forget the geriatric cowboy, a rubber-boned gangster, and the rugby-playing Marilyn Monroes.

But death strikes before midnight. Two of the guests will never go home again. The police arrive to investigate. Will they blame Helen for the tragic events? And what if it wasn't the accident it first seems, but a callous and cold-blooded murder?

Fancy Death
At
Merangs
CAROLE MARPLES

The Ace-some Awards

The **Murder Above Merangs** was the first book I wrote, and it's all due to Scribophile that it ever got finished. Scribophile is a wonderful critique site, and it soon slapped me down and put me in my place. Thanks to all my regular critiquers. Additional aces to Leslie and Sylvia for keeping in touch, and also to Cozy Christa Bakker[1] for being my writing buddy.

Thanks to eagle-eyed Lee from Bookediting.co.uk [2]
and Tiffany from @writenowcreative

---

1. https://cmbakkerwrites.wordpress.com

2. https://bookediting.co.uk